The Young Centaur

Book I
The Life of Kheiron
Wise Centaur of Ancient Greece

ALARIA Z BLISS

The Young Centaur
Book I
The Life of Kheiron
Wise Centaur of Ancient Greece
Text and Cover Art Copyright © 2013, 2014 and 2015
by Alaria Z Bliss

Sea Turtle Press
P.O. Box 942, N. San Juan, California
kheironthewise@gmail.com

ISBN 13: 978-0-9912102-3-7
ISBN 10: 0991210239
Library of Congress Control Number: 2014902506

Printed in the USA

About the Book

The Young Centaur is a highly researched novel that closely follows Classic Greek mythology. In this first book, we meet Kheiron's *naiad* mother, a fresh water nymph who is assaulted by Kronus, the god of Heaven and Earth. She soon discovers that a strange creature is growing in her womb, one that may have two spines, and maybe even two heads – another unusual immortal like the giant *cyclopes* or *hechatoncheires*. She wonders how she could ever love such a strange child, conceived in violence. She didn't know then that her baby's kind nature would melt the hatred she felt, nor did she know that he would become the greatest blessing in her life. Indeed, her deformed baby was destined to be a healer, a foster father and mentor to many of our greatest heroes and heroines.

When Kheiron's mother disappears, he finds himself abandoned and alone. He wanders the hills of Mount Pelion and meets Apollo who teaches him the power of healing, the meaning of dreams and how to divine omens. They visit Artemis and her band of orphaned daughters who teach him hunting and the value of working together. Kheiron falls in love with Kallisto, the beautiful one, but Zeus the most powerful god of heaven and earth, wants her for himself.

In the end Kheiron discovers his immortality, but will he be able to save Kallisto from the consequences of breaking her solemn vows?

Mt Olympus

Vale of
Penios River Tempe

Mt Pelion

Gulf
of
Pagasae

THESSALY

Euboea

Mt Parnassus
(Delphi)

AEGEAN

SEA

PELOPONNESOS

DELOS

THERA

ANCIENT
GREECE

CRETE

MT IDA

The Early Titans

Chaos

<u>Eurybus</u>   <u>Nix</u>   <u>Hemera</u>
(Eternal Darkness)   (Night)   (Day)

Nix, the Dark Bird of Night, flew through the darkness of Chaos and laid a golden egg. When it hatched, Protogonus (Eros) the creative urge was born. And the two halves of the broken egg were Gaia (the earth) and Uranus (the sky).

Protogonus
(Eros)

<u>Gaia</u>   <u>Uranus</u>
(Earth)   (Sky)

Influenced by Protogonus Gaia and Uranus procreated. Their children were the Titans or elemental deities of the natural world

<u>Kronus</u> <u>Rhea</u>   <u>Coeus</u> <u>Phoebe</u>   <u>Hyperion</u>
(Time) (Mother of the gods)(giant) (Shining One)   (Sunlike)

<u>Theia</u>   <u>Crius</u> <u>Eurybia</u> <u>Oceanus</u> <u>Tethys</u>
(Blue Skies)   (Titan) (Titaness) (Ocean) (Seawinds/tides)

<u>Themis</u>   <u>Iapetus</u>   <u>Asia</u>   <u>Hecataoncheires</u>
(Eternal laws) (Titan)   (Titaness)   (hundred hand giants)

<u>Cyclopes</u>   <u>Mnemosyne</u> <u>Asteria</u> <u>Leto</u>   <u>Eos</u>
(one-eyed giants) (Memory)   (Dawn) (Titaness) (Titan)

<u>Helios</u> <u>Seline</u> <u>Atlas</u>   <u>Promethos</u> <u>Epimetheus</u>
(Sun)   (Moon) (a giant)   (Forethought)   (Afterthought)

The Second Generation of Gods and Goddesses

Children of **Kronus** and **Rhea**:
              (Time)   (Mother of the gods)

<u>Hestia</u>   Demeter
(Goddess of the hearth)   (Goddess of the flowering Earth)

<u>Hera</u>   Zeus
(Goddess of Heaven and Earth) (God of Heaven and Earth)

<u>Hades</u>   Poseidon
(God of Underworld)   (God of the Seas)

The most recognized children of Zeus:

Zeus with Metis <u>Athena</u>   Zeus with Demeter Persephone
(Goddess of wisdom)   (Goddess of the underworld)

Zeus with Hera Hephaistos   Zeus with Hera Ares
(God of the forge)   (God of war)

Zeus with Leto <u>Artemis</u>   Zeus with Leto <u>Apollo</u>
(Goddess of the moon and hunt) (God of the sun and healing)

Zeus with Semele Dionysus Zeus with Maia Hermes
(God of the Vine)   (Messenger of the Gods)

with Mnemosyne 9 Muses with Themis The Seasons
(Goddesses of the Arts)   (Goddesses of the Seasons)

with Themis The Moirai
(Goddesses of Fates)

Kheiron's Family Tree

Chaos

Nix
(The dark bird of night)

Protogonus (aka) Eros
(The creative urge)

Gaia
(Earth)

Uranus
(Sky)

Oceanos
(River that covers the earth)

Tethys
(Sea winds & tides)

3000 Rivers & 3000 Oceanides
Oceanids were the three thousand fresh-water nymph daughters of the earth-encirling river: Oceanus. They were nymphs of springs (*Naiad*s), clouds (Nephelai), cool breezes (Aurai), meadows (Leimonides) and groves (Alseides).

Philyra with Kronus (son of Gaia and Uranus)
(a *naiad*)   (King of Heaven and Earth)

\

Kheiron
(the wise centaur)

Chiron, Kheiron, Cheiron, or Xeiron?

There are several different spellings for Kheiron, none of which are right and none of which are wrong. In written Greek there is no C or Ch. Thus the traditional English spelling for Chiron is a phonetic translation using Roman letters. The sound is translated from the letter X, pronounced "ch" as in chaos –closer to the sound of "H" or "kH." If the various spellings of the Greek characters in this book offend anyone, I apologize. The Greeks write it Χείρων.

For those of us root word enthusiasts, it is interesting to note that the Greek prefix χειρω (kheiro or chiro) means hand. In English we have Chiropractor (one who practices healing with the hands), Chiromancer (palm reader) and Chiropodist (a doctor who specializes in hands). Thus, we may surmise that there is something special about our hero's hands. . .

Acknowledgments

Thanks must be given to the amazing writer's groups that have helped me realize that not everything I write is worthy of greatness, but some things are…

To Claire Braz-Valentine, poet, playwright, columnist, and my mentor, who offers writer's workshops in Butte County, California as well as previously in women's state prisons. She knows that one way to heal a broken heart and soul is to stitch them together with a pen and paper.

To my comrades in the group, you are part of me, my people, those who are still here on Earth, and those who have already gone on. I love you all.

To the Sierra Muses, Writer's Workshop, I am honored to be one of you. We are awesome!

To my dear friend and editor, Yakshi Vadeboncoeur. Thank you for your time, knowledge and insights. I hope our friendship lasts forever.

To Katy Height for your time and patience in doing the layout for the cover.

To my family and circle of friends who have supported me to follow my bliss. Life can be difficult, but when those you love stand behind you, what seems impossible can germinate and bloom like a magic seed.

You are all blessings in my life!

May your wounds become a source of healing and strength.

Contents

Contents

Contents

Prologue

4000 years ago, between 2500 BC and 1600 BC, the ancient world that we now know as Greece was sparsely populated with sea farers, fishermen and small agricultural communities. From time to time they were terrorized by invaders who came from the north and northeast, some by land and some by sea. Little is known for certain about the languages and actual history. What we do know was passed through oral traditions. How much is true, one can only speculate. However, the stories, myths and plays preserved by the later Greeks are the tales on which our western cultures were built.

Many of us have heard the name Akhilles, the greatest fighter of the Trojan War. Some too, are familiar with his father King Peleus of Phthia and the beautiful sea nereid, Thetis. Legends live on of Jason and the Argonauts, Orpheus the great musician, Asklepios, the god of medicine, Aristaios, the god of agriculture – names that have survived throughout history.

Common threads tie these particular heroes together, weaving them into a time and place, each in their own right, on Mount Pelion, Thessaly, Northern Greece and into the life of a centaur known as Kheiron. Kheiron was a mentor, teacher, foster father, grandfather and even great grandfather to many of these heroes. Kheiron, himself was a misunderstood immortal, half man and half horse, ostracized because of his physical appearance. Centaurs in the ancient world were known for brutality, carnage and cannibalism. They ate whatever they wanted, taking pleasure in the kicking, screaming and blood that spewed from their victims who were not yet dead. Centaurs were feared beyond all other wild animals. Children, warned by their parents, did not to go out into the forests alone where the centaurs lived.

Some would leave such creatures to the realms of myth. But to generation after generation of wide-eyed listeners, around the evening fires, these stories were as real as the person who sat next to them. These myths explained the changes brought about by nature and the invaders as the whims and wars of the immortal gods and goddesses.

Relatively new to the landscape, horses came to the ancient world of Greece with the invading Aegeans of Eurasia, and stories of half-human, half-horse centaurs emerged as the strange four legged creatures with men on their backs rode into small, isolated, agricultural villages that had never before seen a horse. These new beasts killed indiscriminately and took what they wanted.

Along with horses, the invaders were accompanied by earthquakes and other natural disasters. Mount Thera, in the Aegean Sea erupted, sending debris and tidal waves all over the Mediterranean. Ash clouds blocked the sun and coastal fishing villages flooded. To the ancient people such chaos could only be described as a war between the elemental gods.

It was during this time that tales of Kheiron surfaced. And if he was a real character, he may have been one of the mounted invaders. But as the mythology goes: he, like the other centaurs, came from the Mount Pelion region. Unlike the others, however, he had the ability to heal the sick, guide the lost, provide for the hungry, and defend the weak, tendencies he undoubtedly inherited from his mother, the fresh water *naiad*, Philyra.

Despite Kheiron's gifts, his life was filled with loss and suffering. But, the Gods watched over him and taught him things never before revealed to humankind. It was because of this divine relationship that he became a master in the arts of medicine, herbology, divination, hunting, music, strategy and fighting, necessary skills 4000 years ago. He had the blood of divinity in his veins. Son of Kronus and half-brother of Zeus, Kheiron was conceived during the almighty war between these two powerful gods. They were dark times, but it is important to understand the circumstances that surrounded the good centaur's conception and the trauma from which he was born.

We must start first with Kheiron's grandfather, Uranus, the god of the heavens and lover of Gaia, the earth. Between heaven and earth, Uranus and Gaia, many children were conceived, but few ever saw the light of day.

"No one should have to look upon such deformities," Uranus told the beautiful Gaia as he shoved another creature with one hundred arms back into her belly. He made the earth cry. She wanted to give birth, to feel her children climb the hills and valleys of her vast body, to hear them breathe and laugh and live. But Uranus, her heavenly lover, would have none of them. Instead, he forced them to live deep in the darkness of Tartarus, the underworld. That was until that fateful day when Gaia gave her son, Kronus a scythe and told him what he must do.

Sneaking out through one of the long underground tunnels, Kronus surprised Uranus in the act of making love to Gaia. Quickly, before Uranus understood what was happening, Kronus sliced away his father's manhood. The sky stood naked, stripped of his creative force.

Kronus took the writhing member in both hands, raised it above his head and threw it, with all his might, into the sea where it foamed and frothed, ending his father's rule forever. That act elevated Kronus to king of the heavens and earth.

Kronus, afraid of losing his power and warned by Gaia that one of his children would overthrow him, took all of his babies from the arms of his beautiful wife Rhea and ate them. Zeus, the last baby, should have been in his belly too. But unbeknownst to him, the Moirai, the fates, rolled out their strings of destiny, and a mother who longed to hold her own child in her arms, tricked her husband and wrapped an infant sized stone in swaddling clothes. Rhea, Kronus' wife, feigned great distress at the very notion of having to give up another one of her children, but after a terrible argument and many tears, she gave in and handed the stone to Kronus to gorge himself on. He didn't seem to notice that it didn't move or cry like a baby should. He swallowed it whole, blankets and all just like all his other children. Rhea wept and rejected him as before, but this time she made a promise to herself: she would never bear Kronus a child again, not ever.

Secretly she hid her infant, Zeus, on Crete, in a cave on Mount Ida where he was raised by the two nymphs born from the blood of Uranus' castration, Adrastia (necessity) and Ida (the mountain). They cared for him and shielded him from Kronus. They fed the baby with honey and the milk of Amalthea, the sacred goat, Rhea's dear and loyal pet, whose teats dripped with milk that formed in Rhea's own breasts. The mother would have given anything to feed her own child, but her mere presence on Crete would have made Kronus suspicious.

As added protection and to block the sound of her child's cries, Rhea led the Kouretes, a tribe of warriors from Euboea, an island along the eastern coast of southern Thessaly, to Crete where they could live and practice their war games noisily near the cave. These warriors made a terrible cacophony as they sparred and fought, clanging their spears and shields, dancing and howling near the hidden cave. Kronus, who could not bear them, plugged his ears and stayed far away from their inhabited island.

Zeus, however, surrounded by lovers of war, learned quickly as he watched the Kouretes battling, tricking and plotting how best to overcome their enemies.

When Zeus surprised his own father Kronus in a carefully planned attack, it put the heavenly king in a position where he could do nothing but comply with the demands put upon him. Zeus wanted the liberation of his brothers and sisters. So Kronus disgorged the other children from his bowels. Painfully, he threw them up one at a time, liberating Poseidon and Hades, Hestia, Demeter and Hera from the darkness of his belly. They were freed to fight and make war against him, the king, their wicked father.

With freedom and loyalty to their brother, Zeus, the circle of allies increased, strengthening the forces of immortal gods and goddesses against the old king.

The war between Kronus and his son Zeus was long and bitter reaching new heights of destruction. This war, destined to last for ten, long years, involved all the ancient gods and ravaged the contours of Gaia's body. Where there were valleys, craggy peaks pushed through her skin. And where tall mountains once stood, sunken calderas sloshed with rushing seawater.

Brother fought against brother, sister against sister, water against fire, light against time. This elemental battle between the primordial deities and the new generation of gods divided the ancient forces of nature. Everyone was dragged into the fight, known then and now as the Clash of the Titans.

v

You can imagine the war as lightning ripped the sky and the sea swelled into giant waves that crashed over the land like monstrous hands. Surprise hurricanes blew in, wrenching up trees and snapping them like twigs. The elemental deities tore up the known land and displaced every living creature. Just when the sky turned blue and the sea began to lap gently on the sand, tremors and volcanic explosions disrupted the peace once again.

Obscured by ash, the sun hung in the sky like a poisoned apple while molten missiles screamed overhead. Forests were set ablaze. Grandmother Gaia's blood spilled hot down into the sea while rocks and land crumbled into fissures. Whole meadows, rivers, mountains and landmasses disappeared.

This chaos was a war for power, heavenly, divine power. Zeus challenged his father, just as Kronus had challenged Uranus, and they fought, one against the other for the life of a supreme Deity.

Fear and terror destroyed any sort of equanimity even in the simplest and most peaceful of places.

In the meadow on Mount Pelion where a spring bubbled up from the earth, Philyra, a *naiad*, lived in her own watery world. She was troubled by the quaking earth, the obliterating ash and fires, but not to the extent of others, not until that day when Kronus, in the guise of a horse, brought the pain of war and changed forever, life as she had known it.

Thus, may it be known that from that unfortunate day of great of hardship, came one of the greatest blessings: Kheiron, the wise centaur of Ancient Greece.

1

The Horse

It could have been snow, the way it fell so lightly from the sky, grey bits of volcanic ash that danced slowly from side to side as they made their way to the ground and covered everything. It was quiet, too, just like a snowy morning, overcast and silent.

Philyra sat near her spring on Mount Pelion, gazing at the drifts of ash as they landed silently upon the surface of her pool. She watched as they rested like leaves on the smooth surface before succumbing to her moisture.

Here her spring still flowed, bubbled up from the depths of Grandmother Gaia. Her water tumbled over stones and splashed the air. Philyra was the spring, a *naiad*, the water nymph who gave life to the plants and trees around her mountain home. Water was her essence, her splash a sound of hope in a world where the volcanic explosions of the elemental Titan war changed the world in a matter of moments.

The conflict between Zeus and his father Kronus daily tore up the land as they each fought for the right to exist. The forces of Heaven and Earth battled – fire against water, light against sound.

But here, in Philyra's pool, sunlight, subdued by the haze of ash, shone through the droplets that sprayed off her rocks. Tiny rainbows, tinged by the red sun, brightened this unusual spring, pushing away the lingering color of destruction.

A bird sang, a frog croaked, a fish came to the surface to snatch a mosquito. Here was a haven, filled with lush, green herbs, a moment of happiness and peace, where the sound of Philyra's laughter broke through the oppressive heaviness that permeated the land. Drifting like a hypnotic melody on the wind, her song drew the attentions of Kronus, God and King of the Heavens and Earth.

As Kronus approached the innocent girl, he saw the naked naiad with dark, flowing hair singing to her water creatures, calling them to come out and play in the snow-like ash. She was singing to a frog and to hidden birds among the branches of a nearby fig tree.

Because of her, the colors in the meadow seemed as if rain had just fallen with droplets of dew that scintillated in the grass. The succession of long, dark days had been a constant burden upon every living thing. But here, in this glade, near this spring, it seemed as if those harsh days had never been.

Kronus watched from the shadows of the forest, hidden in the thicket, as Philyra stood up, a tall, willowy figure, that danced to the rhythm of the gushing water and croaking frog.

What makes her that way? Kronus wondered. *How can she laugh? How can she sing?* He couldn't understand, but she stirred something in him – desire and passion for things he did not have. He wanted nothing more than to forget the conflict with Zeus, his errant son, and listen to this girl's songs.

Why had it gone on so long? This war? – seven years, eight already?

When Kronus stole the ruler-ship of the heavens and earth from Uranus, his father, it had been quick, a simple castration of the aging king. But this war seemed to go on forever. Kronus had been stirred up by Gaia's prophesy that one of his own children would overcome him and take the ruler-ship of the heavens and earth.

In his attempts to maintain his throne, Kronus took every precaution and ate his children so that none of them could challenge his authority. But the Morai, the fates, decreed the future, and Rhea, his wife, tricked him into eating a rock instead of his last born son. Now he was engaged in this seemingly endless battle with Zeus.

Damn Rhea, Kronus thought. *In spite of her efforts to save Zeus, I will not give in. I will destroy the earth. I will rip the heavens to shreds before conceding to that wild-haired son of mine.*

But here, he thought, *now, in this meadow, by this spring, I want to forget all that – with this naiad girl. Let the War of the Titans disappear for a while.*

Filled with a selfish notion that he could have whatever he wanted, no matter the cost or resistance, feelings moved through his body and mind. Desires tingled up his thighs. He wanted the naiad, not just her songs, but her body – her happiness. He wanted her to make him forget ...everything.

How, he wondered. *In what form should I appear? As a man or an animal?*

Without any evident cause, the birds stopped singing. The frogs stopped croaking. The music of the spring became silent. Philyra looked around, but nothing stirred. The only clue of what was about to happen was a shiver that ran down her back. Impulsively, she reached for a mossy dress.

At the sound of hooves, Philyra glanced across the meadow and saw the horse. Ordinary in color, his black mane and tail rippled in the wind. His muscles moved gracefully under his dark, shimmering coat.

Oddly, she was attracted to this horse. He was magnificent, and Philyra stood in admiration as he ran toward her, circling the spring, before coming to an abrupt stop. Tufts of grass flew as he dug his hooves into the ground.

Philyra giggled at the power of his presence, and timidly said, "*Kali meera*, Good morning." In response, the horse threw his head back and shook his mane, whinnying loud and deep.

Philyra touched his withers but suddenly realized what the horse wanted and slowly backed away.

"I am not a horse," she whispered, as the stallion stomped the ground. The earth trembled with his power, and much like the disturbed surface of a pool, fear rippled through Philyra's body. She turned and jumped over the stream, but the horse followed. She ran for the trees, but he ran after her. She scrambled up a prickly cedar as he burst through the brush. The horse had powers beyond any other known creature, and the tall cedar that Philyra climbed shrunk to the size of a sapling. Once she was on the ground, the horse pinned her mossy dress to the dirt. The bright green weave tore from her body, and she narrowly escaped.

The horse seemed crazed and madly chased Philyra wherever she ran. She ducked under branches and skidded around boulders, ran down ravines and over a creek. But he would not stop. And she could not hide.

He horse finally cornered the naked naiad in a small gorge where she could neither climb up nor down. It was then that she finally screamed, "Stop." She spoke in the language of all beasts, but he did not seem to hear her.

Philyra's throat and nostrils burned with dust. Her eyes watered, but the horse didn't seem to notice or care.

Her muffled call for help echoed in the gorge.

Such things are not spoken of, and harder yet to imagine, but he took her as if she were a mare. When he finished, the naiad fell into a lifeless clump whereupon he nuzzled her almost sweetly, as if that could atone for what

4

had happened. Then he disappeared, leaving her where she had fallen.

Aching pain seared through Philyra's body, and she wondered if she were dead. But a nymph is incapable of perishing. He left her in the gorge, broken like a shattered pot that would never be whole again – broken, but not dead.

"*Me-te-ra,* " she called, "I need you."

As softly though she said it, her mother heard her. Tethys, the Goddess of the sea winds and tides, mother of the three thousand rivers and the three thousand *oceanids,* nymphs of freshwater springs and streams, Tethys heard her daughter's tears falling on the earth. The goddess roused herself from that mystical place where the sun sets in the far western sea and came to her daughter's aid.

In the gorge, she found Philyra covered in her own watery blood. The crimson liquid spread over the soil like the juice of a smashed pomegranate. The goddess moved like a gentle sea-breeze swirling around the girl, trying to comfort her and yet disgusted by the scene of violence.

"My child," Tethys said in quiet abhorrence, "Who has done this to you?"

"A horse, Metera, it was a horse."

The goddess lifted her daughter's naked body from the ground and held Philyra against her chest. Then she carried the girl to the nearest pool, where she stepped into the water.

"Denarae," Tethys called to this pool's *naiad,* "help me bathe and heal your sister."

In response, the waters churned, and Tethys submerged both of them into their natural, healing element. Bubbles erupted from the bottom, swirling, cleansing Philyra's skin, flowing softly and gently, moving around and inside where the greatest damage was done. Water cooled the wrenching, burning pain.

"Sleep child," Tethys whispered to her ravaged daughter. "Sleep," and as she commanded, Philyra fell into a deep sleep, where everything slipped away as if it had all been a terrible nightmare.

2

The Monster Within

Though Philyra's body began to heal, her mind and heart did not. Her mother Tethys stayed with her for a while, but the sea called, and like the tides and winds she came and went.

Alone, Philyra looked for dark places where no one could find her, and instead of sleeping in the water, as she used to, she burrowed into a nearby cave.

Anger and fear, bitterness and terror churned at the slightest unusual sound. She used to meet the wild horses when they ran through the meadow, even welcomed them to her spring for a drink, but now she trembled at the sound of hooves upon the rock and hid deeper in the shadows of her cave. From there, she watched who came to her pool, but she no longer played in the bubbles, swam, sang, or laughed. Like a plant she withered without water. Indeed, everything under her care became shriveled and fewer in number and barely clung to the weakened life force that emanated from her spring.

It is the deepest nature of a fresh water naiad to care for life, nourish fauna and flora and help them thrive, but now, Philyra had nothing to give. Even the young animals that normally drank in her pool took only a sip and then scurried away. There was a heaviness, a palpable discomfort, that made everyone want to leave, everyone that is except To-nero, a young frog.

The frog watched over Philyra especially when she was alone. It was a gloomy job since she no longer played with

7

him. Yet he kept guard, watching as she sat at the mouth of the cave, a naked body camouflaged in a mass of tangled, dark hair, dry leaves, thistles and twigs.

To-nero noticed when she slept, or when her eyes peered from the cavern, and he stayed near, hopping from stone to log, always knowing where she was, croaking, singing for her, for the water and all the life that normally thrived. He hoped to lift her spirits and bring back the naiad who crouched in the deepest recesses of Philyra's soul. But even when he breached the distance, offered her a tasty fly, or even tried to untangle her knotted hair with the pads of his toes, she turned away from him.

Inside her heart, Philyra wanted to protect To-nero and her spring, but now knew she could not. No one was safe from the horse.

In her cave, Philyra didn't notice whether the sun shone or the sky was grey, if it was day or a night that glowed with the unnatural light of an erupting volcano. They all melted one into the other. The war continued to rage in the naiad as much as in the world. Sometimes she was terrified and at others angry. She wished she could say that her father Oceanus, the great waters that covered the earth, was so incensed about the horse taking his child's virginity, her happiness and laughter that he would do anything to make sure it would never happen again. But her father was not a fighter, and his failure to be so only made her detest him as much as the horse. Why didn't he care? Why didn't he even try to discover the beast's identity?

Philyra did not know then, that the horse had been Kronus in disguise. Her mother Tethys asked about the strange animal. It was out of character for grass-eating horses to attack naiads. But no matter how often she inquired, no one seemed to know. That in itself seemed odd because there was always someone, another *naiad* (a fresh water spring nymph), a *dryad* (a tree spirit), a *nephelai* (a cloud sprite) or other elemental being of land, air or water who watched, observed and knew. The goddess was beginning to wonder if those who had witnessed the atrocity were somehow silenced, especially since so many seemed familiar with what had happened.

"Poor Philyra," the other naiads would say when they saw her. They meant to comfort the girl, but it had the opposite effect. Instead she felt embarrassed and ashamed.

"Poor Philyra," she heard the cloud *nephelai* whisper as they passed by, and even her fig tree openly lamented, "Poor Philyra."

She was sick of it. "Can't you just leave me alone?" she said to the fig *dryad*. "Let me suffer in peace!" And she crawled deeper into the darkness of her cave.

Despite her rebukes, To-nero, who took his duty of caring for her seriously, did not give up. Even when she was rude, he tried to comfort her. And though she would not admit it, he knew her as others did not.

On the days when she was curled up in a ball, catatonic, wanting nothing more than to die, he would hop up and sit next to her, touch her forehead with his webbed fingers and croak. His guttural sounds were soothing. When he sang, the nightmares went away, and she felt safe. But, when he paused or stopped, she would sit up quickly, looking around for the horse that invaded her sanctuary.

To-nero was as important to Philyra's healing as anyone could be. And even though she rarely spoke or even acknowledged his presence, she scanned the meadow for him every morning when she woke up, and he knew it. Though not obvious to an outside observer, her breathing changed when he was close. It became even and steady.

Philyra's large family consisted of Oceanus, her father, Tethys, her mother, her brothers the 3,000 rivers of the world, and her sisters, the 3,000 *oceanids*, which were the spirits of springs and pools *(naiads)*, clouds *(nephelai)*, meadows *(leimonides)* and groves (alseides).

Philyra's sister Denarae, another freshwater *naiad*, bathed in her own pool close by. She floated on her back, watching the *nephelai*, the soft clouds pass overhead, and asked out loud, "Who was that horse that hurt my sister?" It was a question not asked of anyone in particular, but simply asked in a pondering sort of way as she went about her leisure swim. In fact, she quite forgot that she even asked a question, when all of a sudden bubbles, hot bubbles, came up from the bottom of the pool. The earth was speaking. Grandmother Gaia was whispering, and Philyra's sister listened.

"It was Kronus," the bubbles hissed. "My son Kronus was the horse."

The *oceanid* was amazed. Grandmother Gaia rarely spoke, but when she did, it was always significant. The answer to her forgotten question made the *naiad* shiver uncomfortably, and she crept out of the water peering warily at the sky where Kronus lived. Quickly, lest he see her too, she covered herself in a willow branch.

When Tethys learned the truth about the horse, she was angry, much angrier than Oceanus. She screamed at Kronus, creating furious little storms and making it rain for weeks on end. From her the winds howled in rage, adding to the already noisy tremors and thunderous explosions from the sky. There was no peace in her realm, and Kronus felt her vengeful bite, though it made little difference in the overall war.

Joining in Tethys' tirade, Rhea, Kronus' wife, was equally angry with her husband, though she had different reasons. In her mind, the hateful god refused to let her have a child, and yet he would go about sowing his immortal seeds upon other women, impregnating them, letting them have children. Indeed, with the swelling of Philyra's belly, all were aware of her condition.

Tethys, the mother of the three thousand rivers and the three thousand *oceanids,* a goddess of fertility and birth, asked Philyra to let her feel the distended belly.

Philyra lay down as Tethys palpated her abdomen.

The wise goddess pressed gently discovering the distinctive head, and then, another one? She thought, *Twins? No.* Something did not feel right, and she deftly followed the soft spine with her fingers and noticed that it made a peculiar angle where two spines seemed to attach. She could only guess at the strange deformity of Philyra's baby. Her furrowed brow and somber gaze exposed her concern.

Honest and blunt, she finally said, "It will be another unusual immortal."

With the understanding that Kronus' grotesque child grew inside of her, anger broke loose, and Philyra, who had held in the feelings of fear and self-loathing since the violence, was now filled with unbridled hostility for the god who ruined her life and innocence.

"Hateful," Philyra growled, reading her mother's facial expressions, "deformed and hateful, just like its father," and she spat on the ground.

"Why would he disguise himself like a horse? She hissed, "Did he think that we wouldn't find out? How could I ever love anything that came from him? – he whose vile nature has destroyed everything. I will never love this child like a mother should. I hate this baby just like I hate its father."

No one blamed her. But a sad thing happened. Her heart closed to the baby, and she wanted nothing to do with it.

11

Unfortunately, she was stuck, physically attached to the malignant creature that grew inside her.

How could she get away? How could she free herself? The only reasonable option was through her mind. She could pretend to live another life, one without horses, or parasites inside her body.

But fantasies were only a brief escape from her situation, and when the creature kicked her bladder, she was reminded of reality and the demon who would eventually emerge into the world and be hated by all.

"I wish I could be like you," she said to a fruitless *dryad*, whose leaves rippled in the wind, "unable to bear a child."

Tethys listened to her daughter and shuddered, "We all have our places, Philyra, our places and our purpose. You have no idea. All that seems terrible now may change and become the greatest blessing you have ever known."

"How could that be, *Metera*? There is an abomination growing inside of me, a monster that will call me *Metera*. No, what seems bad, now, will only get worse."

"How do you know that, Philyra?" Tethys answered in her wisdom. "All that is terrible bears a gift. That is your work now, to discover the gift, whatever it may be."

Philyra scowled, but in the same moment, a cloud passed over the sun, and the cave became darker.

A gust of wind scented with honeysuckle displaced the dust on the floor. Philyra shivered as a soft glow illuminated the interior of her cave. The goddess Rhea, queen of heaven and earth, wife of Kronus, stood before them.

Philyra stared at the goddess, who was dressed in rays of moonlight and crowned with honeysuckle blossoms. Why she had come here? Philyra didn't know, but when the goddess spoke, her voice tinkled like bells.

"Are you all right Philyra?"

Philyra scowled. It was a stupid question to ask.

"I am sorry for the actions of my husband," Rhea said. He does not know the misery he causes. Truly, I am sorry. If you need anything, anything at all, please let me know."

Still angry and disgusted by her condition, Philyra asked, "Can you take away this child? Let me be as I once was, whole and happy? I don't want this monster. I hate Kronus, and I hate this loathsome creature."

As enraged by her husband as she was, and as much as she detested him herself, Rhea was jealous and did not want to hear of Philyra's hatred. Rhea's upper lip began to twitch, and the sweet, honeysuckle look of concern distorted into an awful grimace.

"Wicked, ungrateful girl! You do not appreciate what you have. Kronus gave you a child that you will be able to keep. Whereas mine, my beautiful babies that grew warm and ripened in my belly, that I birthed into the world, perfect in every way, he ate. You should be grateful that the king of heaven and earth gave you a child at all. I would gladly rid this world of you and your unborn baby, but that would be too kind. Instead, you will suffer, Philyra. Suffer for tempting my husband. Suffer for your ingratitude." The pitch of her voice heightened to a scream, "Bear his imperfect monster of a child, Kronus' child."

Her rage swirled, making a whirlwind of fury in which the goddess disappeared.

"Arrgh," Philyra growled. "I don't want his child."

Angry and hurt, the water nymph trembled and began to cry.

To-nero, who sat by her side croaked angrily.

"How dare she!" Philyra hissed, and then finding strength in the injustice called back, "I did not bring this on myself. Just because someone is a ruler does not mean that

13

he is wise, kind, or caring. How can you blame me? What is my crime?"

From the wind blew the Goddess' response, "Revel in your misery."

Tethys, surprised by her sister's wrath, had kept quiet during the uproar, but now comforted Philyra.

"I don't know why she bothered coming here," Tethys said. "Normally she is gentle and thoughtful. I should have spoken up, stopped her, but provoking her anger more would not have been prudent."

At that moment, Philyra didn't care. Big sobs escaped her lips. "How can she be so cruel?"

"She is crazy with grief," Tethys tried to explain. "Gaia prophesied that a child born of her and Kronus would destroy Kronus and take his throne. Rhea has had six children by him, beautiful, and perfect, as she said. She even named them. Let me remember...the first three were girls: Hestia, Demeter and Hera, and the last three, sons: Hades, Poseidon, and Zeus.

"Rhea is so beautiful and majestic that Kronus loved her and still does, in his own brutal way, even though she betrayed him. He gave her children, but then he ate each one like a lamb. Poor goddess, how can you blame her for hiding the last child Zeus? And now the prophecy is coming true. With the help of his brothers and sisters, Zeus will overthrow his father. We have all been victims of Kronus. He is an evil ruler, and one that we cannot abide." She said the last words quietly, knowing that Kronus could be listening, even here.

The heart of a naiad is compassionate, and with these words Philyra felt sorry for Rhea. None the less, the goddess was unreasonable. Couldn't she see that temptation was not an issue? Didn't she know that Kronus spied on her in secret? And now in this tangled mess of violence and displaced emotions, Philyra had to live not only with Kronus' deformed, immortal seed growing inside her, but with Rhea's jealousy as well.

Emotions of sympathy mixed with anger, all simultaneously churned inside the naiad. It was an unfamiliar state of delirium, like standing on the edge of a precipice where at any moment she could fall.

3

The Cave

As Philyra approached the time of birthing, Tethys returned to her underwater home to fetch sea medicines. Alone, Philyra grumbled on her mossy bed, but To-nero hopped into the cave, excited because the day was overcast and rainy. There was no smoke, no orange sun or oppressive lack of air. Everything was damp and fresh, the type of weather he loved.

Before that fateful day when the horse destroyed the equanimity of her spring, Philyra and To-nero used to like exploring. Together, she and the frog would go places they had never been before, or rediscover a glade, tree or rock, different and new because it was raining.

Today, however, Philyra didn't care about the weather.

"Rrrit," To-nero called to her, "Come out and play in the wet."

"Not today," Philyra answered. "There is something horrid in my belly."

"Rrrrit," he said again, trying to encourage her. But this time, she pretended not to hear. He hopped into the rain and let the droplets land on top of him. Then he looked over his brown-green shoulder in an attempt to coax her out. "Rrrriiitttt."

Philyra saw and heard him, but did not respond. Even if it was raining she did not want to risk going outside where the horse might yet return.

But her loyal friend did not give up. He turned over a blue rock, azurite, and pushed it toward her. He knew that she liked the beautiful, blue stones.

"Rrrit," he said again. "Rrrrit, come outside with me."

Despite her fears, the rare blue stone, as always, enticed her, and she left the darkness of the cave and dragged herself out to pick it up. Without meaning to, she followed the little frog out into the wet day.

In the overcast light, the stone seemed bluer. She marveled at its beauty. It wasn't shiny or clear, just azure, like the evening sky, a hue that made her take a deep breath.

If I could drink blue, she thought to herself, *it would taste like the purest, sweetest water that ever existed.*

But just as she was forgetting her worries, a squirrel jumped onto the fig tree and startled her. The sound reminded Philyra that she was not safe. Terror and the memory of that bad day when the horse destroyed her life came alive as if it had just happened, or was about to happen again, and she ran for the safety of her cave.

To-nero, encouraged that she came out at all, followed her back in. If she would not stay outside, maybe he could get her to do something else, somewhere where she did feel safe. But first he had to console her.

Back on her mossy bed, To-nero croaked and sang, reminding her that today was different. There were no horses outside, no smoke, only the beautiful rain, and he sang the rain song, just for her.

"Rrit-rrit, rrit-rrit, rrrrrit.

Rrit-rrit, rrit-rrit, rrrrrit."

Slowly, when the light in Philyra's eyes started to come back, To-nero hopped to the dark corner of the cave where there was water. "Rrrit," he called to her.

He did not ask her to come outside, but instead simply to follow him – just touch the water.

Lured by the element that flowed through her body, Philyra moved slowly toward the place where moisture dripped down the cave wall.

Her whole being was made of water, and when she caressed the moisture, there was an immediate effect. It made her sigh and taste her fingers. Sweet –nourishing enough to drink, and soon she found herself licking the cool, damp wall.

The water healed her, not completely, but for the moment. It was filled with magnesium, the healing mineral that calmed her body and soothed her mind. And for the first time in weeks, Philyra smiled.

"You are right, To-nero," she said, the corners of her lips still turned upward in happiness. "Water is wonderful." To-nero's name meant the water, and it suited him because he knew water like she did. He knew that it washed away the troubles of the mind and heart, that it cleansed the body and the soul. Water, cool and fresh, pure spring water could fix anything.

It was amazing how much better she felt, rubbing against the wall, splashing in the puddle, getting the dampness all over her. She forgot about the horse and the creature growing inside.

Her temporary joy lifted To-nero's spirits. They loved water in the same way. It was magic. It pushed away Philyra's fears and made her interested in life, as well as in the spacious interior of her cave, which only now did she begin to see.

Lit with only the reflected sunlight from the opening, it was dim inside. Yet the longer she stayed in the darkness, the more she saw. There were little places, nooks and openings, mostly open mouths that sank into darkness, but on careful investigation revealed smaller caves, each one another place to explore.

She and To-nero had been to similar caves, some on land but mostly underwater.

Underground there was a whole system of subterranean rivers and creeks, pools and caves formed by the heat and water of the earth and etched into the marble and limestone. Here, in this cave, except for the one wet place, everything was mostly dry.

Bats lived here, and at night, Philyra often listened to their high-pitched squeals as they spoke in their own language, one to another. During the day they slept, but at dusk, the small furry creatures with leathery wings would come alive and swoop out to catch bugs. In that regard they were like To-nero, preferring flies and mosquitoes for their meals.

As Philyra stepped into a cavernous nook, with To-nero by her side, the pungent smell of urine filled their nostrils. Then she noticed the piles of bat droppings that covered the floor. She looked above the dung heap, and saw hundreds of bats nestled on the ceiling. A cockroach scurried out from the pile and To-nero quickly jumped out of its way.

The dung pile was the cockroach's home, his source of food, not a place for frogs or water nymphs. But curiosity had infected the two of them, and they went on to explore yet another corner of the cave.

They found small animal bones crushed and scattered in an old den. Many of the bones were those of small animals that had once sipped from Philyra's pool but now were nothing more than the remains of a hungry wolf's dinner. Philyra knew because of the scent he left behind.

They went on, following a small shaft of light that shone through a crack in the roof. In that small ray, particles of dust sparkled like shimmering stars as they passed into the light, and Philyra smiled, again.

In the darkness, they felt their way with fingers and toes. The rocky tunnel walls, smoothed with years of trickling water, were now dry with nothing more than a lingering dampness. To-nero hopped forward, eager for something he instinctively felt ahead. Philyra's innate sense of direction noticed the variations in the floor and walls, and she knew when they descended even lower into the earth. When they came to a fork in the tunnel, To-nero stopped and listened. Quiet came from each direction, but To-nero followed his instincts and hopped toward the left. Philyra followed, her protruding belly only slightly hindering her movement.

They knew they were going deeper into Grandmother Gaia. They could feel and hear the changes. Eventually the echoing of their footsteps told them that the tunnel had expanded into a large cavern.

Here in the darkness, they stopped and sensed the open space around them.

Philyra explored with her feet and felt the silt and rock left behind by the ancient river. With her hands, she discovered a huge boulder in the middle of the dirt floor.

A naiad understands channels of water, feels them in her bones. The remnant essence of the ancient stream made Philyra feel at home. However, what intrigued her most in this place was the overwhelming sense of peace. It came over her as if she passed through a tangible veil and into a holy place. Even her curiosity melted, and she felt impelled to sit down in reverence and awe.

I could stay here forever, she thought, as To-nero jumped onto her knee.

"Rrrit," his voice echoed in the chamber. He felt the peace here, too. Philyra lay back in the dry silt - darkness all around her. The baby pressed against her spine, but not intolerably. She had focused so much resentment on the creature, but now here, even that intense hatred seemed to diminish.

To-nero folded his legs on Philyra's chest, resting his cool body against hers as they listened to the only sounds in that womb-like place, their own breathing.

Philyra did not feel frightened, angry or scared as she had for the past several months. "I feel safe," she whispered, "as if everything is all right."

"Rrrrrrit," To-nero answered, "safe," his voice reverberated into her womb.

Suddenly Philyra became aware of the baby inside of her and that she did not feel anger or hatred. The baby had a presence of his own, and the three of them rested in the cavern together, To-nero, Philyra, and the creature, listening to the quiet hum of Gaia's heart.

Hours went by, maybe even a day, as they lay in that timeless place, suspended in darkness.

Hunger eventually forced them to make their way back toward the pool. But climbing the gentle slope was not as easy as the descent. It wasn't that they got lost or because it was steep, but because Philyra's hips were becoming loose and her gait awkward. In addition, the baby wanted to walk and so kicked inside Philyra with what seemed to be many feet.

When they emerged into the cave, Philyra collapsed on her patch of moss and closed her eyes. To-nero went to the pool and brought back flies to share. Out of character, Philyra ate them. Normally she preferred plants.

After the excursion to Gaia's womb, all the hatred that Philyra felt towards the monster in her belly disappeared. More importantly, she began to communicate with her baby.

It responded to her voice and the pressure of her hand. The creature, whatever it was, had a presence of its own, and it wasn't vile, or hateful. Philyra found herself caressing the roundness of her abdomen feeling the tiny curved protrusions that could be a head or two and the odd angles. She had sworn enmity to everything that came of Kronus, but this baby now seemed so gentle and kind. It was not in her nature to hate, more to understand, and instead of rejecting it, as she had promised to do, she found herself bonding.

"You are not his," she whispered to the baby. "You are mine. It is my fluids and my bones that feed you."

She sang water songs and gurgling melodies, talked to the baby as if he were an old friend. She even introduced him to To-nero who croaked lullabies for the unborn child.

"Unlike your father," she told the baby inside, "you will be more like the healing waters of Mount Pelion. You will be kind and gentle, wise and compassionate. You will sing and understand the language of all animals."

In her heart she knew that the baby was a male, and she didn't want him to be bullied or weak. "And," she said musing, "You will be a fighter and a champion for those who are vulnerable. You will be a healer and a friend to all, even the plants and the insects. You," she said, "will be respected and remembered, not for your aggression, but for your righteousness, for your kindness." She didn't know it then, but her words were prophetic. It may be that the baby was destined to be all those things, or perhaps the mother's blessing made it so, but the cavern walls heard what she said, and the roots that hung above her bore witness.

In response, a little round hand pushed against her belly from the inside, ever so softly, as if to say, "I hear you *Metera*." Her child, whatever strange deformity it had, listened and understood.

23

4

Kronus Returns

Filled with the peace of Grandmother Gaia, Philyra became more confident, daring even to go to her pool again. In the water she swam and drank and splashed with To-nero as she had before. Sometimes, but not as often, a startling sound would remind her of the horse, and shivers would run through her body, but those times were becoming fewer and farther between.

As her sense of safety increased, Philyra strayed from her pool to gather the wild greens that grew on the hills, especially the young, tender dandelion leaves and flowers. They were her favorite, but she also liked mallow and amaranth, violets and mint.

She brought back the greens to her cave where she nibbled on them throughout the day. Much like a grazing animal, Philyra had subsisted on water and wild lettuces for as long as she could remember, but something strange came over her with this pregnancy. She had an unnatural craving for meat. She had never eaten it. She had no desire or need, and the idea of killing an innocent creature that she was meant to protect, filled her with disgust and sadness. Yet as she sat near her pool watching a fat bird run through the brush, a foreign thought surprised her – an impulse to catch the bird and eat it.

Then again later, while swimming in her pool, another impulse took hold of her, and she reached out to grab an unsuspecting fish. She threw it on the grass and watched as it thrashed about gasping for air. "I'm sorry little fish," she whispered, but her need for meat was stronger than her desire to protect the cold-water animal.

When the fish finally lay still and she was sure that it was dead, she picked it up by its tail and carried it over to the cave. There she poked and prodded and finally took a bite. Unfamiliar with which parts of the fish she should eat or what to look out for, bones got stuck in her throat, and, when she bit into the intestines, a nasty taste filled her mouth. Scales stuck between her teeth, and the texture of the flesh was chewy and dense and would not disintegrate in her mouth like leaves or flowers. Finally, she just swallowed the flesh, gagging and regurgitating the awful taste. Yet her body craved this unnatural food. Eventually she learned that some parts were more edible than others.

To catch fish, she soon found herself exploring further and further downstream. She didn't want to eat them all from one pool, and they seemed more abundant the closer she got to the sea. She was a natural fisher, fast and astute and knew their habits and hiding places under the rocks and in the shadows.

Once, she caught two fish and left one in the sun. During the day, the dead fish warmed, cooked slightly, and when she finally ate it later, the flesh was softer and easier to eat. She repeated that experiment and found the sun-baked fish to her liking. She discovered also, that by using a sharp stone, she could cut open the fish's belly and take out the bad tasting intestines and other organs that filled the abdominal cavity. As time went on Philyra learned that she could embellish the flavor of the fish by rubbing it with certain roots and herbs like garlic, onions, oregano, basil, thyme, and mint.

What is this strange craving? She wondered. *I have never been a carnivore. I have never wanted to eat flesh.*

Perhaps it has something to do with the baby? Could he be some type of meat-eating monster? She placed her hand on her abdomen, and the small creature inside again responded by gently pushing his tiny hand against hers. She had no more distain for him since that time in the cavern, and so she resigned herself to the strange cravings. "You must be a carnivore like some of the animals that come to my spring," she told her large belly. "Maybe you need flesh to make you strong."

This new diet made changes in her as well. Sometimes, she found herself laughing, forgetting that the world wasn't really safe. And she felt strong, almost defiant as if she could thwart Kronus herself if ever he should come back. Philyra kicked the water with her feet and rubbed her enlarged belly.

One bright day the scent of honeysuckle flowers floated on the breeze. She stiffened, associating the scent with Rhea, Kronus' wife. Philyra didn't know what to do. She stood up quickly in an attempt to retreat into her cave, but when she looked up, a man stood between her and the cave opening.

The man was holding a bouquet of honeysuckle flowers, and he smiled.

"Such a sweet fragrance," he said, stepping toward her with the flowers held out. "They are for you."

"Who are you?" she asked timidly.

"Don't you remember me?" he answered with a horse-like whinny.

Philyra caught her breath and whispered, "Kronus."

"King of the Heavens and Earth. Of course you don't recognize me like this, but I wanted to see how my little lover was doing. Growing I see."

Philyra began to shiver, but Kronus kept talking.

"Thanks to my unnerving mother Gaia, everyone now knows that you are carrying my child. No secrets around here. Rhea is terribly jealous. But you were just too beautiful to resist."

Philyra's teeth chattered, and she wanted to run, but when she turned away, looking for another escape route, he appeared there too.

"Leave me alone," she said, picking up a big stick to hit him with if he got too close.

"You have no reason to fear," he said, laughing and taking the stick from her hand. "You are not enticing to me in your present state. And you must remember, I chose you Philyra. You are blessed."

As he spoke, an unusual audacity came over Philyra. She didn't grasp the part about being blessed. Being ravaged and torn apart even by a god was not a blessing. She spoke boldly.

"I'm glad I'm not enticing to you. I would rather be hideous and scar myself so that you would never look at me again."

"Silly girl," Kronus taunted. "You think that would stop me? I can have whomever I want, whenever I want. You are nothing but an afternoon's play, and if I wanted you again, there is nothing you could do to stop me."

To-nero heard Kronus' voice, and wanting to protect Philyra, even if it was against the most powerful god in the world, he hopped forward. He didn't really know what he was doing, but he wanted to hurt Kronus and make him go away.

A dead branch swung loosely in the fig tree above Kronus' head, and, without thinking, To-nero jumped onto the tree and offset the balance of the huge, hanging branch. It fell onto Kronus' head.

The unsuspecting sky god lost his balance but regained it quickly. He looked at the annoying frog.

"You are making enemies with someone who can utterly destroy you," Kronus growled.

A frog's life meant nothing to the king of Heaven and Earth, whose irritation was turning to anger.

Philyra felt the wrath of Kronus building like a huge storm, and just before lightning burst from the god's fingertips, emotions, that she did not know she possessed, gushed up from inside her and a huge geyser exploded from the spring. There was a loud crash, and To-nero was nowhere to be seen.

"Enough for now," Kronus said looking around for the water naiad who had disappeared as well. Kronus transformed himself back into a larger than human deity. "I am the Lord around here. No one shall question my authority."

The situation made Kronus uneasy.

He glared at the pool, wavering like an illusion until he dissolved into a fine mist.

Philyra held To-nero in her watery hands, angry and relieved. Kronus had tried to kill her dearest friend.

Powerful sounds came up from her gut like an angry torrent, and the spring spewed unusual noises. "I hate you Kronus!" She was not accustomed to such battles of will.

To-nero chirped quietly to console her. "Rrrriit, rrrrriiiiiit, you were very brave, Philyra. Rrrrrittt."

Two ravens flew over the top of the hill and swooped toward the east from where the day began, from where life started anew. "You escaped death," Philyra whispered."

"Rrrriiiittt," To-nero croaked, and he sat next to her on the rock and watched the last golden rays of the sun illuminate the clouds with orange and purple.

Philyra now knew that Kronus could show up at anytime. She had thwarted him, but trouble rippled through her mind. What if Kronus decided to kill her baby, especially now that she wanted it?

That night, as Philyra slept on the mossy bed in her pool, the *oneiroi* sipped from the moving surface of her spring. They were the dream spirits of the unconscious underworld, issued forth from Grandmother Gaia. Like bats, they came by the hundreds, swooping over her head, dropping thoughts, images, and ideas into her sleeping mind.

Philyra saw Kronus vaporizing frogs and eating babies. Then she saw him come and take her unborn child. "Noooo!" she screamed.

She saw Rhea hiding something in a cave. Rhea!

Philyra awoke and urgently lifted her head out of the water. Brilliant stars shone above in the moonless night. *Rhea knows what to do,* she thought. *She knows how to hide babies and keep them safe.*

Philyra whispered into the dark, "Daughter of Gaia, Goddess of the heavens and earth, mother of Zeus and Poseidon, Hera and Demeter, mother of Hestia and Hades, I need you."

Calling the goddess brought calm over Philyra's pool, and the naiad sunk back into the water where she slept until the blue light of morning.

5

Rhea

"Rrriiiit."

Philyra opened her eyes to see a wet fly hanging above her head. Her lips parted, and To-nero dropped the wriggling fly into her mouth.

The little frog saw life in a simple way. He didn't seem to understand that Kronus had tried to kill him. He loved Philyra and only wanted to see her happy. He didn't understand that they were no longer safe.

If Kronus was going to return, it would do no good to hide, so Philyra returned to her spring. To-nero followed.

Why does Kronus want to hurt us, she wondered. *What did I do?*

She needed her ancestral element to overcome the turmoil in her mind. Her pregnant body lunged into the waiting embrace of her spring. She splashed water on her face and sunk underneath the surface.

In the pool her worries dissolved, and she imagined herself like a giant pregnant frog, swimming around to find the right place to lay her eggs. But then reality snuck in, and she realized that there were no frog eggs in her abdomen. Her baby was something much larger.

What kind of creature has a spine that bends at such strange angles? She wondered. *How many feet does it have? How many heads?*

Almost as if in response to her questions, a little foot pushed from inside. It was soft, as if saying, "Don't worry, *Metera.*"

Philyra pressed back, but what she felt was a curving hoof. *It is deformed*, she thought, and sank into the pool with a fearful sob for her future. But again, the water soothed her spirits.

When she saw a grouse scratching in the brush and thought, *I wonder how to eat a bird?*

Strange, she thought, *these cravings,.* The unborn creature seemed so gentle, and yet did he have this carnivorous passion? She looked at the bird and wondered how to bite through feathers. Was a bird like fish on the inside with the intestines and other organs neatly contained in an abdominal cavity?

Philyra was pondering these questions when the scent of honeysuckle drifted through the air. The small hairs on her neck rose in fear. She know new that it could be Kronus or Rhea, and she slipped into her pool, ducking behind the reeds.

A glowing form stepped onto the cold grass, and Rhea stood before the cascading waterfall.

Feeling the goodwill of the goddess, Philyra rose in a bubble of air and blinked at the radiant form.

Star-bedecked long, red curls fell below the beautiful goddess' waist, and Philyra gasped.

Rhea's voice carried on the wind like tinkling bells, "You called me?"

"I don't mean to annoy you," the naiad said, pulling herself awkwardly out of the water.

Disregarding Philyra's words, Rhea looked at the pregnant, naked girl, and said, "You've grown." Then she paused and took a deep breath as she evaluated the sprite's condition.

How could Kronus desire such a ragged little nymph? she wondered.

Leaves and twigs, thorns and feathers stuck out from Philyra's knotted tresses. Her sun-browned body was scratched and smudged with clay. She looked like a strangled weeping willow with a large burl in the middle and a giant nest on her head.

Philyra, on the other hand, admired Rhea's sparking robes and smooth, red-gold ringlets that fell about her face so elegantly.

"You are a mess," Rhea said. "Perhaps I will take care of that later. For now you need marjoram so that your birth will come in due haste."

"Marjoram?" Philyra asked. She was skeptical, but the goddess seemed to know more about these things. "Will it be safe?"

"You eat it all the time," Rhea laughed. "I have used marjoram with each one of my children, and it has caused no harm. Well," Rhea's voice heightened, and a look of rage, mixed with grief, spread to the corners of her eyes, "unless the flavor added pleasure to Kronus' palate as he ate them." The goddess forced a smile and chased her feelings away. She knew Philyra's worries, "It will all be fine, and Kronus won't eat your baby. The prophesy that one of Kronus' children would overthrow him was only for a child born of our union, not yours."

Philyra inhaled, "How much marjoram should I eat?" she asked.

Rhea smiled, "Don't worry. I will get the proper amounts."

In a soft breeze, the goddess disappeared, and Philyra meandered back to the cave where she reclined on her mossy bed.

Because of the baby's pressure on her spine, she had not been able to lie on her back for a long time. Instead, she lay on her side until Rhea returned holding a handful of marjoram.

The goddess' cheeks glowed rosy. She loved the land and took every opportunity to walk the hillsides of her mother's nurturing body, especially when the weather was cool and fresh. It made her feel invigorated and happy.

"For you," Rhea announced, holding the bouquet toward Philyra's nose.

The marjoram scent was strong but comforting.

"We'll make soup," Rhea said, and a big smile spread across her lips showing her white, symmetrical teeth.

"What if the baby is too big?" Philyra questioned the goddess.

"I will help you."

"And you are certain that Kronus won't eat or harm it in any way?"

Rhea shivered. "Trust me, he has nothing to fear from any of *your* children."

Under an overhang, near the mouth of the cave, Rhea dug a fire pit and placed a huge granite stone so that the fire would burn underneath it. Any mortal would have struggled with the weight of such a rock, but Rhea, being a goddess, put the huge slab in place without any trouble. The flat stone would absorb the heat of the fire and make a hot surface where she could cook *psomi,* flat breads made of wild barley, chestnuts and amaranth.

Rhea blew and a tiny, ephemeral flame took hold of the twigs on her new cooking hearth. Soon a healthy blaze burned in the fire ring. The goddess clapped her hands and a clay cooking pot materialized. She set the pot into the side of the fire, filled it with water, and then she herself disappeared.

When the goddess returned, she carried a dead grouse. Philyra recognized it as the one from the brush. "You will need this for fortitude," Rhea told the nymph, and dunked the fat bird into the boiling water. Within a few moments, she lifted it out and began pulling feathers.

With a new batch of water, along with the gutted bird, Rhea added marjoram, wild garlic and onions to the cooking pot.

Long shadows cast across the cave floor as savory, delicious smells filled the air. Philyra watched the goddess glide with the ease of a gentle wind as she went about her work. In fact, her feet did not touch the earth. She left no footprints at all in the dirt.

Rhea hummed a song that echoed in the cave, and, from time to time, she would smile at nothing in particular. Philyra understood that the goddess was volatile, sweet as honey one moment and explosive the next, but the *naiad* promised herself that she would not allow Rhea's rage to hurt her.

She knew, from her mother's explanation, that Rhea's out-lashings came from loss, jealousy, and misplaced resentment. And for those reasons, Philyra pledged to be Rhea's friend, no matter what cruel words the goddess might say. However, Rhea showed no unkindness –none at all.

Eat," the goddess said, as she handed Philyra a bowl of soup. "It will help make the birth come quickly."

Philyra looked into the clay bowl filled with chunky bits of flesh, herbs and roots, and again, out of character, ate it hungrily. Its texture was not unlike that of fish. But the bird was soft, tender from cooking, and she swallowed it, gagging only slightly. Rhea smiled and offered her some flattened bread that she had cooked on the stone.

"Psomi," she said, breaking off a large piece. "When you are done, we will walk, and then you will sleep, for in the morning your labor will begin."

"It will?" Philyra asked in surprise.

"Yes," the goddess answered.

But Philyra didn't want to walk outside, rather in, to that special place that she and To-nero had found. She told Rhea about the cavern and asked, "Do you mind if we walk there?"

Rhea seemed uneasy. "Into the earth? Why don't you want to walk in the open? It will be better for you."

"I feel safer there," Philyra answered.

Like a cloud passing in front of the sun, the goddess' sweetness distorted. "What are your intentions, Philyra? Are you trying to trick me?" She glowed angrily. "I spent years in my mother's belly when my father, Uranus, would not allow us to see the light of day. I know the dark depths of Gaia all too well."

"No, No," Philyra stammered. "I'm not trying to trick you. I just thought that..." Her voice lowered, and she beckoned Rhea to the back of the cave. "Grandmother Gaia's peace is in the cavern. She is so wise and reassuring."

Irrationally, Rhea's face twisted into a strange and beautiful smile, and Philyra wasn't sure if the goddess was going to explode or laugh.

Instead the goddess shook her head and spoke in a strained, deliberate voice, "I don't know why you are doing this, Philyra. Perhaps Kronus put you up to it? Are you helping him? Do you love him after all? She looked at Philyra with piercing eyes, but remembered the nymph's ordeal.

Switching her tone, she whispered. "I apologize. Your heart has pure intentions. I trust you . . .Show me this cavern. I will go."

Still, as Philyra lead her into the obscure tunnel the goddess protested.

"Darkness? I think not." Quickly Rhea returned to the fire and scooped embers into her clamshell. She held the shell with the fabric of her dress, a barrier between the intense heat and her delicate, yet powerful hands.

Light illuminated the cavern, worn smooth by the ancient river. Philyra slowed her pace so that she could look at the colors on the walls. They had been invisible before in the dark, but now were alive with patches of red, orange, yellow and even green.

"Beautiful," Philyra whispered.

Again in the cavern Philyra felt that overwhelming sense of peace. The nagging fears at the back of her mind about the coming birth and the disfigurement of her child – all melted.

In the flickering light of Rhea's embers, the walls seemed friendly and inviting. Philyra touched the rock. "*Yiayia,*" she whispered, "Grandmother."

Rhea bowed reverently and put her hands together in honor. "*Metera,* Mother." The goddess moved in a graceful dance and knelt onto the silty floor. Then she placed her forehead on the ground.

Silently the goddess communicated with her mother, talking inaudibly and listening. At one point she tipped her head as if to hear a whisper. Then a smile lifted the corners of her lips, and she laughed. "Of course. . .the *hekatonkheires*, my brothers with one hundred arms. They will end the war once and for all. Thank you, *Metera.* Thank you Mother."

Rhea rose from the ground and lowered her head to Philyra. "Truly, you have helped me and, indirectly, the world.

Philyra blinked in the muted light.

"You have, of course," Rhea said, "heard how I hid Zeus in Ida's cave."

Philyra nodded affirmatively.

"By keeping Zeus away from Kronus' gullet, I committed treason," Rhea confided. "And now, Gaia has told me how the war can be ended: with the help of the hundred-handed *hekatonkheires,* the giants with fifty heads, and our other brothers, the one-eyed *cyclopes.*"

Rhea stopped suddenly, realizing that she may have said too much.

"Kronus must never hear of this," she said. "Do you understand? Or all could be lost. Promise me that none of this will ever pass your lips."

Perhaps Rhea should not have shared her secret with the young naiad, but there in the sanctuary and presence of Grandmother Gaia, she had a valid knowledge that Philyra would keep her word, but a secret has a smell, especially to gods, and knowing about the *hekatonkheires* put Philyra in grave danger.

Too late, Rhea understood this and regretted the future, but the damage was already done.

"Everyone has a purpose," she said, repeating Gaia's words. "Even the hideous *hekatonkheires* and *cyclopes.* They," she told Philyra, "will dethrone Kronus. They will win the war. In the beginning when Kronus avenged our unjust imprisonment, castrating Uranus and banishing him to the nighttime sky, he did not liberate us all from the darkness. He was afraid of our giant brothers with the hundred arms and those with only one eye. They were so much bigger, and so much stronger. He left *them* underground, locked in the realms below Gaia, in Tartarus. There Campe the monster keeps guard. Gaia just told me that they are the key to Zeus' victory. They will dethrone Kronus."

Philyra gave a delighted clap, "What can I do?"

The goddess smiled at the naiad's naivety, but reassured the innocent girl that just bringing her to this place was help enough. "Soon," she added, "thanks to Gaia, the war will be over."

Philyra was now a co-conspirator in the plot to overthrow Kronus. She knew the secret and also that it was treason, but she had no remorse. She had lived in happiness near her spring until that fateful day when Kronus left her in a puddle of her own watery blood. He did not care about life or any suffering that he caused.

Here, in the cavern, below the light of day, Philyra held out her hands to Rhea and said, "I promise that no word of this shall ever pass through my lips."

Rhea gave her ready smile, but emotions distorted the beauty of her knowing.

"I am afraid, Philyra, that Kronus may have suspected me – that he was searching the earth for a possible child. Do you understand? I am confessing to you that it is because of my actions that Kronus came here on that unfortunate day. You must forgive me if saving my son brought Kronus' unwanted attentions upon you."

Philyra could hardly grasp what Rhea was saying, yet spontaneous tears welled in her eyes as her emotions flooded with understanding.

Before the horse came to her meadow, she had never even seen Rhea, and yet the events of their lives merged together, so that Philyra now carried the ripening fruit of Rhea's husband.

The young naiad trembled as she squeezed the goddess' hand and smiled through wet eyes. She was a gentle nature spirit.

"This is a heavy burden," the goddess whispered, "and just as you are about to give birth. I will stay and help in any way I can. I owe it to you."

In the flickering light, the two women held hands, and the baby, warm in his mother's womb, snuggled down in contentment.

Though Philyra said nothing, Rhea sensed the slight pain in the naiad's lower back.

"We must return to the cave," she said, helping Philyra stand.

To-nero croaked, "Rrriiiiiit," and began leading the upward journey.

When they emerged from the tunnel – the naked *naiad* with wild hair, and the resplendent goddess – they were greeted by Philyra's mother Tethys, who instinctively grabbed her daughter from Rhea's grip.

The goddesses were sisters, daughters of Gaia and Uranus, two of the twelve titans.

Accusations flew from Tethys' lips, and her eyes flashed with mistrust. "How dare you torture my poor daughter. She has suffered enough at the hands and hooves of your husband. How dare you return here to slander and double the harm already inflicted!"

Caught in the moment, Rhea was surprised and speechless, but Philyra tore away to shelter Rhea from the onslaught of harsh-winded words.

"No harm was done here today, *Metera,*" she told her mother. "Rhea has helped me and been only kind."

"Then why are you so pale? Why are you out of breath? What magical potions did you put into this poisonous soup?" And she kicked over the cooking pot so that it spilled like a wave over the dirt floor. A hurricane formed on Tethys' brow and sprayed Rhea with spit.

The Queen goddess, newly emerged from the safety of Gaia's cave, wiped the spittle from her face.

"She is helping me, *Metera*," Philyra interjected.

"She has tricked you, Philyra," Tethys seethed. "Rhea has deceived you and poisoned you. Get away from her," and she pulled her swollen daughter away from her beautiful sister.

"Go Rhea," Tethys demanded, "and leave my daughter alone."

"You don't understand," Philyra shouted again.

Rhea recomposed herself and stood tall, shining like the goddess she was. She took a deep breath and whispered calmly, "Philyra is my friend, Tethys, and no harm was done before you injured the equanimity. You will be sorry for your words when you know the truth."

The cave hummed with the sound of a thousand angry bees, and Rhea was gone.

6

The Birth

Believing that the soup had been poisoned and unable to comprehend that Rhea pledged friendship to Philyra, Tethys had to find an antidote. Philyra was no help to her mother in this regard. The naiad wouldn't even explain why Rhea had come in the first place.

With her mother's accusations and misunderstandings Philyra felt anxious and worried. In her heart she knew that Rhea had been honest, but perhaps Tethys knew things that she did not, and doubt began forming in her mind.

"Rrrriiiiiit," To-nero chirped.

"You are right," Philyra assured the frog, then faced her mother.

"*Metera,* Rhea told me that the baby would come in the morning. I think that it may be true."

Tethys quickly looked Philyra up and down with her astute knowledge of childbirth, and then nodded her head affirmatively. "I may have been wrong," she told Philyra. "In which case, you will need to rest while you can."

But Philyra could not rest or sleep, and she crept outside into the dark evening. There in the cold night air, she looked up to see the winter stars. Her eyes rested on the brightest.

"Sirius," she whispered to the glowing star that stood out amid all the others. "In the morning my baby will be born. Please, watch over him."

The well-being of her baby was now of utmost concern. Somehow, despite Rhea's reassurance, she expected that Kronus would, at least, try to hurt him. In her worry, she invoked everyone's protection: all of the water and river spirits -- *oceanids* and *nereids*, sprites of fresh water and sea, her sisters, the cloud *nephelai*, as well as the bat-like dream spirits, the *oneiroi*; tree *dryads*; breeze *aurai;* and meadow *leimonides;* all the gods and goddesses, especially Grandmother Gaia, *Yiayia*. They would be her baby's family.

"Please," she asked, "Yiayia, may you and all your children and grandchildren, including the moon and the sun and the stars, bestow your blessings upon my baby."

As Philyra returned to the cave, she noticed a small sprig of marjoram dropped on the ground. Crouching low, she picked up the herb. The strong-scented leaves were familiar and edible -- something she ate often with her other wild greens.

"This is not poisonous," she whispered and rubbed her belly. A small hoof pushed softly against her hand.

As if talking to an old friend, she told her abdomen, "You will be fine. Whether or not you are glad of it, you are Kronus' son, just like Zeus. I hope that you will never have to be part of this war and that our family will teach you everything you need to know."

A few bat-like *oneiroi* swooped past her head as she looked once more at Sirius before returning to the cave. Once inside she handed the herb to her mother Tethys.

"This is marjoram *Metera*, not poison."

Tethys sniffed the herb and nodded, and Philyra went to her moss-covered mound where the high-pitched, comforting tones of the *oneiroi* lulled her to sleep.

A strong cramp awoke Philyra from her soft, green bed, and she found herself face to face with a girl she had never

44

seen before. The rich scent of pomegranate fruit emanated from the strange girl.

"My name is Hera," she said, smiling timidly.

"Philyra," the naiad answered with a reciprocal smile. Another cramp diverted her attention, and Hera watched with curiosity.

"It's beginning," the girl said. "Your mother says that water spirits are easy to birth, they just gush out when they are ready. Perhaps it will be so with you."

Philyra hoped that to be true and thought excitedly about the baby that she would soon be holding. She didn't care now that it might be deformed. Even if it did appear like some kind of monster, she knew, without a doubt, that she would love this child no matter what it looked like.

Another cramp followed, and Hera alerted Tethys while Philyra instinctively crawled toward her element, the pool. Tethys, the goddess of sea winds and tides, joined her in the water.

"Think of it as a wave Philyra, you, the spring nymph of Mount Pelion. You understand waves. Move with them, and soon it will be over."

Philyra floated in the water, the pain mounting, passing and receding, similar to waves. It was easy to feel them as such, but as they progressed, she found herself battling them and ducking under the water, trying to escape.

"Meet the wave," Tethys reminded her. The goddess' voice droned through the water as Philyra crouched under a rock among timid fish. The waves came on with more intensity and She came to the surface to listen to her mother's voice, calm and knowing.

In the middle of one contraction Philyra looked at her mother and growled, "These are rough waves." Unfortunately, they got worse.

Wanting to learn the art of midwifery, Hera crawled into the water with Tethys and Philyra.

Tethys supported Philyra's back with one hand while massaging her protruding abdomen with the other. "Here," she told Hera, "you can you feel the head or at least one of them." Then the muscles tightened in Philyra's belly and the contours of the child disappeared. "That is the womb squeezing around the baby to push it out," Tethys said wisely.

As for Philyra, the clenching contractions were becoming less like waves and more like jagged mountains. There was nowhere to escape, not even under the water. The birds were silent, and Hera's eyes were big with worry. Tethys' brow furrowed.

"This is not a water child," the goddess sighed as Philyra's high-pitched screech seared through the air. None of Tethys' children had ever been so difficult to birth, and she felt uncertain how to proceed.

In desperation, Philyra called out, "To-nero!"

But Tethys said, "Stop screaming, and use your strength to push."

Unable to get away from the pain, Philyra obeyed, and turned all her energy into bearing down. Only for brief moments between contractions could she close her eyes and rest for a few breaths before the next one twisted her body in its attempt to expel the baby.

To-nero swam under Philyra's arm and climbed onto her head while Hera ducked underwater to see the dark, round head starting to show between Philyra's legs.

Two pushes brought the baby's head and upper body out, but then all progress stopped.

"Don't push," Tethys told Philyra, realizing that something much larger than the head and torso was coming next.

Tethys looked at Hera. They had planned for this unfortunate event, and the young goddess retrieved a small bowl and handed it to her mentor. It was an unguent of fish tallow, ground seaweeds, and many wild herbs including mallow, purple loosestrife, quince, marshmallow and sage, all simmered down and strained so that it made a thick healing mass intended to help Philyra stretch and her baby come out.

Philyra pulled herself partially out of the water, and held onto a grey rock while she bore down with every bit of effort she could muster. It was not enough.

Tethys' brow creased, and she wrapped her hands around the baby's slippery chest and under its arms. It looked up and met her gaze. The baby was stuck, halfway in and halfway out.

Philyra, exhausted and wanting nothing more than to give up, gave her last bit of strength while Tethys pulled with the power of a goddess.

A loud snap seared the air as the baby slipped out. Philyra gulped a breath of air and sunk under the water.

The naiad groaned in deep agony as Tethys pulled her up. Then she cried, but not from joy, as the newborn creature was laid across her sunken belly. Through watery eyes, Philyra saw that the baby was indeed deformed with a body that was half horse and half human.

Hera looked at the horse's lower abdomen and said, "It is a boy."

The little creature stared at his mother, taking no notice as Tethys wrapped a warm, sea otter blanket over his damp body. Half of him was covered with skin while the other half shimmered with black fur.

"This is your son," Tethys whispered as she put him near Philyra's breast. He instinctively rooted for the nipple and began suckling.

To ease her pain, Tethys gave her daughter a piece of dark, opium latex to chew. Bitter and sticky, the narcotic medicine would soften the deep ache that she could not otherwise control, and the baby would get the effects through her milk.

Every movement Philyra made hurt, so she could do nothing but let the poppy medicine do its work while she lay next to her baby inside the cave.

When Philyra awoke from her induced nap, Tethys was holding the new baby. His horse legs dangled below while his upper body towered above his grandmother's head.

"Look at him Philyra," the proud grandmother said. She didn't care that his body was strange. Three of Tethys' own brothers were born with fifty heads. In comparison, this baby was not so unusual. "Here," she said, giving him back to Philyra.

As the horse-baby hungrily nursed, he looked at his mother's face. His dark eyes stared at hers. This was her child, deformed as he was, and Philyra loved him.

"You were both hurt," Tethys told Philyra. "Normally horses stand when they are born, but his front horse shoulder is not right. Don't worry though, you will both mend."

"Your child has our blessings and our love," another voice came from the mouth of the cave. Philyra looked up and saw Rhea standing with Hera. Mother and daughter, they looked very much alike. Rhea brought a bowl to Philyra. "Drink this," she said. "It will help you heal and return your strength."

"What is it?" Philyra asked.

"Algae and kelp broth."

Philyra looked questioningly at her mother. There seemed to be peace between the two goddesses.

"It is all right," Tethys said with a knowing smile, "Rhea has told me everything. She sincerely wanted to help you, and I apologize for my rash behavior. We are sisters after all. We must stand by one another."

The naiad smiled and turned her attention to her new baby. She touched his face and ran her fingers down his back to the angle in his spine where his skin became fur. Then she gently touched his horse shoulder where it was broken.

"We are both hurt, Little One," she whispered. "But we have goddesses to wait upon us." Again she looked at his body, unlike any other child or nymph she had yet seen, but to her he was not deformed. She looked into his face and met his eyes, so present and beautiful. She felt a powerful force flowing through him. She had sensed it in the cavern, a feeling that made her at ease and brought peace to her spring.

7

Healing with the Goddesses

Covered in otter furs, Philyra and her unusual baby lay inside the cave near the fire. The glowing warmth added a softness to Philyra's already foggy mind. When the opium wore off, the ache in her hip peaked and made movement near impossible without agony.

In nature, broken hips are a death sentence, but Philyra was immortal. She had to endure the profound ache whether it healed or not. However, the naiad was fortunate. There were three goddesses determined to ensure her healing and the welfare of her baby. Among them she felt safe, and she nestled under the otter furs, where the skin of her new baby rested against her bare chest. Another dose of opium gum soothed the pain.

Her new baby had not only one, but two torsos, one with the smooth skin of a man-child, and the other with the fur of a horse. He had two arms, ten fingers, four legs, four hooves, one set of genitals and a tail. Gratefully she thought, *he has only one head.*

His deformity was certain, but would it inhibit his ability to walk? Would the unusual proportions disrupt his equilibrium? Would he think like a man or a beast? Already Philyra's hunger for fish disappeared, and she knew that it had been the baby's craving and not her own.

I wonder, Philyra thought, *will he terrorize my spring and the animals that come to drink?* Questions hovered in her mind, but only the unfolding of time could answer them. Here and now, it was hard to imagine this baby, who watched her so adoringly, to be a carnivorous animal.

At first glance, his loving eyes appeared brown, but on closer observation, copper and blue, green, black and grey could be seen in the unusual patterns of his iris. His eyes reflected the colors of both the earth and the sky. Philyra gazed at him.

"Who are you?" she asked her horse-baby.

In response, he lifted his head. However, he made no sound. In fact, from the moment he came into the world he made no noise. He only watched and observed.

When Philyra tried to sit up to eat her mother's seaweed stew, the pain in her hip made her gasp, and the baby's tail switched sympathetically.

Philyra chewed black opium gum to ease her own discomfort and vicariously administered the pain-killing opium to her baby via the milk, which eased the pain in his broken shoulder as well.

Attentive nurses, Tethys, Hera and Rhea tucked soft otter skins under the mother and child and took turns at cleaning up excrement and urine. They washed the furs, rubbing them together at intervals as they dried so that they would become soft again.

From time to time, they carried Philyra and the baby outside, so they could breathe the fresh scents of spring and let their bedding air out. Often, mother and son would lie side by side in the meadow. And, perhaps coincidentally, the little horse-baby would gently rest his warm hand over his mother's broken hip.

"He seems to know where it hurts," Philyra told To-nero, "and his hands radiate a warmth that eases my discomfort. I wonder what name I should give him?

It was a cold, early spring day, warmer in the golden rays next to the pool. Philyra picked up one of the rare, blue rocks for her dark-furred baby who lay peacefully in the sun.

An unusual sound caught Philyra's attention, and she tilted her head slightly to hear what she thought was Tonero. Instead something new came from the pool. Water was part of her body, her thoughts and emotions, and she knew every sound that her spring made, but this new melody, bubbled up from the bottom and crackled the surface of the water with a "khei, khei."

Philyra observed, wondering what kind of creature was about break the surface, but instead another sound erupted, "iirrr, iirrr."

She tilted her head in the other direction to listen more attentively, and it changed yet again. "Ooonnn ooonnn." She began to realize that it was one of those moments when Grandmother Gaia was speaking, and she tried to make sense of the bubbles.

Hera came out of the cave, and took note of her water cousin's smooth hair. It had taken her hours to disentangle the ratty mess, and the sad thing was that Philyra could care less. Hera sighed, yet she felt proud of the looped braids and the long strands that curled into ringlets. *I wish that she had let me put shells in her hair.* But Philyra preferred feathers and dried, green moss, and she had no desire to wear clothes.

Hera looked down at her own drooping dress. Living in the world sullied her raiment, but Tethys, the wise sea woman whispered, "Remember who you are. The draping of a physical life obscures the light of your divinity, but they cannot take it away." "Shine, Goddess. Let your divine light shine."

Hera smiled, even now, as she cleaned her cousin's bedding and repeated her Aunt Tethys' words, "Shine, Goddess, Shine."

Philyra smelled the scent of pomegranates and knew that Hera was behind her. "Look," she said and pointed to the bubbles.

The pool was continuing to make the unusual sounds.

"I was just thinking about what name to call the baby, and the pool said,'Khei khei iirr iirr oonn oonn,'" Philyra imitated. "Khei khei irrirr onnonn. Khei irr onn. I wonder what it means?"

Hera sat down next to her cousin and listened to the water.

"Khe-ir-on. . . khe-ir-on. . . khe-ir-on. The sounds played in Hera's mouth, but when the syllables came together, and she said the name, "Kheiron," the baby stirred and looked at her. "Is that your name?" she asked him.

Both Philyra and Hera watched as she repeated the name. "Kheiron." The horse baby looked at her in anticipation, as if waiting for her to tell him something important.

"I think that is his name," Hera said staring at the horse-baby.

"Kheiron," Philyra repeated, and the unusual child looked at his mother.

"You know," Hera said, "kheiro means hand. Perhaps there is something special about his hands." They both looked at the small human hands on the upper part of the baby's body.

Philyra shrugged her shoulders, "Undoubtedly," she told her child, "your name is Kheiron – Kheiron with the warm, healing hands."

He stared at her with comprehension and nodded his head, as if confirming this discovery. Then, contentedly he rested his head in the grass to absorb more warmth from the sun.

Dry leaves began to stir, and a honeysuckle breeze blew gently against their faces. All turned toward the shafts of light that streamed through the budding fig tree. Rhea emerged.

"I have something to tell you," she announced in her high, bell-like voice. "The message from Grandmother Gaia has reached Zeus, and we should expect more tremors as the hundred-handed hekatonkheries and one-eyed cyclopes are released from their underground prison in Tartarus."

Indeed, no sooner had she spoken than the whole world began to shake. Rocks fell from the precipice above the cave. One of them smacked the ground close to Kheiron. A head appeared in the sky, followed by forty-nine more. It was one of the monsters with fifty heads. It had one-hundred arms, and each of its hundred hands held a boulder that it launched toward Kronus in the sky. No sooner than one was released, then it grabbed another. No wonder Kronus feared these creatures. One alone was massive, blocking out the sun like a huge storm and invoking terror.

Kheiron stared at the giant beast, who, feeling his small gaze, turned one of his fifty heads toward the horse boy. The intensity in the giant's eyes made Kheiron cry, and that sound brought the attention of all the other forty nine heads. The creature starred at the horse child lying near the spring on Mount Pelion and tried to discern if the horse-baby was a friend or a foe.

However, Hera raised her majestic voice to a roar that stirred up winds and disturbed birds in their flight. "Don't frighten the baby!" Her voice seared through the sky, "Look, you have made him cry!"

She startled one of the most terrifying warriors ever to walk the earth. The hekatonkheire shivered, as the young goddess demanded "Stay away from here." Then she scooped Kheiron up in her arms and held him close for reassurance.

Tethys responded in like manner, moving like a wave across the soil and lifting Philyra to the safety of the open meadow just before the retaliation from Kronus sent another surge of unsettled earth crashing near the pool.

"He cried," Philyra said, reaching out for Kheiron. "That was his first cry," and she wiped the tears from his face as he suckled her breast for comfort.

The hekatonkheire, now aware of the goddesses and their keep, thundered away. He meant no harm to anyone but the god of heaven and earth, Kronus. He must have informed his two other brothers about the goddesses and the horse-child, because afterward, all three of the giants made sure to keep a respectful distance as well as maintain a circle of safety around Mount Pelion.

Everyone hoped that the hekatonkheires would quickly put an end to the war, but intermittent earthquakes and flashing, torrential storms indicated that their hopes had not yet been fulfilled. Through it all, Philyra kept Kheiron close to her as they slept, ate and healed. She often worried that when left to her own devices, unprotected and alone, that Kronus would return to snatch her boy. This fear froze the water in her veins until the warm, reassuring hand of her half human child melted any anxiety.

Her baby had an unusual power. One could say that it was coincidence, or that a child with two hearts would tend to be particularly warm. But when she grimaced, he would look at her face and understand, instinctively placing one of his hands over the exact location where the shards of bone grated one against another. His warm hands made all

Philyra's hurts go away. Yet his own horse shoulder still caused him discomfort.

The other goddesses could have healed both of them in a moment. But they stayed as guardians, nurses and cooks for the naiad and her child. They provided a safe and nurturing environment in which the baby and mother could discover their own skills and cure their own wounds. They had reasons for the actions they took, as well as for the things they left undone.

Kheiron still nursed at his mother's breast, but one day after a short nap in the safety of the cave he woke up and, seeing shafts of light, wanted to be outside. His horse shoulder was not entirely mended, but determination made him stand and make his way toward the mud and grass. Whatever healing was needed occurred instantaneously. His bones knitted into wholeness, and the stiffness in his muscles melted into strength.

Philyra caught sight of her baby and clapped her hands. Kheiron wobbled slightly, but stood, and then walked toward the meadow. Without even thinking about it, he was done with the broken shoulder.

"Look," Philyra called.

The goddesses delighted in his accomplishment and stood by as Kheiron took his first steps, shakily walking on all fours like a young colt should, and then he ran.

"Well, if he can do it..." Philyra said, encouraged by her son's achievement. She attempted a few steps, and, like her son, released her trauma and walked. Soon, mother and son ran in the meadow side by side.

It was their first move toward independence, and Philyra knew that before long she would have to rely on herself.

She went for longer walks, taking hand-woven baskets that the goddesses had made from the branches and reeds that grew near her spring. She gathered, not only the rich and varied fresh *ta horta* greens, but she also learned new plants to eat from Rhea: salsify and beets, rock samphire and tassel hyacinth bulbs, asphodel and wild carrot roots, acorns and chestnuts.

The goddesses gradually performed fewer and fewer tasks, and as the summer months progressed Rhea showed Philyra a small stand of young, wild okra, *bamyes*.

"These make you strong," Rhea told her, and popped one into Philyra's mouth. It wasn't bad, but later, the goddess made some into a slimy stew. "Eat it," Rhea demanded when Philyra wrinkled her nose, "It's good for you." Then she made another dish like it the following day. Soon Philyra found herself actually enjoying the slimy *bamyes* and cooking them for herself.

Kheiron said his first words: "Eat it." He liked the force behind Rhea's demand and the shudder it elicited from his mother. "Eat it," he repeated. Philyra was uncertain whether to scold him for talking to her in that tone or to praise him for his first words.

Kheiron waited for her reaction, which usually came as an explosion of laughter.

"Let's eat it together," she said.

Kheiron never turned his nose up at any food. As he explored and grazed, he ate anything and everything that was edible, uncannily he knew what was poisonous and instinctively avoided it.

He ate *bamyes* raw or cooked, had fun repeating his Auntie's words: "Hungry?" "Dinner," "*Bamyes*," "Eat it," everything to do with food. It may have been because he had two stomachs, two gall bladders and two livers, but his appetite outdid them all.

Tethys, the sea goddess, made frequent trips to her salty home, coming back with treats from the ocean: octopus and cod, *ahyini* (sea urchins) and sardines. These she turned into a stew that she called "*kakavya*" (fish soup). Kheiron curiously sniffed the fish and then, not sensing anything evil, devoured them hungrily.

"Good food makes the weak, strong, and the strong, stronger," his Auntie Rhea told him, and he proved it by running circles in the meadow. He carried heavy loads of firewood, wild berries, roots, leaves, nuts and grains over his back or on his shoulders. Food and snuggling were his favorite things, but he had other interests as well.

Sometimes he stood perfectly still, watching birds and other timid animals that came to the spring to drink. Once he heard To-nero croaking loudly near the pool and came to see what was going on. Fat little fish came to the surface like bubbles. Philyra joined him to see what he watched, and she smiled. There were tadpoles in the pool. "Those are To-nero's children," she told him happily.

"Rrrriittt," Kheiron croaked, imitating To-nero.

Philyra no longer ate poppy gum. It made her mind groggy, and she wanted a clear head so she could keep alert and make sure her baby was safe.

Her overwhelming urge to eat flesh had passed, but the little horse boy's instincts were beginning to show. She would watch him stand still as a tree and then, all of a sudden, dash out to corner a small rabbit. He would look at the creature hungrily but not harm it. He was curious and, through his observations, began learning the habits of the visitors – what they ate and where they lived.

One day, he returned from the lower meadow holding a dead grouse in his hands. It was then that Philyra knew his true appetite was taking over.

"We will cook it," she told him and filled the cooking pot with water to boil. First he would have to learn to pluck the feathers and clean it as Rhea had taught her. He was so young, yet, already so capable of taking care of himself.

59

8

The Oven

One warm summer night, after a meal of boiled chestnuts and squid stew, the goddesses lay in the meadow under a darkening sky. The music of a hundred frogs filled the air as Philyra's spring gurgled and splashed over contented rocks. Above them, stars twinkled amid the deepest blue.

Crickets began to chirp, and Hera whispered with the gentleness of a summer breeze, "It's a magical night."

"They know," Rhea said listening to their high trill, "that the barley is nearly ripe."

They all understood that she meant days of hard work ahead. But there was another subject they all avoided. Tethys breached the silence.

"Soon our paths shall separate."

No one said anything. Their time together had become precious, and no one wanted it to end.

"Let us do something special," she suggested, "something that will last for a long time. The barley grains will be yellow within a month. Let us build an oven."

The next day, Rhea led them into the gorge where the earth was soft with sticky clay. They dug with fingers and hands, muddying their dresses and skin, until Tethys decided to have some fun and threw a handful of the reddish mud at her sister.

At first, Rhea became angry, her shimmering complexion splattered with clay. However, she surrendered to the moment and scooped up a large handful of the wet mud, which she flung back at Tethys.

Clay flew in all directions and no one was spared.

"You look like you have some strange rash," Rhea yelled at Tethys.

The sea goddess snorted, "Well, you appear to have been rolling in cow dung."

Each developed spots and smears, gloppy hair, and fits of laughter before toting the heavy piles of wet clay back to the meadow.

There, inside the cave, they built the oven where over many years, it would become an integral part of many hearty meals as well as provide warmth during cold winters.

The heavy lifting and hard work to create the oven was so human, but to the goddesses, the toil was enchanting.

A platform was created with rocks and mortared together with clay. They used willow branches which they covered with a thick layer of mixed clay, sand and pebbles. The oven took shape with a dome and a chimney that rose through a natural hole in the ceiling. In their eyes, the oven was like a womb where the fire could burn and where bread could be baked and eventually birthed.

When their work was done, they transported an ember from the cooking fire and set twigs and sticks ablaze inside the dark chamber. A large stone cover was placed over the opening. It burned for several hours and glowed with heat. When the stone was removed, hot embers lay on the oven floor, and the willow framework had burned away. The oven was complete, ready for generations of baking.

Tethys scraped out the ashes and left some of the hot embers toward the back. Then she pushed a fermented dough onto the oven floor. It was the maiden bake, and they gathered around to drink in the wafting aromas.

They all sat silently on the cool floor of the cave. Kheiron felt the uneasiness and rested his head on his mother's lap for comfort.

When the *psomi* was done, Rhea pulled it out with a long flattened stick and broke it into hot steaming pieces. They ate quietly. It was their last meal together. Tethys passed a clay cup of mint-sweetened water saying, "You are a woman now, for you have birthed your first *psomi*." She was talking to the oven, but she winked at Philyra, meaning her as well.

When Kheiron ate the last bite of bread, he spoke a short sentence like a two year old, "*Yia sas*, goodbye." Each of the goddesses smiled at him in their own way, and then, as they had always come and gone, they disappeared in a honeysuckle breeze, a sea mist and a vapor of pomegranate dew.

9

Disappeared

"We are alone now, you and I," Philyra said, taking her son's hand and walking toward the meadow where they laid in the grass and watched the cloud *nephelai* pass overhead. It was a place of comfort outside of her pool.

"We will be all right," Philyra reassured Kheiron. "We can take care of ourselves."

Life with his mother was very different from life surrounded by attentive goddesses. Philyra loved and cared for Kheiron, but she spent a lot of time in her element talking to the frog To-nero and now his hoard of children. Kheiron tried to get her attention by calling, "*Metera*," but her eyes were partially submerged in another watery world, and Kheiron had to entertain himself, tasting plants and watching the wildlife. Occasionally, he who would become one of the greatest hunters of Aegea caught a bird or rabbit that came too close to his quiet hands, but he never tortured an animal. When he was hungry, he twisted its head quickly, snapping the vertebrae so that death was swift and painless. If an animal suffered, he felt its pain profoundly. Food was food, but unnecessary suffering could be prevented. Wounded creatures that he had no intentions of eating would, instead, receive his primitive doctoring – calendula poultices or various herbs to eat.

At night Philyra came out of her pool and rested under the stars with her son. He no longer needed the nourishment of her breast but still nursed for short periods of time just for comfort. They laid side by side in the meadow while she told him stories about the animals that came to her pool – their silly antics and absurd happenings that she had seen in her life as a naiad. And then she pointed to the stars.

"Look," she said, "they are alive, each an immortal being of light with a power of its own." She showed him the star in the north that never seemed to move, and then she pointed out constellations that followed one another from east to west.

"See that bright one," she said, pointing her finger at a large star. "It moves at a pace all its own, moving from one group of stars to the next. It is a planet and others like it are the children and grandchildren of Chaos."

"Who is Chaos?" Kheiron asked.

"Chaos is the essence of all things, the beginning. She gave birth to the first born, Gaia, Uranus and Protogonus."

"Who is Protogonus?" Kheiron asked.

"The urge for life," she answered. "It was his influence that came over Kronus when he took me for his pleasure."

"Pleasure?" Kheiron asked.

Philyra shook her head. "There was no pleasure for me." Silence followed for a moment. She would never forgive Kronus, but she loved Kheiron, the product of the great god's assault.

"Protogonus, is lust," she whispered. "Perhaps he is the true father of all living creatures."

Philyra pointed to a very bright star on the eastern horizon, "His name is Sirius, the dog star. He is part of that constellation that looks like a wolf. When he first reappears in the nighttime sky after the hot summer, the rainy season will soon begin. Watch for him. When the rains are meager and food seems scarce, Sirius' watery grace is the key to abundance and good harvests."

"Who told you that, *Metera*?" Kheiron asked.

"Gaia," she answered patting the earth.

66

"There are messages in the stars," she told Kheiron, "and if you watch them carefully, they will tell you things not spoken of."

Her stories piqued Kheiron's curiosity, and he watched the sky trying to understand something in the unusual patterns. He stayed awake late into the night, certain that he might miss a shooting star or some other important omen.

Even though Philyra spent a lot of time in the water, she also enjoyed doing things with her son. In fact, he was as much a comfort to her as she was to him. One of their favorite pastimes was singing gurgling, hissing water songs that Kheiron learned to emulate. Truthfully, he imitated many songs of the forest and spring, so much so, that woodland creatures were deceived by his calls. Squirrels stared at him strangely, baffled by the odd shaped, half-naked animal who spoke their language.

Philyra would have accompanied Kheiron more often, but she was confident in his abilities to care for himself. And as he foraged on his own, he often gathered more than enough food for the both of them. Already he was a marvelous provider and collected not just for himself. He wove his own baskets from willow and cattails that he strapped over his back. And when he was out, he filled them with herbs and *ta horta* (wild greens), grapes, pears, plums and figs that they dried into sweet, leathery snacks and shared with the wild animals.

The goddesses had taught Philyra and Kheiron how to make pots with moist clay and how to bake them in the oven to make them hard and sturdy. They used the pots the goddesses left behind and made more for storing dried foods. Kheiron cooked his meat over the flat cooking stone, and Philyra ate wild plants as she had before.

"Unusual," she thought, "that a grass-eating horse craves flesh." But she loved Kheiron anyway.

*****

Kheiron, with the mind of a seven year old, met another season of falling leaves with his mother and a myriad of frogs. Cool weather, as heralded by the bright star, Sirius, brought the rains, and Philyra sat with Kheiron husking chestnuts and storing away a winter's supply of food. A gust of wind blew up from the sea, and displaced seagulls screeched as they attempted to out-fly a storm. Lightening split the sky, and a loud crack of thunder rattled the air. A surge of unsettled clouds obscured the sun. Philyra heard hooves clattering on the rock. She stood up and looked through the misty fog where a stallion came into view. It might have been the leader of a small heard, but the hairs on Philyra's neck prickled.

This was the moment she had feared for a long time. "Hide in the cave," she told Kheiron in a commanding voice.

Kheiron didn't understand. He felt her emotions, but she had never told him to go into the cave, not without her. He looked at his mother and stood tall. "I don't want to *Metera*. I want to stay with you." But Philyra pointed adamantly toward the dark cave. The horse was approaching too quickly.

"Now!" she demanded, and Kheiron reluctantly followed To-nero, who led him inside.

Philyra turned to the stallion and rippled with fear. She would protect her child, no matter what the cost to herself.

She recognized the same white lightening down the horse's muzzle as he galloped toward her. She quaked like a linden tree, oblivious of her nakedness. This time she would not run nor cower.

"What do you want Kronus?" She tried to sound brave in her tremulous voice.

Kronus varied in shape between horse and god. She saw him sniff the air with a snort. Then his booming voice rang out, "Where is she? Where is Rhea?"

"Not here," Philyra said loudly.

"She was though," Kronus said sarcastically. "I smell her, and I smell her secrets. Where has she gone?"

Philyra shrugged her shoulders as if she didn't know.

"You know more than you are telling," Kronus sneered and cornered her between the cave and her stream. "A secret has a smell, and I smell secrets all over you. Where did she go?"

"I don't know," Philyra shivered. "But if I did know, I would not tell you, you who take what is not given, you who do not care what harm you cause."

The sky god thundered, "Ungrateful, Philyra. I gave you a child that you love. Deformed as he is, you love him. Is that not a gift of good fortune from your benevolent god?"

"Benevolent? Cruel," Philyra whispered, "You are cruel, Kronus."

"So," Kronus bellowed, "you will not tell me about Rhea, nor, I suppose, her plans."

"I do not know her plans," Philyra responded defiantly, and in truth, she did not.

Kronus took the shape of a very large man and loomed over the naiad. "You really are ungrateful, Philyra," he told her. "The fruit of your womb is an abomination of immortality. And you are ungrateful for the gifts of my love."

"Love?" Philyra questioned. "You have no love."

Violent winds stirred up and shook the fig tree, snapping its branches. A growl churned from Kronus' belly, and a look of rage distorted his face.

69

A strength surged through Philyra's feet as she spoke almost inaudibly at first, but not so quietly as to prevent Kronus from hearing. "You invoke fear and terror, anger and hatred."

Clouds surged around Kronus as his anger mounted. He starred hatefully at Philyra, who stood between him and knowing Rhea's secret plans. His anger turned into a blinding, jagged light that he turned upon the small naiad.

Philyra saw the blast coming, and like a field mouse that looks into the wide, round eyes of the owl before sharp talons sink into its flesh, she could do nothing but scream to Kheiron, "Protect yourself!"

Her scream echoed into the cave and startled Kheiron, who instinctively ran toward the place where he last saw her.

"*Metera*," he called, galloping into the meadow where Kronus stood, smoke rising from his hair like a smoldering fire.

Kronus watched the horse-boy advance down the hill. This was his son, and his face twisted into an unnatural smile.

"Come here boy," he called.

Kheiron stopped in his tracks and scanned the area for his mother.

"Where is she?" he asked.

"She has left," Kronus answered off handedly. "She said you were an abomination to her sight, neither god, nor horse, nor man – a deformity, a monster. She said she didn't want you. You can come with me, though. I am your father, Kheiron. I will care for you. There is a mighty battle raging, and I could use your help, your skills, my son."

"Your son?" Kheiron questioned. He didn't believe a word the man said. "Who are you?" he asked and where did my mother go?"

"That doesn't matter," Kronus answered. "I am the high god of the heavens and earth, your father. Come with me and forget her."

Turmoil ran through Kheiron's mind. "*Metera*," he called louder looking in all directions, "Where are you?"

"Foolish child," Kronus spit. "She hates you. Don't you understand? She was sick of looking upon your disfigurement. You don't need her, boy." Kronus held out his hand to Kheiron, but the horse child trembled inside. He, who instinctively knew the smell of poisonous foods, did not trust this God, and he ran toward the pool calling, "*Metera!*"

"Stupid child," Kronus sneered, "Search for her if you like, but you will not find her."

Kheiron stood silent and still near the pool as Kronus turned into an angry wind and blew over the hills.

Rain pelted down and desperation took over as Kheiron followed the grass worn trail around the spring, looking and calling for his mother.

"*Metera*, where are you?" He looked into the bottom of the pool and under the rocks. He splashed through the water and turned over boulders with an unearthly strength, certain that she must be there, but she wasn't. He went to the *bamyes* and to the gorge that she normally avoided. Anxiously, he came back to the cave and searched the dark corners, wiping tears from his face, calling over and over, "Where are you, *Metera*?"

That night, he slept in the rain, near the pool, under the drizzling fig leaves. When he woke up, he looked for her cool, wet body. He whinnied, "Where are you?" and wept when there was no response.

10

Alone

Kheiron walked aimlessly. He had searched every place he had ever gone with his mother but could not find her. His two stomachs growled, but he ignored the pangs.

I have to find her first, he thought, *then we can eat together.* He had hope, but Kronus' words kept replaying in his mind: *She hates you. You are an abomination to her sight, a deformity and a monster. She doesn't want you.*

"Kronus is a liar," Kheiron said out loud. "She loves me. She has always loved me."

He remembered how she scratched his back saying, "What a beautiful boy you are." He remembered how she smelled his scalp and kissed the top of his head.

She did love me, he told himself. *She does love me.*

He thought about the last sound he heard from her: that scream. Kronus must have hurt her or even killed her. Kheiron was familiar with the lifeless bodies of animals. Now with a gnawing fear, he searched the meadow, looking for traces, smells.

Despite the knowledge that his mother's love had been sure, he began to have doubts. *Maybe Kronus was right. Maybe she didn't love me. Maybe I am deformed. Am I really a monster?*

Kheiron stood near his mother's pool and asked To-nero and the other frogs, "Have you seen her?" But To-nero and the hungry chorus only croaked back at him, echoing the same question: "Rrriitt, rriitt, Have you seen her?"

Remembering his aunties, Kheiron called Rhea, Tethys, and Hera, the goddesses who promised to hear should he supplicate their names, but days went by without even a sea mist or a honeysuckle breeze to acknowledge his calls.

He tried to sleep in the cave where the familiar sound of rustling bats and high pitched squeals made him think that his mother's absence was just a nightmare dropped by the *Oneiroi,* the leathery-winged dream spirits.

When he did fall asleep, standing near her mossy bed, his own guttural sobs woke him. Hot tears slid down his naked chest and disappeared into his thick fur. Only moments of disturbed unconsciousness got him through the long nights.

Before the light of dawn, singing birds announced the imminent rising of the sun, and Kheiron walked outside where he looked into the nighttime sky and saw the brightest star. It appeared on the eastern horizon at the end of summer and disappeared on the western horizon toward the end of spring.

"Sirius," Kheiron whispered. "Where is my mother?" But even after a long pause, there was no answer.

Kheiron stomped on the earth and thought, *Perhaps Yiayia will tell me Yiayia,* Grandmother Gaia was his last hope.

Philyra had taken Kheiron into the deep, cavern sanctuary of the cave a few times. She thought it was a holy place where Gaia spoke clearly.

He picked up a pine branch with pitch over one end made for going into the tunnel. Unfortunately, there was no fire to light the staff, and he stood over the white ashes, stirring them in hopes of an ember.

Like a gift from some unseen benevolent friend, a small orange glow no bigger than a chestnut surfaced. With renewed courage, Kheiron fed the ember with twigs and sticks, and then watched as it blossomed into a flame. Out of habit, he placed a log over the fire and lit his pine staff. Now he could walk into the darkness and see.

She could be here, he thought as he entered the long tunnel in the back of the cave. *She could be sick, or hurt. Yiayia Grandmother Gaia will tell me. Yiayia will help me find her, and I will make her well. I will bring her food and water and herbs, and I will take care of her and make her better.*

"*Metera*," Kheiron called hopefully into the obscurity, his voice echoed down the long corridor of the cave. "I'm coming."

Once in the deep cavern, Kheiron saw bundles of grain and dried flowers, offerings left for *Yiayia* by his mother and Rhea. He remembered watching them kneel in the dry silt as they spoke to the wise earth.

His mother always talked of that sense of peace she felt here. But just now, anxiety raced through Kheiron's body, and he could not hear the permeating silence that tried to comfort him.

"*Yiayia*," he called, "*Grandmother Gaia*, you who know everything, you who see everything, tell me where my mother is."

Kheiron waited patiently and listened attentively, but the walls were silent. The sand, the boulders and the dirt below his hooves, quiet.

Frustration mounted as Kheiron's voice echoed, "Why don't you speak to me, *Yiayia*? Why won't you answer?" But there was still no response, and after a while he yelled, "Am I so deformed that no one will talk to me now? Is there no one left who cares? No one who loves me? *Yiayia*!" he screamed at the silence. "Answer me!" He waited for something, anything. Aggravated, Kheiron

75

smacked his staff against the wall. The impact snuffed out the flame.

Darkness filled the empty space around him and he reached for the sides of the cavern wall. "You must not be my grandmother," he told Gaia. "You do not hear me, and you do not speak. I am alone." He touched the cool, damp rock and stumbled forward. He would have to find his own way, even in the dark.

11

Whispers of Her Voice

Under his familiar blanket of stars, Kheiron listened.

He knew his mother wasn't coming back, and yet he heard whispers in the wind, soft breezes that lifted the hairs down his back, and he heard what he thought were her songs.

In the darkness of early morning, he stood still. Where did that melodic sound come from? Using all his senses, he focused intently on determining the origin. Whether awake or asleep, he knew his mother's voice anywhere, but the sounds he heard were elusive – here and there, and not there.

In frustration, he followed his well-worn path around the meadow and finally stopped under a small tree, watching as dawn began to swallow the nighttime stars.

I heard her, he thought, *but what did she say? And if she spoke, that means she is alive, but where?*

In his young but adept mind he tried to understand as his eyes scanned, keeping alert for anything that moved.

Something stroked his back just like her touch, and he turned quickly, but it was only the branch of the tree brushing against him.

Odd, he thought, *she seems so near.*

As the sun illuminated the earth, one star remained above the eastern horizon.

"That star reminds us to have hope," he remembered her saying, And he repeated her words, "Hope. Hope. Don't give up hope."

Under this tree, he watched the sun rise and set. He heard the creek splash as it flowed downhill. He felt his mother's presence even if she were nowhere to be found. It was a place which he would come to love, and where he would have stayed only hunger forced him to go to the cave for food.

The storage pots were full, ready for a long winter. There were baskets woven with willow and reeds that he had made. These carefully crafted containers lined one of the back caves where it was cool and dry, and they overflowed with barley, carob pods, dried grapes and figs, chestnuts and acorns, bitter almonds and fermented fruit in vinegar. He had lots of food that would keep for many months, so long as it remained dry. Some had required salt to stay preserved, while hard pears and small apples, stayed fresh in cold storage simply packed in herbs.

With his belly full of dehydrated *psomi*, meat, fruits and a few carob pods as well as some extras that he tucked into the rabbit-skin bag over his shoulder, Kheiron felt new inspiration to search the lower parts of the mountain. He had heard his mother's voice and that had given him hope that she was alive somewhere, but in which direction?

Near his hoof, half buried in the soil was a small, blue stone with a pointed edge. He leaned over to pick up the azurite with his human hand. It was the color of water and sky, one of the blue stones that Philyra loved.

"Where should I go?" he asked the stone and tossed it to the wind. It spun and turned mid-air, then landed softly in the grass, pointing west, downstream. Without forethoughts or provisions beyond his snack, Kheiron galloped west.

To-nero, the old frog climbed into the linden tree and watched him run away. "Rrrrit," the little frog chirped, but Kheiron didn't hear him.

Doing something, going somewhere, lightened Kheiron's heart. His inner nature led him forward, and despite the barrenness of winter, there was a power in the land that rustled through the trees, lifted the wet undergrowth with unusual fleshy fungi, and filled his nose with the musty scent of living soil.

For several hours he followed the stream as it coursed downhill. He nibbled the snacks in his bag as he walked. He picked his way through steep terrain and cascading waterfalls that plunged into green pools. At one such place he stopped to feel the spray on his face. Certainly a *naiad* lived here. Kheiron tried to find her, but she did not reveal herself to him. Instead he watched a cluster of fish darting across the sandy pool bottom. He, with two stomachs, one human and the other horse, started to salivate.

He remembered the stories of how his mother had caught fish with her bare hands and how at first, she had eaten them raw.

He stepped slowly into the shallow end of the pool, so as not to disturb the water too much. Then he waited. An unsuspecting fish darted by, and he reached out to grab the sleek body. The finned creature slipped through his waiting palm just as the five, pale digits of his other hand tightened around the fish and pulled it out of the water.

Kheiron had an uncanny ability to catch animals, but now, for some reason, he released the fish while the others hid in the shadows and under the rocks.

Kheiron's hooves slipped on the wet stones as he climbed out of the pool.

Why didn't I eat the fish? he wondered. Perhaps the reason was that his mother no longer ate fish. *Like her*, he thought, *I can eat ta horta*. But the small winter grasses and herbs that grew on the hillside were in a dormant stage and not abundant enough to satisfy his hungers. He thought of the food stored in the cave. *I could go back*, he thought, but something inside refused. Instead, he walked on, taking note of the trees and bushes that clung tenaciously to the earth. Some trees had been knocked over in the storm and lay on the ground with their roots turned up, as if they grappled for their lost sense of stability.

He followed a well-trodden path that ran near the creek and noted the tacks of numerous animals. Patches of crumpled grass and piles of droppings told him where the various animals slept, ate and drank. Gullies and rivulets fed into the creek. There was water everywhere. He noticed new scents, flora and fauna unique to these lower elevations. What he saw, he remembered and in the future would know where he had seen it, smelled it or heard it. If ever he wanted to return, his sense of direction, amazing as it was, would lead him back.

12

The Baby Goat

Kheiron cupped his hand for a drink at a small rivulet and heard a weak staccato moan.

His eyes followed where his ears led, and a small path became suddenly evident.

Curious, he jumped the creek. When he landed, his back hooves clattered against the rocks.

I must keep quiet, he thought to himself. But then he heard the sound again. *Naiad?* He wondered. *Dryad? Or Animal?*

Ahead, in the middle of the path and surrounded by fallen rocks was a small goat, a baby, no bigger than his arm. Above, standing near the edge of a sheer cliff was another goat, bleating.

The mother perhaps, he thought.

For a natural hunter, a small baby animal mortally wounded from an evident fall could have been an easy meal. But Kheiron saw the nearly lifeless baby with its umbilical cord still wet, and, instead of twisting its head in a fast and certain-to-kill manner, he knelt down and stroked the soft, white and black fur.

"You want your mother don't you?" he whispered.

Using both hands, he gently lifted the tiny animal and cradled it in his arms. "I will take you to her."

The rugged path up the cliff was not easy as he attempted to keep his balance and ensure that the tiny goat was not jostled. More than once he slipped, but dropping his precious cargo was not an option. He would protect the baby goat at all costs.

Near the top, he saw the mother who had retreated to her herd. Excited, Kheiron ran towards her, happy to reunite her with the baby. But the goats ran when they saw him. Certainly the mother would come back once she saw her baby, and Kheiron held it low in open view.

Still the mother and herd, accustomed to large hunting animals that preyed upon them, only paused when the kid bleated weakly. Self-preservation was stronger than motherly protection.

So focused on reunification, Kheiron was slow to realize that it was he who scared the herd. *Maybe if I leave the baby in the grass and go away,* he thought. He hid himself in the bushes, camouflaged by a low-growing oak, and waited. Cautiously, the herd did return, each coming over to smell the wounded kid before going back to nibbling weeds. Only the mother stayed near, eating grasses and leaves.

Why doesn't she do anything? Kheiron wondered. But in nature, if a herd animal cannot stand on its own, it is left to die. The others may simply stand near, mourning for a short time, but then continue their foraging.

When the long shadows of afternoon crossed the grass, the goats moved on, and the mother followed. It was an instinct of survival, stay with the herd. What Kheiron saw, however, was the kid goat left alone.

The small creature panted painfully, still alive, eyes closed. So Kheiron, the horse-child, folded his four legs to the side and sat next to the tiny creature, gently stroking the fragile body to offer comfort. The little goat refused Kheiron's attempts to give it water. Later, when Kheiron was older, he would come to understand that in the throes of death all creatures refuse nourishment.

82

However, Kheiron's own body was not beyond hunger, and he nibbled on the few provisions in his sack until they were gone. Even then he stayed by the baby's side. He refused to leave the kid as its mother had.

Into the night he sat vigilantly with the goat, yet watched the stars as they came out. He was beginning to recognize stellar patterns and see images in their arrangements. He even picked out a goat shape with the tail of a fish. All the while his hand rested gently on the goat baby, and he was acutely aware as each laborious breath became shallower and shallower. In that position, Kheiron fell asleep.

Early in the morning Kheiron awoke, his hand still on the kid. But there was no warmth, nor breath.

"No," he whispered, stroking the soft fur and lifting the tiny, stiff body to his chest. Maybe he could make it warm again.

He held the little goat until daybreak, until the star of hope, the last bright star on the horizon, disappeared. Hungry again, Kheiron watched as robins alighted in the meadow and pulled worms out of the ground. The goat was dead. He could eat it, build a fire as his auntie Rhea had taught him, with a drill and hearth, but he could not bear to eat *this* baby goat, not now, after keeping vigil over the small creature who like him, had been separated from his mother.

As he watched a robin pulling a fat worm from the ground, hungry, Kheiron began to reason, *If birds can eat worms...* He followed their example and used his fingers to dig in the soil until he discovered a large, plump wiggler. With only a moment's revulsion, he popped it into his mouth.

Unusual. The texture was gritty with soil, but the flavor, not bad, and neither was it poisonous. He had discovered another source of food and ate until his hunger subsided.

Like an attentive parent, he tried to share with the baby goat, but realizing the silliness of it, said, "You wouldn't like them anyway," and he laughed.

Kheiron wove a wintry garland of thyme sprigs and placed it around the small kid. The fragrant herb grew prolifically all over the mountain, even in winter. Thyme filled the senses and reminded him of happy moments with his mother, when she placed such wreathes upon his head.

He should have left the carcass for others to feast upon if he couldn't eat it himself, but instead Kheiron carefully arranged the dead baby goat in his empty rabbit skin sack. It was nothing he could explain, but keeping the tiny thing close to him was important, as necessary for him as looking for food. It may seem odd, but he put wild onions and the roots of asphodel and carrot, black salsify and garlic-moly, dandelion and chicory, in the sack, right next to the dead baby goat.

He took a long drink in the stream then went in the direction that the goats had gone. He had no one waiting for him and nothing else to do. He could go where he wanted. Looking for his mother was always in the back of his mind, but the urgency had gone. He knew that he was alone except for the baby goat.

With the mind and body of a ten year old, Kheiron followed the herd. After many attempts of calling to them with the bleating cries of their own kind, they still refused to accept him. So he struck out on his own, discovering and exploring new places on Mount Pelion. In fact he soon knew every stream and meadow, every outcropping of rocks, every cave and pool. He wandered to the inlet bay in the west, followed the peninsula that curved out like a crippled finger to the southwest, and stood in awe when he saw the wide-open sea toward the east. He discovered sea urchins and crabs in the tide pools – more sources of food. In a rocky basin, he found salt, where trapped ocean water had evaporated. The sparkling crystals caught his eye, and he instinctively smelled and tasted them. His Grandmother Tethys, the goddess of the sea winds and tides, had taught him that salt was used to preserve food and add flavor.

He dug his fingers into the salt and saw that the heavier sand had a distinct line below the white salt. All he had to do was scrape the upper layer into a little pile and collect it. This discovery made him happy, and he wrapped his new treasure in a scrap of leather, sprinkling some around the baby goat that was starting to decompose in his bag. Of course, the goat smelled bad and had for a while, but Kheiron's nose soon became accustomed to the odor.

Salt might help, he thought as he sprinkled more over the sunken eyes. To an outsider, clinging to the carcass may seem strange, but what was most important to Kheiron was keeping the baby close to him, not abandoning it.

Kheiron looked over the rippling turquoise sea. The vast expanse of blues and greens and white-capped waves scintillated in the morning light. The waves undulated as if they were alive. Images of bright colored sea vegetables, shells and unusual fish filled Kheiron's mind as he remembered the stories his grandmother Tethys told him of her underwater home. She had cultivated a rich imagination in her grandson, he who could not swim but loved to play in the cold water. He ran on the isolated beaches, drummed his hooves in the shallow surf, laughed and splashed in the salty water. Just beyond the swells, dolphins jumped and somersaulted through the air. Being near them made him feel invigorated and happy.

The living, aqua-colored water was his grandfather, Oceanus. He knew this to be true, but the wise sea never spoke in words that Kheiron could understand, though it wasn't because Kheiron didn't ask or listen. Certainly the all-encompassing Oceanus spoke in whispers as the waves crashed and dragged pebbles back into the slurry of water and sand. And though Kheiron couldn't make out what his grandfather said, he gathered some comfort as he stood up to his waist in the surging waves. He felt at home, with his family, as if everything were all right, at least for the moment.

13

Wandering the Hills

Occasionally, Kheiron encountered humans, but never had the chance to speak with one. He would have been delighted to make a new friend, but, at the mere sight of the horse with the upper body of a man, any humans he met usually screamed and ran or stood ready to fight for their lives.

Sensitive, at first Kheiron cried, devastated that these people who looked so much like his mother would run from him, but he learned to keep his distance, realizing, that as Kronus had said, to them he was a monster.

He ate worms, sea urchins, fish and tender fresh greens, and on that simple diet actually gained weight and grew. He could no longer bear to kill animals with big, pleading eyes. His mother, who cared for all living creatures, frowned on such things, and she was always with him, in his memory and thoughts, directing his motives to care and help.

Vultures tried to take his goat more than once when he set the carcass on a rock to dry out, an act they were sorry for, because Kheiron defended it with an uncanny ferocity that left the scavengers terrified. Once they did tear it open and exposed the putrid innards. Reluctantly, Kheiron scraped out the rotting flesh and left it for the birds to devour. Over time, the carcass became nothing more than dried skin and bones, but Kheiron still kept it with him.

When deer and wild horses ran franticly and rabbits became aggressive, Kheiron learned to expect earthquakes, especially near the full moon. Sometimes he watched as one of the giant, fifty-headed *hekatonkheires* hurtled a boulder or mountaintop. The horse-child was so much smaller than them, yet they always seemed to know where he was.

When not in battle they would wave at Kheiron and bellow, "*Kali meera*," good morning or "*Kali spera*," good evening. At least they were friendly, if not friends, and Kheiron knew that when they appeared grey smoke would soon fill the skies and volcanoes would erupt. At such times, he would often return to his cave near his mother's spring where the air seemed clearer.

Sometimes at night Kheiron would stand in an open meadow overlooking the bay. From there he could watch the stars and draw pictures with his imagination, so that the sparkling eyes of heaven turned into the characters from stories his mother, aunties and grandmother had told him. He remembered each of the stories, and, in his imaginings, under the blanket of night, all sorts of animals appeared: fish and lizards, bulls and horses, people and gods, a myriad of relatives and friends who came out in the evenings to visit with him, sing and tell more stories. They watched with him as he observed the lightning battles between Kronus and Zeus with jagged streaks that illuminated the sky and spread from one horizon to the other.

As spectacular as these conflicts were, Kheiron learned that they could be just as deadly, especially when the blinding, livid spikes hit the forest. Then fire would blossom amid the brush. Not only were the trees and bushes destroyed, but also food sources, nesting glades and lives.

Kheiron walked in the aftermath of the fires discovering scorched animals, some not quite dead. These he took home to the cave and nursed with the healing foods and herbs of his mountain.

"I'm just going to bathe you in this calendula flower and marshmallow root," he would say, as a wounded fawn kicked at him in fear. In his short life he had learned that calendula flowers, which bloomed most of the year, together with marshmallow leaves and roots often made a positive difference in the healing of flesh. He made them into an infusion, or soup as he called it, washing the exposed tissues and feeding the creatures the cooked mash. Crushed yarrow leaves he sprinkled into bleeding wounds, and that alone would often staunch the flow of blood.

He rescued terrified animals, enduring painful scratches and bites as he cared for them, but he never gave up. He sang water songs and cooed to them in the familiar tones of their own language. And after a while, those that survived learned to trust the strange creature who doctored and fed them, and smelled of rotting goat and wild thyme.

Many of his patients did not live, often because they were far too injured. None-the-less, he stayed by their side, sang softly and tried to make them comfortable. When a rabbit or deer, bear or owl took its last breath, Kheiron cried like a baby, abandoned again.

Despite his inclination not to kill, Kheiron had a strong instinct not to let fresh meat go to waste. And though he grieved for the dead animals, meat was food, not to be scoffed at or discarded wantonly. He left some for scavengers, among which he counted himself, and with a sharpened horn cut and tore the remains of his dead patients to share with the wildlife. In this way, he became familiar with the internal organs of each animal. He compared them to organs he had seen before and tried to figure out where they were on live animals, including himself.

He discovered the internal systems of bones and muscles and how they related to structure and motion. He observed the digestive tract, the lungs and breathing, heart, veins and arteries, liver, gall bladder and kidneys. It was all very interesting to him. Naturally, food was always in the back of his mind, but, curiosity taught him which herbs and foods affected which body parts. One thing he noticed in living animals was that if they were ill, injured or traumatized, there was often a misalignment along the spine or muscular spasm that distorted it. He taught himself to massage and press the muscles with his warm hands until the spasms released. Sometimes this would be all an animal needed, and in this way, some of his patients got better quickly, became strong and ran off into the forest.

Alone again, Kheiron held his sack with his precious desiccated goat and went back to eating and preserving his own food.

Sometimes, just for comfort, he would stand in the meadow near his mother's spring and lean his side haunches against the trunk of the small linden tree. With his eyes closed, he listened to the soothing rustle of leaves as they made a watery sort of music, like familiar lullabies.

14

Apollo

A flock of swans flew in from the North. Big and white with black beaks, they advanced toward Kheiron's meadow, honking as they soared in concentric circles above him.

He watched, counting seven, flying gracefully in formation. And then, out of the blue, as if attacking, they dove straight at him. He rushed to the side to avoid a collision.

They came in and touched the ground with quick little steps that established their footing. They seemed fearless and did not even give him a suspicious sideways glance.

In their midst, a flash of light distorted Kheiron's vision. At first, it seemed as if a star had alighted with the flock of swans, but the light assumed a form. It was a man with long, dark, curly hair, and he radiated, almost glowed. He wore nothing but a loincloth to cover his body.

Over one shoulder hung a long, curved, shiny staff, held together with sinew. Kheiron would later recognize this bow made of gold. Over the other shoulder hung a long sack which contained sticks with feathers on them, a quiver, he would later learn, filled with arrows. The white feathers, the only visible part of the sticks, shimmered with rainbow colors and turned from blue to purple, red to orange, yellow to green. The strange man smiled warmly and in his presence Kheiron did not feel fear or anxiety.

"What do you have there?" the man gestured with his glance at the small bit of desiccated fur that hung out of Kheiron's bag.

At first, Kheiron said nothing.

"I see you are shy," the man continued. "Did you know that the war is over?"

"The war?" Kheiron spoke quietly.

"Yes, the war between Kronus and Zeus. Kronus is defeated." The man pointed toward a mountain in the distance where Kheiron recognized a giant *hekatonkheire* with one hundred arms who reached out to balance himself as he jumped into a fissure of the earth and disappeared.

"Don't worry about them," the man said. "They will never harm you."

But Kheiron already understood this because of their friendly gestures toward him. "Strange," the man said, "that such terrifying creatures can be so harmless to the innocent and vulnerable. They are beasts of the earth, children of Gaia and now, under the world in Tartarus, they will guard the prisoners and rebel Titans."

The land shook in response to the *hekatonkheire's* activities, and the man smiled again. "The doors of Tartarus are shut for eternity. Only Zeus may reopen them."

Kronus is defeated? Kheiron thought to himself. *Kronus, my father. Kronus who made my mother go away.* He didn't say a word, but the man responded to his thoughts.

"Yes, Kronus. He is defeated and will never harm you nor anyone you love again. I myself cannot claim any assistance in his downfall, but my father has fought him for nearly ten years. It was the hundred-handed Giants," he indicated the place where the *hekatonkheire* disappeared, "they and their brothers the *cyclopes'* who tilted the balance. Kronus is now imprisoned in Tartarus, and I am going to meet my father."

"Your father?" Kheiron mumbled.

"Zeus," the man answered.

He looked at Kheiron, studying the horse-boy's strange form, his human head and torso, and his unusual horse body with four legs.

"I know that Kronus hurt your mother," the man said.

Kheiron responded with a shudder and clutched the dried goat closer to his side.

"There is nothing anyone can say to take away the pain of losing her."

Kheiron felt uncomfortable, but the man continued.

"All the grief you've ever felt connects you with others who find themselves in the depths of despair. It is because of this familiarity with pain that you will be able to lessen the suffering of others."

Kheiron squinted at the man with curiosity, and then remembered what he had originally asked.

He opened the sack and said, "It's a baby goat."

"Tell me about your mother?" the man asked ignoring his response.

Kheiron looked away, but whispered, "Her name is Philyra. She is a beautiful water nymph." A smile spread across Kheiron's face as he pictured her stepping from the pool, water cascading down her face and black hair, her long, lithe body shimmering in the sunlight, her wet toes wiggling at him as if to say *Kali meera*. "Her name is Philyra," he said louder.

The man knew Kheiron's heart and memories, everything about him. "You think that Kronus killed her, don't you?"

This man asked too many questions, and Kheiron became nervous.

"I am called Apollo," the man said, sensing his tension, "the son of Zeus and Leto. I am the twin brother of Artemis." He spoke as if Kheiron knew all these people, but he didn't. "I just spent a year with the Hyperborans of the north," the man continued, "where I studied the mysteries of the universe. And now, I am going to fight the Python and establish the new oracle at Mt. Parnassus. When I am done, I am going to Mt. Olympus to meet my father, the victor of this Ten Year War, your brother, the king of all the heavens and all the earth, Zeus."

"My brother?" Kheiron questioned. "How can Zeus be my brother?"

"Are you not Kronus' son?"

Kheiron nodded his head affirmatively.

"Well then, you are Zeus' brother."

"Can I come with you?" Kheiron asked without hesitance, but then he thought about the animals he had been taking care of. They were all either dead or healed, and none were left at the cave. Then he looked down at the tattered goat, "But I can't leave him."

"Look, Kheiron."

The man knew his name.

"Our meeting is destined, and I have things to teach you. Sometimes we have to let go of people, animals, mothers, goats. It is never easy, and it hurts. But it hurts more to hold on. Can you see the goat? Not as it appears, but as he is?"

Kheiron watched as a glowing light appeared near the small scrap of fur. It hovered slightly to the side, in the crook of his arm.

"You have kept it in bondage by clinging to its life and its death. Your little goat is mortal and you must let its spirit go in peace. He needs to romp with other departed goats. It is his right and his pleasure."

Kheiron knew that what the man said was true, but letting go was difficult. He could never leave the little goat alone. Now, however, it appeared that he had no choice. The time had come. In this man's presence, Kheiron reluctantly kissed the stinking carcass.

"Good-bye," he said under his breath and tenderly laid the tattered skin in the grass. A luminescent form bounded off, leaving an ache in both of Kheiron's hearts, his horse heart and his human heart. He grieved like a child. Tears dripped down his hairless chest as he pawed the dirt. Letting go was difficult, but he had clung to that ragged piece of departed life for much too long, and he knew it.

With nothing left to hold on to, Kheiron, a young adolescent, turned bravely toward an uncertain future.

"Mount Olympus," Apollo said excitedly. "I have other business to attend to first, but you can come. In fact, it is your destiny, Kheiron."

"I am looking for my mother," Kheiron said, not forgetting his ultimate mission in life.

"And you shall find her, but not for a very long while."

"If I go with you, will you help me find her?" Kheiron bargained.

"I cannot make what is destined come any sooner, but I will help you find her when the time is right.

In his mind Kheiron heard his mother's voice, "Trust your instincts."

With this man, he felt safe. "I will go," Kheiron agreed, and no sooner had he said that than the swans gathered around.

"Why swans?" Kheiron asked.

Amid the noise of flapping wings, Apollo yelled, "They take me where I want to go." Then he grasped Kheiron's hand in a firm grip, and together, they were swooped into the sky.

15

Mount Parnassus

With their light colored feathers reflecting the brightness of the sun, the swans transported Apollo and Kheiron. When Apollo first took Kheiron's hand, the horse-boy's palm became hot, not burning, but enough to make him let go.

The golden god laughed above the sound of the swans' beating wings, as Kheiron examined his fingers to see if they were scorched. "You will be known as a great healer," Apollo smiled.

Kheiron rolled his eyes. This god said strange things that didn't always make sense to him.

"Seriously," Apollo laughed, "all that I say will come to pass. Prophecy is my gift. You and I, our destinies are entwined. I will help you and your progeny, and, in turn, you will help me and mine."

Kheiron wasn't sure how to respond, but Apollo changed the subject and pointed to the south. "We need to go to Mount Parnassus first. You don't mind, do you?" It was a question not meant to be answered, because, as Kheiron would learn, Apollo did what he wanted to no matter what anyone else said.

The horse-boy watched in awe as they glided over a narrow sea, "the sea of Euboea," Apollo called it. "This is one of Oceanus' many arms."

"Oceanus, my grandfather?" Kheiron said excitedly.

"Yes," Apollo answered. "The big river that covers the earth, Oceanus, father of all the rivers and *oceanids*, water sprites and *naiad*s like your mother."

"Do you think he knows where she is?" Kheiron asked.

Apollo laughed. "You may ask him, but remember that you are meant to discover some things on your own and in their right time. Trust me. Your mother is alive, and you will find her someday."

Kheiron smiled as he grasped the idea that eventually he would find her.

They continued southward in a glow, moving like clouds over hills and valleys until Apollo pointed his large hand toward a mountain that stood out above the others.

"Mount Parnassus," he said, "once the Oracle of Gaia, then her daughter Themis, goddess of Divine Law and Justice, and later passed to my grandmother, Phoebe, goddess of light."

They approached the southern slope, and the swans back beat their wings to land near a small stream surrounded by bright, white stone. Dry and desolate, the earth was barren, with no greenery or any form of life.

A toxic scent filled the air, and Kheiron stared at a cave with a stream that spilled from its crumbling mouth. Orange slime undulated from side to side in the slow moving current. *I would not drink from this spring,* Kheiron thought wisely, as an unfamiliar, acrid odor emanated from the water.

"It is the stench of Python you smell," Apollo said, holding his nose. "Python is the one who has poisoned these waters."

As if trying to rid their beaks of annoying flies, the swans shook their heads to dissipate the air-borne fumes. Unsuccessful, they deposited Apollo and Kheiron, honked, and flew off to find better air.

Kheiron's hooves clattered as he followed Apollo up the steep incline through the white limestone. They mounted the dirty creek and stained rocks until they came to the cave, an open fissure that gaped like a wound in the earth.

Apollo stopped at the entrance and opened his arms, "I am here at the Oracle of the goddesses!" he shouted to the sky. "I am here, Gaia, the first mother of creation, Phoebe, my grandmother, goddess of light, and Themis, my aunt, goddess of justice and prophesy, she who, at my birth dripped holy ambrosia into my suckling mouth.

"Illustrious Phoebe, Themis, goddesses who are one with the ancient mother Gaia, you who speak the laws of nature, provoke visions of future events, you who deliver justice, here upon these white rocks where you have inspired mystic visions, I have followed your guidance and come to take control of the Oracle. It is you who brought me here to honor the power and listen to the divine wisdom that issues forth from the bones of Grandmother Gaia."

Apollo knelt in the dust and whispered the holy names with reverence, "Gaia, Themis, Phoebe, Gaia, Themis, Phoebe. . . goddesses of earth, prophesy and light."

Then Apollo got up saying, "They have abandoned their sanctuary. Themis gave her life, her loins, and powers of prophecy to help Zeus win the war, as did Phoebe and Gaia. They are no longer here. Besides, our duties are to him now. The father rules in this new era. All the gods and goddesses pay obeisance to Zeus, the king of the heavens and earth. The oracle passes to me now. Henceforth, it is mine and shall speak the will of Zeus, my father, and no other. It is in his name that I claim this spring and the land around it. But first I must kill Python."

Apollo walked the area of the spring inspecting everything, from the putrid water to the rocks that tumbled down the mountain. There were several fissures, unusual openings in the ground, from which invisible gases seethed into the air. These were not the rank airs of Python, but a deeper gas that rose up from the earth. Apollo stood over one of these crevasses, straddling it with a foot on either side and took a deep breath. A smile spread over his lips.

"Yes," he said, as his eyes rolled back in a euphoric state. "Yes. . . Can you feel it, Kheiron? –that power that surges here? I will call this place my own. The Oracle of Gaia, Themis and Phoebe, Delphinios, the womb of the goddess, and me, the dolphin god." And he played with the words, "Delphinios, Delphin, Delphi. . . Yes, when Python is gone, the oracle will be known as Delphi, Oracle of Apollo."

Kheiron stood near another fissure, breathing the silent, ethylene fumes. He began to feel odd sensations – tingling in his limbs, light-headedness. Thoughts flowed into his mind as if someone else spoke. *Beware of the snake, the guardian of this place.*

Foggy-headed, Kheiron looked around. Who spoke and where was the snake? Apollo caught his eye with a knowing glint.

"It'll be here soon enough. But look at this place, Kheiron. This has been a center of divine inspiration since the earth first came into existence. Gaia has spoken here. Themis, Phoebe, Zeus, Apollo, we all speak here. It is *Ismenion*, the seat of prophecy that knows no lie. It is *Ompholos*, the belly button of the world."

Apollo took a deep breath of the vapors, but Kheiron's foggy mind kept wandering back to the whispers, "Beware of the guardian, the snake."

"You will see the snake soon enough," Apollo said, kicking stones into the foul rivulet. "And when I am finished with that serpent, she will regret attacking my mother."

"She?" Kheiron questioned, "I thought the serpent was a he."

"He . . . she, whatever it is, is a child of Gaia. And yes, it attacked Leto, my mother, chased her from one place to another so that no place was friendly for her to give us birth –Artemis and myself. It doesn't matter if the creature is male or female. It must be destroyed."

16

Python

Apollo yelled into the cave where the putrid water soiled the rocks. "Dragon," he called out, "You who are older than humanity, you who should be protecting the Oracle, where are you? Where are the neophyte priestesses? The young brides of the goddesses, the oracles embodied? Gone? Frightened away? Did you poison the waters and terrify the pilgrims for your own benefit?" His voice reverberated into the cave.

Turning toward Kheiron, he caught the horse-boy's eyes and pointed to a small plateau above the streambed, "Go there Kheiron, and stay out of the way."

Reluctantly, Kheiron trotted up the narrow path and then, watched as Apollo disappeared behind a rock. When Kheiron next saw him, Apollo was not a man but a glowing light, most definitely a god.

"Where are you, Serpent?" Apollo's powerful voice thundered.

If the serpent was there, certainly the challenge had been heard. But the creature did not respond, and Apollo stood, doing nothing. Time in the life of a god is very different from time as humans know it, and Kheiron watched and waited, falling asleep, standing, as horses do.

When he opened his eyes, Apollo was digging in the dirt with one of his silver arrows. Suddenly, what Kheiron had taken to be a large boulder lifted up of its own accord. It was, actually, the head of a snake and not just any serpent but a giant python.

Not to be rushed by a mere god, the snake's mountainous head rose slowly and turned one big, black eye toward the offending visitor.

"So we meet," Apollo said bowing slightly to the ancient snake. His gestures were reverent, but he spared no insult to the powerful guardian. "You have slacked in your duties and let the Oracle go to ruin. The waters are sullied and filled with your own stench. You were supposed to guard this holy place, but now all that remains is desolation."

Python slithered around Apollo, staring at him with one, large, dark eye while the other kept Kheiron in its view. The enormous head bobbed up and down, and the long, forked tongue flicked the air.

Three times the size of Apollo, the snake seemed to have the advantage. Feeling this superiority, it boldly lunged in aggressive, intimidating advances. The snake did not have the intention to kill but merely to show this small, insulting creature that Python, a child of Gaia, was the more formidable in this match.

"In the name of Zeus, I claim this spring," Apollo declared confidently.

The Serpent laughed in a hissing voice. "Silence, silly child. You cannot steal the ancient Oracle of Themis. She would not allow a slimy male, god or no, to take hold of her sacred sanctuary."

Apollo scoffed, "You, serpent, have failed in your responsibilities. Now, I step forward as the hand of justice, and it is time for you to go."

"It will not be easy, son of Zeus. If fight you choose, then you will lose. In the end you will be sorry," hissed the snake.

"You chased away the Oracle who spoke the prophecies of the goddess."

"She was no Oracle," hissed Python. "She was a saboteur, a human that spoke of my destruction. I silenced her."

"And where is the justice of Themis?" Apollo asked quietly.

"Justice?" replied the snake, "I am the justice."

"You have forgotten your mission of being a conduit between heaven and earth," Apollo scolded. "Drunk on power, you poisoned yourself, your mind, the land."

Python dipped its head angrily and lunged at Apollo's knee, this time not in threat.

The golden god stepped quickly out of the way.

"I could take you easily with my bow," he said, "but I would rather give you a fair chance. Let Themis' law prevail. We will fight to the death."

Apollo liked competition and was not in any hurry, nor was the snake, though both were eager to test their powers.

Gaia's serpent child coiled and turned away, the long, massive body side-winding towards a more open area.

To make the match more even, Apollo threw his golden bow and quiver toward Kheiron. The weapons clattered on the rocks, where the silver and gold arrows fell loose. In the sunlight, Kheiron saw how they shimmered like nothing he had ever seen before. He bent down to gather up the precious bow and arrows and proudly draped them over his own shoulders for safekeeping.

Apollo and the serpent circled each other, both moving, one facing the other. They were poised, ready either to attack or be attacked, the serpent with long, large fangs and Apollo with nothing but his hands. Around and round they went, anticipating the other's intent, ducking, striking, grabbing, missing.

Kheiron watched anxiously unable to turn away as Python wrapped a powerful tail around Apollo's ankles and dragged him to the ground.

Apollo glanced at his bound legs. He was trapped but not yet defenseless. Python took advantage of the god's averted eyes and coiled higher.

Things did not look good for the golden god. Kheiron paced. He wanted to help, but Apollo had commanded him to remain out of the way, and so he stayed on the plateau above, watching helplessly.

"I fight for Themis," Python hissed, tightening around Apollo's body. With mouth open, anticipating Apollo's flesh, Python readied to squeeze the life out of the god and end this silly battle once and for all. But when Apollo liberated his hands and grabbed the snake's head, Python was startled. Apollo dug his fingers into the massive head, and kicked his feet against the dirt. This action propelled him and the Python against the marble stone. The massive head protruded slightly beyond his own and smashed into the solid wall.

The serpent was stunned, and Apollo took the opportunity to slam both of them towards the rock again.

Kheiron gasped as the suffocating grip around Apollo's body loosened slightly.

The golden god dug his strong fingernails deeper into the tough flesh behind the serpent's skull. Then, shaking the neck with unrelenting strength, Apollo rammed the head one last time.

Python stiffened and shuddered as Apollo yelled, "To the death." But the serpent took a deep breath and grew to the size of a mountain.

"You cannot kill me so easily," the serpent boomed. "I am a child of Gaia."

Apollo turned to Kheiron who immediately understood and tossed the bow and quiver through the air.

Apollo caught them and in a single movement had the bow strung and aimed at Python.

Python lunged at the ant-sized god, but Apollo had already released his arrow which stuck firmly in the serpent's neck.

"You cannot stop me, Apollo," the serpent hissed. "I am the oracle now!! I should have killed your mother before you were born."

Apollo's arrows flew, hundreds of them, without seeming to harm the snake at all. Until at last one shot through the serpent's eye and pierced the seat of primordial thought. The immortal brain exploded from within.

As the snake became limp, Apollo stood up and caught the drooping head in his arms.

On the platform above, Kheiron had his doubts as to the rightness of what he had just witnessed. His mother had taught him to care for creatures or kill them quickly. Why did Apollo want the Oracle for himself? Many questions ran through his mind as he stepped around boulders and made his way to the shimmering god and the body of the long, massive serpent.

"There is more to this than you know," Apollo answered Kheiron's silent questions. "It is not just a matter of stealing Python's home. This is a place of great divinity. Python was given the duty of protecting the cave and the Oracle, but took possession of it for herself, not for the benefit of others. And what is more, Python poisoned and killed wantonly, keeping the pilgrims away. It is my responsibility, Kheiron. Do you understand?"

Kheiron looked at the ground.

"Killing is not appealing," Apollo continued, "but sometimes there is no other way. Death is inevitable for mortals, and sometimes even immortals must be destroyed. War is like that. Besides, this place is important to the gods and must be protected. Even you, Kheiron, will eventually play your part in training the warriors and oracles of our land."

Confusion played on Kheiron's face. Apollo's predictions of the future troubled him.

"So are we going to eat the snake?" Kheiron asked. The scavenger in him tried to make sure that the meat did not go to waste.

"No. I have other ideas," Apollo answered, picking up a tripod with three, long, straight shafts that lay in the dirt.

Kheiron recognized that the metallic staves were made of material similar to that of Apollo's bow and arrows, yet they were darker in color and tethered together in the middle.

"Music, healing and prophecy," Apollo said, pointing to each leg of the tripod, "symbols of my power." Then Apollo instructed Kheiron to open the three legs outward and distribute their weight so that they balanced evenly from the fulcrum.

Once in the position he desired, Apollo twisted Python's body around the three-legged support, adjusting the head so that the eyes looked straight ahead and the mouth hung open as if to speak.

"You have been conquered," Apollo taunted the lifeless form. "Now you will guard the Oracle's seat. You will act as a conduit between heaven and earth. She who speaks the words of prophecy shall never fear you nor any of your kind. And henceforth you will serve Zeus and his virgin mouthpiece." Apollo spoke with an intensity that Kheiron had not yet heard.

"You fought well and hard, Python," Apollo continued. "I honor you for that. But now I am the Pythian god, and you, my servant.

"Speak Python."

The serpent's mouth did not move, but a voice came from within. "The spring is yours, oh Apollo."

Kheiron looked curiously at the body, wondering where the voice came from, but the python's eyes were dark and indecipherable.

With a glint in his eye, Apollo answered Kheiron's thoughts, "Be certain, it is not Python who speaks." He winked and knelt on the earth. "Oh, Zeus," he called loudly, "God of the heavens and earth, Themis, Goddess of Justice, law and order, Phoebe, Goddess of Light, I have liberated this spring from the dragon. This place that was once dedicated to Grandmother Gaia shall become a holy shrine once again, a sacred spring to which the sick shall come for healing and the confused for wisdom and guidance. I ask for your blessings."

A voice echoed in Python's mouth:

"Though you wear the guise of a man,
Golden Apollo,
The work of prophecy shall continue.
With your protection
We will offer succor to the sick
We will give wisdom to seekers.
But first, Apollo, you must heal yourself from
the poison that adheres to you,
Oh dark-haired one,
Fear not the evil in your soul
But find the seed, which you must root
Lest your plans of healing and prophesy be moot.
The pain you wish to heal in others, you must first find
within.

109

For if you know not the depths of suffering,
You cannot reconcile any sin."

"What does that mean?" Kheiron asked, but Apollo was
already searching for the answers, "Something else to be
done, something else?" His ears, not his eyes, led him to
the sullied spring that spilled from the opening in the rock.

"There is more to this place than meets the eye," he said
reaching his hand into the murky waters. His arm went
deep into the mud, and then he pulled out a stone, a
poisoned seed. He put it into his mouth and swallowed it
whole. "A fragment of our dark beginnings," he whispered.

A grimace distorted the god's golden face as the foreign
object wallowed inside his stomach and intestines. He
looked sick as the evil surged through his limbs. Yellow
pus oozed from the corners of his mouth, eyes and ears.

Kheiron began to worry. He had never seen anything
like this before and didn't know what kind of herb would
help Apollo.

When Apollo's eyes rolled back into his skull, Kheiron
flushed with fear. "Why did you eat that strange stone?" he
asked. But Apollo could not answer. Instead he stumbled
forward, coughed, gagged, and fell. In this stupor,
vomiting the contents of his stomach, Apollo seemed more
like a man than an immortal. And though Apollo retched,
the stone did not come up.

In a slow roll, Apollo finally turned onto his back, and a
look of peace spread over his face. Was he dead? No, the
god smiled. Suddenly he coughed. His body shuddered and
then regurgitated the stone. It fell onto the ground with a
thud.

The rock did not appear to be the same one that Apollo
originally had swallowed. Instead, transformed, it had a
golden hue. Apollo opened his eyes serenely, laughed, then

picked up the stone. He dug his hand back into the murk, and buried the golden ball.

Inside the mouth of the cave, swirls of clear water churned and trickled over the putrid rocks. It flowed down the hill and into the pools below. Filth transformed into clarity. Pure water sparkled as if reflecting the light of a thousand suns. Life would again grow and flourish here.

"Taste the water now," Apollo encouraged with a grin.

Reluctantly, Kheiron cupped his hand and reached into the small, clear pool. He sipped cautiously, but the taste was sweet.

"Soon the people in the valley and the few goats and sheep they have left will be dancing and singing," Apollo said with a laugh. "All beings who walk and crawl upon Grandmother Gaia should have the right to drink fresh, clear, healing water."

Apollo dunked his head into the clean pool and shook his dark, curly hair. It shimmered golden-violet as droplets flew in all directions.

Smiling, Apollo pointed toward the sea and said, "Out there is a ship. It is being blown off course as we speak, and my dolphins are guiding the ship to the beach below. In their search for pure water, the people on board will discover this place and decide to stay. They will become my priests and priestesses." His eyes crinkled into a laugh as he jumped along a ridge and climbed the mountain. He traced a pattern on the hillside. "This is where they will build my temple, and here, my altar. Pilgrims will make offerings and sacrifices here. And, where the python now sits, the Pythian oracle, the virgin priestess, shall utter my prophecies."

Kheiron watched as Apollo danced around the barren grounds. "You shall see, my little horse-man. All will come to pass as I say."

111

Kheiron turned his head in the direction of the ocean. It all seemed so strange. He could not see the ocean with his eyes, but with an inner vision he saw the scintillating crests that rolled toward the land and a small dot, bobbing up and down. Could it be as Apollo said? Was that the ship and the pious folks who would come here and build his temple? Apollo laughed. "It is," he answered, reading Kheiron's thoughts. "It is!"

17

Artemis

Apollo and Kheiron stood on the high mountain perch of Mount Parnassus watching the future priests and priestesses of Apollo row to the beach toward the south. Apollo laughed in delight to see his prophecy unfold. In his merriment, he was like a child gagging on his own mirth. But the gag was more of a cough, the cough more of a gasp, the gasp more of a struggle to breathe, and Kheiron watched in horror as Apollo's golden face became ashen, and his internal light began to diminish. "Artemis," Apollo whispered. "I need my sister. . ."

With great effort, Apollo reached toward Kheiron, but as he touched the boy a painful weight entered Kheiron's arm. Instinctively the horse-boy pulled away, but Apollo clutched more deeply.

The sound of wings beat the air, and, as if beckoned, the honking swans alighted next to their failing master.

Understanding that the swans would know what to do, Kheiron, with Apollo still clinging to his wrists, dragged the unconscious god into the midst of the restless birds.

The wing power of seven swans launched Kheiron and Apollo into an empty space that was neither hot nor cold, light nor dark, a place without feeling or pain. Suspended in this nothingness, Kheiron lost awareness.

* * *

The musty scent of rotting leaves made Kheiron's nose twitch. His eyes were closed, but the cold, wet humus seeped into his fur, and he shivered. He moved his right arm, but it felt numb. He squinted his eyes open.

Surrounding him was a thick forest of cedars, so dense that subdued sunlight reached him only through apertures of branches and fronds. Apollo was nowhere to be seen. Kheiron folded his forelegs underneath him and stood, taking note of the wide tree trunks whose tops disappeared far above his head. All around him, young, spindly saplings crowded around the larger trees.

Hungrily, he scanned the ground and saw newly fallen cedar seeds. Cedar seeds are a strong, concentrated food, and he had learned that only a few would satisfy his appetite until he could find something more suitable.

As he chewed, he looked for a trail. He always looked for a trail, where to go next, an escape route. It was part of his horse nature. But the saplings were so tightly woven, one into the other, that no one save a mouse could escape this place. Apollo had brought him to a natural prison, and he felt a sudden sense of panic.

A small viper caught his attention as it wriggled across the matted, forest carpet and disappeared into a rodent's hole near the base of a large black oak. It was the only deciduous tree hidden in the fibrous net of low-growing cedars, and it sheltered not only the viper among its roots, but some other animal which only now began to stir.

After all that he had recently witnessed, Kheiron stood perfectly still, ready to face whatever was about to explode from the soil.

To his surprise, a large, brown hand pushed up like a fungus from under the fallen leaves.

"Apollo?" Kheiron asked timidly.

"Yes," was the weak reply.

"Where are we?"

There was no verbal response, only a groan.

Kheiron dug at the layers of leaves and fronds that covered the god as if he had been there for months, or longer, buried by seasons of fallen debris. Time, as noted before, is very different in the life of the gods.

Apollo's brown, naked body was no longer radiant or gold, but bore the ashen colors of the Oracle's poisoned stream. Kheiron's nature was to help, but whatever afflicted Apollo was beyond the young horse-boy's understanding of food, water, herbs, or kindness.

Behind him, twigs crunched, betraying the fact that someone else was now in the cedar grove with them.

Kheiron looked over his shoulder slowly and found himself facing a tall woman. How she got through the net of cedars, he didn't know, but her long, dark, curly hair was very much like Apollo's. In fact her facial features were so similar that she could have been a replica of Apollo himself.

Her brown skin was scratched from traversing dense brush. And, similar to his own mother, leaves and feathers hung from her hair. However, unlike Philyra's tangles, this woman's hair was braided, plaited into five or six strands, and the leaves and twigs seemed to have been placed intentionally. She wore the skins of several animals around her waist and chest to cover the womanly parts of her body.

This certainly was Apollo's sister, Artemis. Like her brother she carried a bow, only hers was made of a silvery metal, and the arrows in her quiver were fletched with black feathers instead of white. On her brow, a crescent flashed for a moment and then disappeared. A silver light similar to the golden halo of Apollo shimmered around her. Her most striking characteristics, however, were the expressions that passed over her face. Every emotion came

115

and went in shadows and light, showing her thoughts and concealing them simultaneously. There was a friendly glimmer in her eyes, and her mouth lifted into a droll smile that conveyed amusement.

"Artemis?" Kheiron stammered. "I am. . ."

"I know who you are," she responded curtly and stepped over the piles of leaves to her brother's protruding hand.

She grasped his weak and nearly lifeless body with the strength of a bear and pulled him over her shoulders like the carcass of a fallen animal. "Follow me," she said to Kheiron.

18

Purification

The cedar trees opened in front of Artemis, and Kheiron trotted in her footsteps as the trees closed rapidly behind him. He followed on her heels down a long path and up a steep ridge toward a dark opening in the rocks – a cave, he realized.

Just outside the cave, Artemis dropped Apollo onto on a small, grassy knoll in the sun. He landed with his arms and legs spread wide open.

"Just like the newborn babe I pulled from our mother's womb." She spoke with the arrogance of an older sibling in regard to her baby brother whom she had mid-wifed into the world. She had been born only days before Apollo, but again, time in the world of immortals is very different from time as humans know it.

"The oracle is secured," Apollo whispered.

"Of course," she answered. "Otherwise you would not be like this.

She stepped back, taking note of the ashen color of her brother's skin. Then she pulled a long silver arrow from her quiver. She drew the sinew tight and released the arrow from her bow before Kheiron had a chance to yell, "Stop!" which he did, only too late.

Apollo's body shuttered as the sharp point pierced through his chest and stopped in his heart.

"In order to be reborn, you must first die," Artemis whispered under her breath.

"Die?" Kheiron questioned. "I thought Apollo was immortal?"

"He is," she answered, stepping over her brother's body and removing her obedient arrow. "He will never truly die. Just watch."

As she removed her arrow, Kheiron saw a yellow-orange blob, reminiscent of Python's putrid waters, hanging off the point. The huntress shook her weapon, and the amorphous mass flew into a small puddle that Kheiron hadn't noticed before. In the water, small, glittering lights surrounded the blob, attacking it until nothing remained of the mass, and the puddle became clear, reflecting only sunlight.

Strange, Kheiron thought.

"That is just the beginning," Artemis said. "The poison has been removed, but Apollo is still weak. He killed Python, a child of Gaia, a feat for which he must not only be purified, but also for which he must pay. We will rejuvenate him in the pools for now."

Pools, Kheiron thought, remembering his mother's pool and uncomfortably becoming aware of his own arm, numb with a sickening cold. Some kind of noxious transference had occurred when Apollo grabbed his arm, and though he thought about saying something to Artemis, she apparently already knew.

"Stand still," she said, as if anyone could do otherwise. She moved so quickly that before Kheiron could understand what was happening she had one of her silver arrows notched.

The shaft went through his hand with a searing pain that made him howl in agony.

"Don't be such a baby," she smiled. "You are tougher than that." Kheiron closed his mouth, but the pain from the arrow overwhelmed him.

His mind slipped out of awareness, and he dreamed that he was carried by a couple of women who laid him down in a dark cave. The scent of mugwort surrounded him.

"Let it all go," a female voice whispered close to his ear.

He, with a keen sense of hearing, did not recognize the vocal intonations of the person who spoke. Moreover, as he became aware of his body, he realized that he was submerged in water, suspended and held just like when he had been tiny in his mother's pool.

The voice spoke again, "Self-doubt, grief, loneliness, let them go." Kheiron opened his eyes and saw a pale shaft of light shining through a crack in the ceiling. It was much like the streams of light that shown into his own cave. The only obvious difference was that here, inside this cave was water. Someone supported his head, holding it so that he could breathe, and his horse body floated behind him in the deep water. He heard the trickle of a small stream.

"Where am I?" he whispered.

"In the hidden pools of Artemis. I am her servant, Kallisto," a girl's voice answered. "In here you will be purified and healed. The Goddess smiles upon you, divine man-child . . . horse. You carry the burdens of loss and abandonment. Let them go," she repeated.

Kheiron's *naiad* mother flashed before his eyes. "Let go of my mother?" he responded abruptly and turned his body so that his hooves felt the bottom of the pool and he stood, rising above the girl.

In the dim light, her eyes glinted slightly.

"I will not let go of my mother," he told her emphatically. "She is alive, and I am going to find her."

"As you wish," the girl continued, showing no concern at Kheiron's unusual form nor his agitation.

He dropped back into the water, and again the girl supported his head. The scent of mugwort permeated his thoughts as he floated in a calmness that filled his mind and body. He was again transported back to a time when Philyra held him in her pool. He smiled, imagining his mother's face and the frogs that always clustered around her. He hummed one of her gurgling lullabies, "Glurr nana phshhh phshhh."

When he finally breathed peacefully, the girl lifted Kheiron's head and encouraged him to stand up. Then she showed him a dark beach. His hooves felt the sharp edges of the rocks underneath him as he climbed out of the water. From the dark beach, in the subdued light, the underground sanctuary came into clearer view. Roots hung from the ceiling and dripped with water, and he could see a small rivulet that fell from a higher cavern into the pool. The air was cool, the temperature pleasant. Tall rock formations reminded him of people, but they did not move. *Perhaps they are lampiades*, he thought, remembering the stories of sleek, underworld water nymphs that his mother told him haunted the underground springs. Here, among them, he felt that sense of peace that she had spoken of when she was in the womb of Grandmother Gaia.

"Thank you," he whispered to the girl.

"Gratitude brings grace," the girl whispered back. Kheiron nodded as he noticed a golden glow lying on the pebbled beach near him – Apollo?

The sun god stood up and stretched.

"Feeling better?" Artemis' voice came from behind.

"Yes," Apollo answered and launched himself into the pool. His shining light illuminated the underwater stones as he swam across the bottom. When he swam back to the beach he lifted his hand. In his palm was a rock he had collected.

"A prism," he said, handing a quartz point to Kheiron. Even in the pale light of the cave, tiny rainbows shone just for a moment.

Next to Kheiron, Artemis spoke, "You should hold onto that rock. It will help you concentrate the healing power of the earth when you do your work." And she passed him a leather bag to keep it in.

"My healing work?" Kheiron asked. "What do you mean?"

Apollo stared at Kheiron with a trance–like gaze as if looking across a wide distance. "Healing of the body, mind and soul –not just for yourself, but for others. It is in suffering that one learns compassion. It is in harming and realizing the consequences of your actions that one begins to learn forgiveness. It is in living that you will come to know the skills needed by men, and it is to you that they will come for learning."

"That doesn't make any sense," Kheiron answered.

Apollo looked away from whatever it was he saw and laughed. "Prophecies don't always make sense, but when time runs its course the pieces settle together, and the vision is revealed. Sometimes not as you first imagined, but, nonetheless, it reappears like a forgotten dream."

Kheiron shrugged his shoulders, and Artemis smiled. The girl from the pool kept her eyes trained on the goddess and smiled when she did. Kheiron was to learn that Kallisto and the other loyal followers of Artemis were sworn virgins and declined the company of men. Apollo, being Artemis' brother was excluded, and Kheiron, as he would later wonder to himself, didn't count because he was half horse, not a man.

"Kallisto," Artemis called to her devotee. "Shall we hunt?" Kheiron perked up at the word.

"You like hunting, don't you?" the goddess said to him. He wasn't sure how to respond. He did enjoy the hunt but struggled with the notion of killing, especially now. He preferred to be a scavenger. None-the-less, he had learned how to trap wild birds, and he could catch rabbits with his bare hands. In fact he was quite good at it. He was a hunter by nature and quite adept at providing for himself. And the fact remained that he loved the taste of meat. When he was unlucky enough not to find any animals that had died of natural causes, he had eaten a lot of earthworms recently, but he decided not to mention that. It was an ongoing source of consternation and confusion whether to satisfy his hungry belly with the flesh it longed for or to follow his conscience and let all creatures live.

"Sometimes I like hunting," he answered.

Artemis laughed understandingly, "To care or to kill? A thought I often ponder. Yet we are hunters, Kheiron. It is our nature to kill, even while it is our nature to protect."

Artemis looked up at the dark roof of the cave. "To reconcile this dilemma, I have learned to kill quickly and with the least amount of suffering to the animal. Bleeding out is the sweetest way to die. The animal simply falls asleep when there is not enough blood in the system, whereas, if the windpipe is severed, there is a lot of distress and fear." Her gaze met Kheiron's and a look of understanding passed between them. "We will hunt together," she said with a smile, "we who understand one another."

Kallisto," she called to her maiden, "an extra bow and quiver for our young friend." Artemis turned and walked out of the cave, Kallisto right behind her.

Young friend? Kheiron thought to himself. I have lived eleven seasons. I am not so young.

"Go ahead," Apollo called from where he lay, lounging on the gravel beach. "Go have some fun. As for me, I am going to stay here. Soon enough I will have to pay retribution for killing Python."

Kallisto called back, "Follow me Kheiron, I'll show you the way."

Curious to see how Artemis hunted, Kheiron followed Kallisto and the goddess out of the dark cave.

19

Bows and Knives

Kheiron caught up with Artemis and the girl just outside the cave, but as he emerged from the tunnel a growl made him stop. Four wolves circled him. Artemis clicked her tongue and gestured with her hand. In response, the four beasts stepped back and became quiet.

"They are Artemis' hunting wolves," Kallisto said, petting the largest one on the head. "She has taken care of them since they were pups when their mother was killed by a foolish hunter. Now they are part of our family."

Kheiron nodded slowly, watching the wolves who eyed him suspiciously. Under Artemis' gaze, they made no attempts to harm him, but he could see in their eyes that if Artemis made the slightest indication of her approval they would rip him to shreds.

"They trust her completely," Kallisto said, as she lifted a wooden bow off her shoulders and handed it to Kheiron.

"You may use this for a while, she said, releasing her weapon with a slight hesitation. "At least until you have made one of your own."

Kheiron ran his hand down the smooth wooden arc.

"It's made of yew wood," Kallisto said, "fabricated with my own hands. Yet it serves the goddess as we all do.

"You will come to know that all yew trees are sacred to *Her*. All of *Her* weapons and tools originate from the yew tree. The stave from which we carve our bows, the shafts of our arrows and the handles of our knives, they are all made from yew trees."

Kallisto bowed slightly to the tree next to her, its reddish brown bark and spiky needles radiated a strong presence. She pulled one of the arrows out of her quiver and showed it to Kheiron.

The shaft had black crow feathers, glued with pitch and wrapped with sinew at the end. What was most interesting to Kheiron, however, were the tips. They were made of shiny metal, different from Apollo's and Artemis', but they were thin and very sharp. He wondered at this strange, thin material that did not break. Artemis read his mind.

"These points are bronze, a mixture of ores scraped from the bones of Grandmother Gaia and forged in the Vulcan home of Hephaistos."

"What is bronze, and who is Hephaistos?" Kheiron wanted to know.

"Too many questions," the goddess answered. "You will learn more about bronze later. As for Hephaistos, he is the crippled son of Zeus and Hera and has no match in the art of metal smithing." She turned her shoulder to show her silver bow and arrows. Then she brandished several sharp blades made of bronze.

"Take your pick of the blades," Artemis said holding them out for Kheiron to choose.

Each of the knives had a wooden handle, carefully hewn by skilled hands. Each was different, infused with the essence of the tree and by the one who carved it. All carried the scent of old blood. They were extremely sharp, much sharper than any stone, horn or bone blade that Kheiron had ever used.

"It can cut through the thickest bear hide," Kallisto added, indicating her sandals that were evidently made from bear paws.

Bear hide, Kheiron sniffed, *that is what this girl Kallisto smells like –bear and wild oregano.* He had come to realize that every person and every animal had its own scent, distinct even from others in the same brood. He sniffed again and took a long draught of this bear, oregano-scented girl. He sniffed in the direction of Artemis and noted yew, cedar and mugwort, indecipherable from the trees and plants that she loved.

Kheiron looked at the knives in Artemis' hand and chose one with a long blade. It seemed huge to him, but later, as he grew larger, it would seem small.

Kallisto smiled. Like Artemis, she wore the skins of many animals and carried leather bags over her shoulders and around her waist. Her hair was straight, almost black and cut short. When she smiled, Kheiron felt warm inside. To him she was beautiful in her own rough way, tough and sinewy like the wolves, but her smile was unaffected and sincere, and she did not look at Kheiron with fear as did every other human he had encountered. Kallisto was human, of that he was certain, but that did not diminish her beauty nor reduce her skills. She did whatever Artemis asked, responding as if the goddess' desires were her own.

Artemis nodded her approval, for what, Kheiron couldn't tell, but Kallisto handed Kheiron a sheath. "It is for the knife, a gift from Artemis," she turned her eyes toward Artemis' feet and the goddess smiled.

Wings beat the air, and a bird swooped down from the sky. A crow landed on Artemis' head, but the goddess seemed undisturbed. In fact she opened a small pouch at her waist and, taking something from it, handed the bird a red berry. It hopped to her shoulder where it turned it's head from side to side and eyed Kheiron.

"He is a friend," Artemis told the crow. But the bird continued looking curiously at the half horse-half man creature before taking the berry. After a moment, it regurgitated the seed and dropped it into Artemis' waiting hand.

"Even the seeds of the yew have great power," Artemis said, rolling the small black seed between her fingers. In their hearts, they hold a poison so strong that, when it hits the blood of its victim, death comes swiftly. Even the needles contain this poison. It is a tree to be respected, honored and used with wisdom."

Stroking the branch of a yew tree Kallisto said, "You are fortunate to have been told her secret. There are no bows or arrows so fine as the ones made by Artemis. Ask for her blessing, and, when it comes time for making your own, she will help you in the crafting.

Kheiron looked at the slender tree towering over them, its fronds pointing side to side in a flat plane. He would learn that this tree made good bows because of its flexibility even when dried and old. He was familiar with tree *dryads*. Like all creatures, each tree had its own personality, and this one, in a gesture of acceptance, scratched his head slightly.

"You will come to know this tree as a friend," Artemis said. "It will find you when you are lost, guide your arrows, and point the direction of your future. Listen carefully, for it has much to teach."

Then the goddess took her bow and, fitting one of the black feathered arrows against the sinew, imitated how she would track an animal. Like a dance she had performed many times, she moved her body and bow as one.

"Follow the prey with your mind," she said. "With your eyes, match its speed and aim ahead. See your point piercing through the heart, right behind the front shoulder . . . and release."

She lowered her bow and gestured to Kheiron to take his turn.

Awkwardly, he placed the notched end against the sinew, aimed at a leaf and released. The arrow wobbled and fell far before its mark. Artemis smiled wryly.

"Kallisto will help you practice. But in the meantime, come with us and watch. You will learn."

20

Hunting with Artemis

Artemis dug her foot into the ground and, not following any trail, leaped into the woods. Kallisto and the wolves followed behind her. Kheiron ran to catch up, but it was hard to match their speed. Despite the absence of a path, they ran, oblivious to the branches and twigs that slapped and scrapped them as they stayed their course.

Kheiron finally caught up on top of a small hill that overlooked a stream. Kallisto raised her finger to her lips, indicating quiet. The wolves cowered and lay down, all the while keeping their eyes on Artemis for her next move.

The goddess nodded toward Kheiron. Her face flickered with shadows and light. She was a creature of the forest and spoke the language of the animals, without words. Her gaze told him to pay attention.

The cool, fresh scent of water, alders and willows filled Kheiron's nose. The breeze lifted the hairs on his arms and told him that the wind blew downstream . . . and there was something more, the musty scent of a buck. Kheiron pointed upwind. Artemis nodded knowingly. Their vantage point camouflaged them from the unsuspecting creatures that came to the stream for a drink.

Within moments, dry leaves crunched just beyond their vision, and the wolves silently stood up to watch.

A roebuck jumped out of the brush. It stood with its ears perked and turned in all directions, feeling that something was different in the quiet.

Her bow already strung, Artemis' gaze followed the buck as it stepped into the water. Without waiting, her arrow sped through the air and struck him in the heart.

Startled and mortally wounded, the buck instinctively ran toward whence he had come.

"She never misses," Kallisto whispered. "Deadly. She doesn't like to make an animal suffer for long."

Kheiron valued that quality in the goddess and watched her as she kept her eyes and ears trained on the buck. Then she looked at Kheiron. Her gaze was piercing and intense, and told him to follow and track the buck . . . slowly.

The horse-boy led the group downhill, agily skirting rocks and trees in his way. Kallisto was right behind him, then Artemis and the wolves after her. The goddess trained her apprentices through example, but then stayed behind to let them test their own abilities.

Kheiron's instincts came alive. His ears and nose twitched as he plunged into the brush, pushing his way through branches into the stream. Water scrambled the stag's smell, but Kheiron noticed a low growing leaf near his hoof, and a small drop of blood. Artemis restrained the wolves.

There was no path, but Kheiron pushed into the thicket – nothing. Doubting himself, he started to turn back, but a cloven hoof under dense brush moved slightly. The dying buck had thrown itself into the thicket in an effort to hide.

Pride filled Kheiron's heart as he shoved the bushes aside and saw the young buck. Only a minute had passed since Artemis' fatal arrow had struck.

Kheiron's pride diminished as he knelt down and struggled with his internal desire of wanting to help and knowing that the buck would be dead in a moment.

The wild creature knew that he was dying, and there was a look of surrender in his dark pupils. His eyes became foggy and his head drooped. Kheiron started to sing. It was a *naiad* lullaby filled with the comforting sounds of water.

"Sleep little one.

The worries of the day are gone.

Kshhhh, daaadaaa, glurrrr, glurrrr.

Kshhhh, daaadaaa, glurrrr, glurrrr."

The buck's head relaxed, and his body went limp.

"I'm sorry," Kheiron whispered. A few tears dripped down his face as he turned his head away and pulled himself out of the thicket. He did not want Artemis or Kallisto to see him crying.

"To kill or to care?" he thought. That is what Artemis said.

The goddess understood the torment in his generous heart. Light and shadows crossed her face. "You are very compassionate, Kheiron. Some hunt with no thought for the life they take. Yet all life is valuable. We give thanks to this buck that surrendered his breath so that we might fill our bellies with his strength. Would you be so generous as to give your life so that others could eat and live?"

Kheiron nodded affirmatively. "I would," he answered.

"As well you should, Little Colt. As well you should."

Kallisto, moving quickly, was already in the bush and dragging the carcass out. She took a knife from the sheath at her waist and with its talon-sharp blade opened a slit between the deer's leg bones. She cut through the muscles of the belly and all the way up to the neck, careful not to sever the bladder, stomach or intestines. "Urine spoils the meat," she said, wiggling the fleshy sac loose. "But we won't let it go to waste. Bladders as well as stomachs make good water containers." Then she cut the wind pipe and pulled the internal organs, from top to bottom, all the way out in one neat package. Finally, she flipped the carcass over. A gift to Grandmother Gaia," she said, as the blood drained onto the soil.

When she was done, she placed the internal organs back inside the abdominal cavity to make transportation easier. Every part of the animal, Kheiron learned, would later be eaten or used for some utilitarian purpose.

Finally Kallisto stood back and waited, indicating that the animal was ready to be moved. Kheiron took her cue and lifted the front legs of the carcass. The head went limp toward the ground. Kallisto took the back legs and lead the way.

As they went, Kheiron thought. Was hunting necessary, or could he just be a scavenger? There was a certain excitement in tracking, losing the trail and discovering it again. He thought of the baby goat and other numerous animals that had died in his arms. They had each become precious to him. Killing was difficult, whether for food or to end the torment of suffering.

Just now, it was the buck's eyes that troubled him most. It had looked at Kheiron not so much with fear as with resignation. Kheiron had not shot the fatal arrow, and yet he felt like he had been looking into the eyes of a friend he had just killed. The deer, however, had not conveyed any indication of remorse. The buck had been a brother of the forest, killed for food that he, Kheiron, would be all too happy to eat, enjoy even. Was it so simple that some needed the flesh of others to survive while others needed only foliage, roots and berries? His mother could not kill. "It was for you," she had said non-judgmentally when she told him about the fish she had eaten in her pregnancy. "You need meat just like wolves and lions."

How could he ever reconcile these two opposite, instinctive needs? How could he heal and kill simultaneously?

He looked at the hunting wolves who pranced by Artemis' side almost smiling for the food they brought home.

21

The Daughters of Artemis

Kallisto and Kheiron followed behind Artemis and carried the roebuck. They walked through the forest until they heard the sounds of people -- clanging and scraping, along with hushed, low voices. And then they were among them, five women and two young girls who now stood silently watching the small hunting party.

It was evident in their gaze that Artemis was loved and respected here. She made eye contact with every woman and girl, and each lowered her eyes and bowed her head as she received this blessing.

Kheiron noticed their glances at him. They did not stare, but took quick looks, trying not to seem as if there was something unusual about him, this horse-boy who accompanied their goddess.

These women were wiry and tough, of various statures and colors, dark skin and light, black hair and red, scratched and weathered. That there were no men among them made no impression on Kheiron. To him that seemed normal, having spent his entire young life among none but women, the only exception being Apollo and on one occasion Kronus.

Apparently the hunting party had interrupted the women at their work. Strips of suspended meat hung over a hand twisted rope near the fire, drying in the smoke. It was a familiar scene to Kheiron, as was the blackened, clay pot that simmered in the fire. The aroma of rabbit meat and wild thyme made Kheiron's mouth water in anticipation of a meal. Two women had been busy cleaning animal skins. One was in the process of scraping the inner flesh from a rabbit hide while the other was stretching a bear skin over a large rock.

One young woman, who seemed particularly muscular, stood over a flat stone. Stacked beside her were roughly wrought ore arrow tips. In her hands she held a tool for pounding, also made of ore. Around her hands and arms she wore thick hides, as if to protect her skin. It brought to memory, Kheiron's grandmother *Yaiyai* Tethys, who used leather over her hands when she pulled the *psomi* out of the oven. However, what was particularly unusual about this woman was that she had only one breast.

Kheiron tried not to gawk at the strange anomaly nor to be too uncomfortable with the other women who seemed unsure how to treat him – as a friend or a foe. He was a male in the company of sworn virgins. Men were not allowed in their midst. But Kheiron did not know this. He sensed only that they were all uncomfortable with him. It was then that the largest of Artemis' grey-black wolves moved in, and without even a growl, licked Kheiron's horse shin. Her approval made the others relax. A few even smiled at their new guest. The she wolf, like Artemis, rarely made shows of affection to anyone, so this gesture gained him immediate acceptance.

"His name is Kheiron," Artemis told the women. "He is alone in the world. Teach him everything. He is a child of the forest and hungry for knowledge."

Catching the sunlight in her eyes, Artemis smiled with a knowing nod. Then she turned, and with her bow and quiver over her shoulders, she ran up the hill, wolves at her heels and crow overhead. No one questioned her. Like

Apollo she made her own plans and followed her own inspirations. Everyone else served her.

Kallisto pulled the dead buck forward. "Follow me," she said. "I'll show you where we need to go."

Kheiron followed in tow, carrying the roebuck's front legs and passing the other women and the campfire with the succulent rabbit stew. Two of the girls ran ahead, and whispers started up behind him.

Distracted by the unusual girls, Kheiron got out of step with Kallisto and almost dropped the heavy carcass. Kallisto looked over her shoulder in frustration, and Kheiron focused his step, moving his right hoof forward just as she stepped forward with her right foot. This kept their walking rhythm smooth and the burden less awkward. Hereafter, he would be careful to pay more attention.

When Kallisto stopped, Kheiron looked around and noticed a cave with animal skins that camouflaged an opening.

Kallisto looked over her shoulder and nodded at Kheiron, as if to say, we are here.

Kheiron watched Kallisto and carefully lowered the carcass to the grass, matching his movements with the girl.

Kallisto gingerly removed the internal organs and set them on a piece of leather. They would be carried to the stream, rinsed and then cooked or used in some other way.

Kallisto did not waste her time or her energy. Every movement of her body had a purpose. "We will eat liver and heart tonight," she said, as she ran a cord through the split bones of the buck's hind legs, "and tomorrow, head stew."

She severed the head with her knife, cut the skin around the ankles and up each leg, then removed the hide in one piece using only her hands and a sharp stone. When the carcass was rinsed and cleaned they carried it into the cave. The other girls had prepared the area by covering the floor with layers of wild oregano and thyme. There wasn't much room, but the air was cool, cold even. Wedged between the walls was a wooden scaffold that was secured into carved notches in the rock. Over this beam, the girls tossed their rope and hoisted up the carcass so that the shoulders hung high off the floor thus making it difficult for wild animals to reach. Kheiron helped by holding the deer's back from underneath while the others secured the rope in place.

He wanted to know everything about how they prepared, preserved and ate their meat. It showed on his face as he watched Kallisto secure the rope.

"So long as it is cold enough," she said, "we age our meat after we skin it." The stiffness comes and goes, and the flavor becomes rich. If it is too warm, we eat the meat right away and then preserve the rest near the fire, with salt and herbs."

She smiled at Kheiron's eagerness. "When the aging is done, the meat becomes dark, and there is a nice shine on it. But it must keep cool," she reiterated, "or it will go bad. That is why we cover the cave door with two rows of hides.

Kheiron knew about bad meat, having experienced the nausea and vomiting that accompany it. He had watched vultures and even wolverines eat old meat, but apparently they could eat things that he could not. In his own attempts to prevent spoilage, he had cooked his meat quickly, dried it or given it away.

A shaft of light shone through the split hide covering over the cave door, and Kheiron wondered what type of animal those large skins could have come from.

"Bulls," Kallisto answered, when he asked. "Big, aren't they?" She pushed them out of the way and urged Kheiron and the girls to precede out of the cave. Then she secured the hides in place with leather lacing.

"These hides keep the cave cold and help prevent spoilage. They also keep most of the flies out so that we don't get too many maggots."

One of the girls appeared as if she intended to stay and sat down at the cave's entrance. Kheiron looked at her questioningly.

"Someone has to guard our meat. We are willing to share," she said, "but not to be stolen from."

Kheiron had never minded sharing with wild animals, though sometimes they did take too much.

22

Orphans

One of the younger girls walked beside the unusual horse-boy, curiously looking at him out of the corner of her eye. "Who are your parents?" she asked.

"Philyra," Kheiron answered slowly, "and Kronus. What about you?"

"I don't know," she answered. "Artemis found most of us. We were abandoned in the forest for various reasons – Perhaps an oracle prophesized some unfortunate tale of our future, or more likely, we were simply unwanted girls – you know, not boys. It is easier to leave a child to the whims of Nature rather than take its life. That's when Artemis found us, as babies or children, alone in the forest. She cares for the orphaned, the young of all animals. That is why I wondered . . . if you were orphaned too?"

Kheiron thought for a moment. "Maybe I am," he answered.

The girl nodded with understanding. It was hard to admit that your parents didn't want you.

Kheiron's attention turned toward thoughts of Apollo, and he wondered where the god might be. When he asked, the girl said, "Don't worry. He is like Artemis. He will find you."

In the camp, Kheiron felt a little timid as the women eyed him. They greeted him with approving nods, though being shy he only returned the gesture slightly. He didn't know then that a man in their midst had limited moments in

143

the world. He was, as of yet, unfamiliar with the vows of Artemis' Daughters.

Kallisto led Kheiron to the smith woman. Everyone was skilled in each responsibility, but this girl seemed to have a way with metal. She was wrapping up her work for the day in a large piece of leather.

"Makara," Kallisto said. "Kheiron is interested in metal and bronze. I trust that you will guide him in his understanding of the craft."

The smith woman with one breast, looked at Kheiron with a sneer and nodded. Yet Kheiron felt awkward, as if she had been commanded to be his teacher and didn't want to. He tried to make her more comfortable by saying, "If there is anything I can do to help you?"

Makara lifted one corner of her mouth in a slight smile, then unrolled the leather skin that she had just carefully tied up. There in the waning light lay her work: arrow tips, thin and sharp like those that Kallisto had shown him earlier. Kheiron looked at them carefully, noticing that each one was unique.

"Can I learn how to make points like these?" he asked.

"As the Goddess wishes," she answered curtly.

Excited at the possibility of making such incredibly, sharp, thin arrow tips, Kheiron eagerly looked for more.

Sensing his delight, Makara reluctantly unwrapped another roll, just a little proud to show the efforts of her labor.

The blades she unveiled were different shapes and sizes. Some were like the knife that Kallisto used to disembowel the buck, but others were curved, pointed, and very sharp for cutting roots.

There was one, in particular, longer and wider than the others, that had sharp teeth like a baby lion's, all in a row.

"This one is used to harvest trees and limbs for our bows," Makara said. "It is the hardest to make and yet extremely useful."

Kheiron touched it carefully. Tools and weapons piqued his curiosity.

"Can I work with you tomorrow?" he asked excitedly.

Makara stared at him coldly. "Unless the Goddess has other plans," she answered.

Kheiron smiled at her, "I am glad to meet human women."

At this comment, three of the girls folded in around him.

Makara postured intimidatingly. "There is something you must understand about us," she said to Kheiron. "We do not abide the company of men, mothers, or family societies. We are not like other human women. We are huntresses. The Goddess has welcomed you among us, perhaps, because you are young and more animal than man. Had you been a man, we would have already cut your throat."

Cold emotions flashed from her eyes, and Kheiron stepped back, feeling the vehemence with which she spoke and the lack of care with which she would just as easily slice his neck at a moment's notice.

The storm of emotion passed, and Kheiron was left puzzled, categorized as an animal, and questioning his own identity. Philyra had called him her "precious horse-boy." And he had seen himself through her eyes, as more of a boy than a horse. Now among these women, or rather huntresses, he looked at Makara and tried to see himself in her eyes. They were blank.

"What am I then?" He asked her.

Makara took a step forward, cornering him with her dark eyes. "You are a deformed animal."

Kheiron shook his head, just as other wild animals do to convey that there is no threat, and Makara stepped away, relaxing her aggressive stance.

"A deformed animal," he repeated. And she nodded her agreement.

Kheiron did not want to show his disappointment or fear. Animals can smell that, so he turned his back to Makara, as if he didn't care and walked toward Kallisto. Hopefully Apollo would find him soon.

* * * * *

Kheiron followed Kallisto as she hurried over an un-worn path that turned and twisted through the trees. In a clearing they came across Artemis, who sat cross-legged upon a large rock overlooking a pool of water. The goddess seemed to be watching the fish as they fed in the twilight. Small, concentric circles spread out from where each fish breached the surface to catch a bug. Their hungry efforts gave the smooth water the appearance of rain.

Kheiron stepped into to the pool to get a drink and heard the honking of swans overhead. They announced Apollo, who appeared suddenly next to Artemis in the last rays of sunlight. Kheiron sighed from relief.

Kallisto bent down on one knee and lowered her head in reverence toward Artemis, and then to Apollo. Kheiron climbed out of the pool and copied her movements as best he could, bending his forelegs and bowing his head.

Artemis nodded in recognition and rose saying, "We will sing tonight under the stars." Then she strode past them, a soft pale glow following in her wake. *The moon and the sun*, Kheiron thought to himself, as he watched Apollo pass in a golden glow.

When the dog star was high above their heads, the other women sat quietly around the fire, whispering if they spoke at all, until Artemis introduced her brother.

"Apollo, my golden brother, has a story to tell us."

The golden god stood up and indicated Kheiron with jovial appreciation. "I found this young centaur wandering in the hills of Mt. Pelion, carrying a dead goat."

The women giggled, and Kheiron's cheeks burned hot as they all turned their eyes to look at him.

"He is very compassionate," Artemis added, "and already shows the skills of a fine hunter."

"He is a brother to our father Zeus," Apollo continued. "He is a son of Kronus."

Kheiron noticed Kallisto out of the corner of his eye. She beamed at him. He didn't know why, yet her smile made him feel warm, and he lowered his head shyly as Apollo recounted the story of his fight with the serpent.

"...Python, the giant snake," he spoke dramatically, "killed the virgin priestesses and took the oracle for itself. The oracle of Themis prophesized Python's death at the hand of one of Leto's children. Since Leto is our divine mother, that would be me, or you, Artemis. Python knew this when Hera sent it to chase and torment our mother during her pregnancy. The beast made sure that our mother would not find a safe place to give us birth. So, as it was, the battle was destined, and my motives for killing Python were not only to reclaim the Oracle for Zeus, but to seek vengeance for our mother."

Apollo described the battle in detail including the aftermath when he ingested the beast's poison and how he purified the waters.

"...Her vile toxicity infected my blood until I was so weak I could not lift my own body from the ground. Artemis healed me with her arrows of purification. And here in the Vale of Tempe, I died. I was reborn in the sacred pools. In truth, I continue paying restitution for Python's death. No one can kill a child of the gods without some sort of payment. Mine will be servitude to a human king, Admentus, who lives nearby. I shall shepherd flocks. Is there no lower occupation than that of a god in slavery to a mere mortal? But that is my restitution."

Apollo glanced at Artemis. "In gratitude for your healing, my dear sister, I bless your Vale of Tempe with opulence for one hundred generations. For now and a long time to come, this land will know abundance." His eyes sparkled with mirth, and the women, like a pack of wolves, howled in a cacophony of exhilarating cries.

23

Stories around the Campfire

Standing near the fire, Kheiron watched Apollo and Artemis. They had the same dark, curly hair that shimmered violet in the firelight. Artemis had the lithe body of a lion, agile and strong, and her brother, likewise, was lean and muscular. They both appeared kind, good natured and happy, but Kheiron had seen the look of death in Apollo's face when he killed Python, and it made shivers run up his spine. He now wondered if Artemis had that same quality. She cared for the young, orphaned creatures, abandoned in the woods, and yet she could kill like the messenger of death - with no remorse.

Now, side-by-side, the brother and sister glowed majestically, each reflecting sunlight and moonlight in the faces of the others around them.

Makara, the one-breasted woman, brought out a clay pot with an animal skin pulled tightly over one end. She began to hit it slowly, creating a steady beat to which the other women moved back and forth.

Kallisto started to sing. It was a chant unlike any Kheiron had ever heard before. His mother's songs were watery, melodious and bird-like in their lilt. But this one was strong and rhythmic and told of the powerful goddess who in her kindness watched over the young animals and women of the forest. Her ferocious nature frightened off those who would do them harm. The goddess' prowess with the bow and arrow was unmatched by any save her brother, the Golden God, Apollo.

"Kind beasts of the wood, beware of the Goddess,
For when she hunts, she hunts.
She will do anything, anything, anything for those
who serve,
But woe to those who break their vows.
Woe to those who cross her.
Death is certain.
Death is swift,
Death is certain
And very swift"

The songs went on into the night, songs of ferocities performed by the Goddess, songs of her hunts and acts of care. One tale told of both Artemis and Apollo, how they sought revenge for their mother upon the Queen Niobe. Kallisto told the tale:

"What human queen dare boast that she had more children than the Hyperborian Goddess, Leto, the sacred mother of our heavenly twins?

"That foolish queen, Niobe," Kallisto said dramatically, "had such audacity that she enraged the Goddess, she from whose womb came beloved Artemis and her sacred brother Apollo. Leto sent the moon and the sun to avenge the queen's haughty insult. Artemis with her accurate aim took down each of the queen's six daughters, and Apollo, with his golden bow, took down her six sons.

"Never was a queen so sad." the women repeated the chant, "Never was a queen so sad,"

Disturbed by this story, Kheiron wondered why the gods and goddesses were so petty as to avenge a mortal's foolish words. Their cruel actions seemed to be ruled by mere vengeance. They were Divine Beings to be respected, but how could he respect those who wantonly killed the sons and daughters of a silly human queen? The song so bothered him that he got up to leave the circle. Apollo and Artemis watched with questioning eyes. Kheiron knew that he could not keep secrets from them. Still he bowed his head in their direction, just as the other women had done when they got up to leave. They both nodded to him, and he started off into the darkness.

Within a few paces, his walk became a trot and then a full-fledged run as he pushed through bushes and trees. He stomped down vines with his hooves and made his way toward the open meadows.

He felt disappointed and confused as he clutched Kallisto's bow to his chest and ran. He had just begun to trust Apollo and Artemis, but now they had fallen in his eyes, and he felt alone, again.

In the obscurity, he could have stumbled into a ditch or ran into a tree, but the faint glow of starlight illuminated his way, and he was able to dodge rocks and jump over rivulets. He galloped as fast as he could until he came to the base of a hill, then he continued at full speed to the top of the crest.

At the summit, breathing hard, he stopped and paced. Sweat rolled down his flanks and his mind finally cleared of trouble. His breath slowed. From this vantage point, on top of the hill, he looked out over the dark valley where he saw the faint glow of Artemis' campfire. Or perhaps, he wondered, it could be the twins themselves? In either case, he looked away. Behind him were more hills, ever mounting, higher and higher. It was warm in the valley, but on the mountaintops amid the clouds that encircled the peak, he could see the soft reflection of snow.

Nature soothed Kheiron's troubled mind, and he sang a little song.

Glurr, naffshhhhhh

Sweet breeze and starlight
Trickling water and moon
Healing heart and gentle flight
The morning will be here soon.
Close your eyes and rest your soul
For tomorrow you will run, my foal
With all your might,
In the fields, my foal
With all your might and strong
Glurr, naffshhhhhh
Glurr, naffshhhhhh

He remembered laying his head in Philyra's lap, while she stroked his curls. The memory brought tears to his eyes, but he kept singing, repeating the song until a sense of peace came over him, and his tears dried. Maybe things weren't so bad after all. Kneeling down in the grass with his legs tucked under him, Kheiron watched his old friends the stars as they glided across the zenith and set behind the western horizon.

24

Under the Stars

Kheiron woke with a start. Darkness was all around him, and the goat constellation had moved halfway across the sky. He noticed a slight glow next to him, "Apollo?"

"I found you," the god answered. "What was wrong?"

He didn't have to ask. There were no secrets with Apollo. "It was the story, wasn't it? How is it that a god whose goal is to heal the sick can kill innocent children?"

Kheiron nodded his head. He didn't have to say anything. And Apollo continued.

"You give us too much credit. Gods are just as foolish as humans. We are slaves to our own emotions and troubled minds, full of ego and pride, jealousy and hatred, vengeance and despair –not always right or just. True, we are powerful and our love is great, as are our boons, but we are fallible, Kheiron. Give us our due respect, but do not expect us to meet your high, moral values."

Kheiron rubbed the sleep from his eyes and shrugged his shoulders. "My high, moral values? I just thought that you would use your great power to help others, not frivolously destroy lives because your mother was insulted. I expected more from you."

Kheiron could see Apollo's bright teeth in the dark as he smiled.

"That's what I like about you, Kheiron. You challenge me to be better. I could take your words as disrespect, but you say them in all honesty and without true condemnation. For such a thing I could kill you, but that would be another year of servitude to someone and besides, I need you and your wisdom."

Kheiron rolled his eyes, but Apollo had more to say, "Suffering and death are simply part of the natural cycle, even for the gods. Our powers pass away. We rule now, as Kronus ruled before, and Uranus before that. It is not that we disappear, but new gods come and take our places, stronger and hopefully wiser. Just as the stars rise up in the east, they set in the west and then rise again, birth, death, rebirth. We all die, mortals and immortals alike, but in different ways and not forever. The gods live on in the stars, and humans continue in the underworld with Hades, or in the Elysian fields, the land of the blessed, as spirits. And all of us are brought to life again as we are remembered."

"Is my mother a spirit?"

"Yes and no," Apollo answered.

"Did she abandon me? Did she think that I was an abomination, a monster? Is that why Artemis accepts me, because I am an orphan?"

"No, Kheiron. . . well maybe. Kronus raped your mother and disfigured her body. I suppose for that reason she hated you at first, but you are a wonder and a blessing."

"She hated me?" Kheiron said, realizing that what Kronus had said was, if fact, true.

"No." Apollo shook his head. "You are very special, Kheiron. Your mother loved you so much that her love glows in your heart and touches those around you."

"Look up there," Apollo said, bluntly changing the subject to get Kheiron's mind off this obsession. He pointed to a group of stars. "Do you see that bird with a long neck in flight, that swan?"

Kheiron studied the configuration of stars. "It looks like it is flying into the west, down toward the horizon."

"Only to rise again tomorrow night," said Apollo in a dreamlike voice. "On Delos, where Artemis and I were born, there are lots of swans, big, white birds with long necks and dark beaks. The males are called cobs, the females, pens. They are magnificent in flight and regal as they float in the water. I call her Cygnus," he whispered, looking at the constellation, "Cygnus, the pen, the female swan. Even Hera, in all her jealousy, cannot destroy everything that is precious to me."

"What do you mean?" Kheiron asked, remembering Hera, the young girl who played with him in the meadow when he was very little.

"Hera, daughter of Kronus, technically your half-sister, I know you think she is kind," Apollo said, "but she hates me and to a lesser degree Artemis. We are the children of Zeus by Leto. And, of course, she hates our mother. I suppose it is natural. She wants Zeus to herself. But Zeus is a lover of many beauties, nymphs, goddesses, even humans. He loves them all, and Hera hates them. She likes Artemis all right, perhaps because she refuses the company of men. When we finally get to Mount Olympus, you will meet Hera as she has become, trite and angry. But before we go, I must watch the flocks a little longer – you know, as payment for killing Python. Then we will go to Olympus."

"Oh," said Kheiron. "What am I supposed to do in the meantime?"

"Study with the Daughters of Artemis, I suppose. Kallisto will teach you some hunting and fighting techniques. Not everyone is as kind as you Kheiron, and you will need to defend yourself and others. You will see, time slips by very quickly, and this year, though it may be eight years in the realms of humanity, will seem like only a few days. Also, you can watch over the sheep with me and we can talk about what you have learned. You can improve your divination skills, and we can discuss healing in its many forms."

Kheiron nodded his head to show that it was all right with him. He trusted Apollo now. "I think she likes me," Kheiron added, thinking of Hera. "She was there when I was born you know."

"You are one of the fortunate few," Apollo answered, tracing the cross of Cygnus' long body in the sky with his finger. A star shot across the lower horizon and disappeared in mid-flight. Apollo smiled. "Yes, time slips by very quickly."

25

Running With the Horses

Kheiron awoke in the cool morning and shook all over. Droplets of dew flew in all directions. Here on the hill, above the Vale of Tempe, the air was sweet.

Kheiron trotted down toward the familiar river where he scooped his hands into the cold water for a drink. When he looked up, he saw a cloud of smoke rising in the west.

Fire? he wondered, but looking more closely, he saw horses running at the forefront of the smoke. The clouds were dust.

Curious about horses, Kheiron jogged toward the Vale floor. He hoped to watch the herd from a distance. However, the lead stallion, a beige, saw him and stopped. The other horses followed suit as the cloud of dust caught up and covered them all in an obscuring mist from which the stallion emerged. It ran full speed toward Kheiron.

Uncertain what he should do, Kheiron shook his head to let the stallion know there was no trouble, but the horse saw him as a threat and intended either to kill or chase him off.

The horse-boy retreated toward the hill from whence he had come, but when he looked back, the stallion was quickly catching up with him. Before he knew it, the other horse had run ahead to block his way. At the top of a knoll, the beige stallion watched then began to circle Kheiron closer and closer. It lunged at him in intimidating advances then snorted and reared as Kheiron backed away. Kheiron could feel its breath on his arm, and he moved quickly out of the way. But the horse stomped the ground.

Just as the stallion swung its head in a quick biting movement, Kheiron backed up and turned quickly to avert the injurious teeth.

He did not fight back, but the stallion bit at him relentlessly until it caught a chunk of flesh from his shoulder. Then it turned and kicked him.

Kheiron moved out of the way, but powerful hooves smacked his buttocks, and pain shot through his leg. Immediately, the stallion leaped forward, lifted its back legs off the ground and kicked at him again.

Instead of standing there, Kheiron ran as fast as he could in the other direction. The stallion chased him.

Kheiron ran to the top of a small bluff with the stallion in hot pursuit,. Once there he stopped and stood, breathing hard.

The stallion was almost on him when Kheiron started waving his arms and yelling, "Horse brained fool. Can't you see that I mean no harm?"

With his arms waving high above his head, Kheiron seemed taller and bigger, and when Kheiron reared up, instinctively defending himself, the stallion backed up – frightened by the strange horse.

Realizing the effect of his noise and movements, Kheiron dropped his hooves to the ground and shook his head near the stallion's eye. He growled angrily.

The stallion looked at Kheiron's wild-eyes then bolted toward his herd.

Kheiron stood alone. He had frightened off the lead stallion despite his own terror.

His laughter broke the air as he made his way toward the river.

Without fear Kheiron ran into the water. He let the current push against his haunches and flow through his fingers. It was cool and brisk, and he shivered all over.

When he stepped onto the bank he felt his full horse nature and wanted to run. He took off at a gallop and could have run forever, his chest pumping with power and strength.

The horses had all run downstream with the stallion and were now grazing, when Kheiron unexpectedly startled them again. However, this time, struck with an idea, he ran toward the herd. They ran too, trying to get away. He didn't care this time and instead ran hard to catch up. Soon he found himself side by side with the slower mares.

When they noticed the strange human torso, they ran faster, but Kheiron matched their pace, and he stayed with the herd, all of them running until they were exhausted. When they finally began to slow down, he shook his body loose to show there was no need for fear. Still they stepped away from him. Once again the stallion tried chase him off. Frustrated, Kheiron started in the opposite direction. Apparently, he would never be accepted by men or beasts.

He ran, but the funny thing was that this time the horses followed him. The stallion condescended to Kheiron's superiority and they ran together -- Kheiron, the stallion and the mares, as one big beautiful herd, hooves pounding earth, breathing hard. Kheiron had never felt such exhilaration, and he made happy horse sounds that were imitated by the others behind him.

When they slowed to a canter, some of the mares drifted toward the river for a drink, snorting as they went. Kheiron stood among them in the water, the animals who where most like him, and watched the sun rise over the eastern hills. For the first time since before his mother had disappeared, Kheiron felt happy.

26

Fire and Ore

After his experience running with the horses, Kheiron walked with a more confident air. By day he apprenticed with Artemis and her daughters and learned more about the codes by which they lived. All of the women wore leather skins around their waists and chests. Each carried a bow and quiver, weapons, Kheiron learned, that every daughter had made for herself. Each girl created her weapon in a ritual act that took much concentration and unfortunately did not always turn out the way she hoped.

Every daughter had knives, some were carefully chiseled stone and some were metal, while others were made of bone or horn. Over their shoulders or around their waists, they carried leather pouches and stomach bladders that contained food and water. They never took anything extraneous with them, but always had what they needed. It was important to be able to move quickly as necessity demanded.

Camp was a place where they stayed for a while, curing and drying meat, making new weapons, or repairing the old ones. Meat was an important part of their diet, especially when they were on a long run. A run could last for months. During that time they ate fresh kill, but the dried meat preserved with salt and oregano, garlic and thyme was a daily staple. Caches were made to store what they could not take with them. These were generally buried in caves and piled over with rocks, camouflaged from unsuspecting eyes or hungry noses. They didn't mind sharing their food with wild animals. That was natural. Humans were another story.

The daughters of Artemis were fast, fast at running and fast in their crafts. They practiced their skills daily, which included sparing and mock fighting. Artemis wanted each of her daughters to be able to not only protect herself, but also the young and helpless. Some of the daughters, as Kheiron had noted before, had only one breast. Makara was one of those. Without realizing any transgression on his part, Kheiron boldly asked her, "Why do you have only one breast?" It was an innocent question, but Makara flushed. Already, having Kheiron in their midst disturbed her.

"It is a small sacrifice to run with the Goddess."

"A sacrifice?" Kheiron asked.

With one swift move, Makara pulled the bow off her shoulder, laced it with an arrow, and trained it on Kheiron's chest. That, along with her deadly gaze, made Kheiron realize that she could easily kill him without regret, and his heart began to race.

"My breast was in the way," she said, "so I sacrificed it."

"Oh," Kheiron responded, shaking his head like a deer in an attempt to dispel her defensive stance. "Did it hurt?"

"Of course," she said sarcastically, lowering her bow. "A sacrifice is supposed to hurt."

"How did you patch it? How did you make it heal?" Kheiron wanted to know.

Makara rolled her eyes, annoyed at his incessant questions.

"With macerated herbs."

"Which herbs, and how long did it take?"

"If you must know, it took a cycle of the moon from the first quarter and then back again. Artemis helped me sew

162

the skin together with sinew, and we used yarrow, calendula and the roots of Althea." She smiled wryly as she remembered Artemis piercing the horn needle through her flesh.

"I know those plants," Kheiron said excitedly. But unimpressed, Makara said, "So you think you are smart?

Kheiron turned his eyes to the ground and said no more.

* * * * *

The next day, when Kheiron trotted into the camp, he felt troubled. He wanted to feel accepted among the daughters of Artemis, but so far only Kallisto seemed to genuinely like him. He looked for her amid the busy girls, but today he was expected to help Makara, a job he did not look forward to, not because of the work, but because she seemed to dislike him so much.

Makara stared at him with an angry gaze when Kheiron walked into her view. He shook his head to show that he had no aggressive intentions, but she plowed into him in an attempt to knock him off balance. With four legs, Kheiron steadied himself easily. Makara was not accustomed to fighting with a horse, or a horse-like creature. "You probably don't even know how to fight," she jeered.

Kheiron shrugged his shoulders and followed Makara who slinked through the brush like a silent lion. Kheiron had to gallop to keep up with her.

At first he had been excited to learn her metal craft skills, but now she didn't speak to him and hardly seemed to notice that he was there. Why do I have to work with her? he thought. Yet Artemis had ordered this arrangement, and everyone did what *She* said.

Kheiron stood silently as Makara gathered leaves and twigs into a pile. She pulled a horn from her waist and emptied its contents onto the dry kindling.

163

A glowing orange ember slipped out of the hollow horn and nestled among the tinder. Makara covered it over like a mother tending her child, then tucked more leaves and twigs over the glowing coal. The ember began to smolder, and within a few moments flames awoke and hungrily ate the small sticks.

"Fire is alive," Makara said, speaking quietly as if to herself. "Prometheus first gave fire to people for warmth and cooking. He hid it in a giant fennel stalk and stole it from the heavens against Zeus' will. In so doing, he sacrificed himself for the love of humanity."

"What do you mean," Kheiron asked, disrupting her spoken thoughts.

She glared at the horse-boy. "He gave humanity fire without the consent of Zeus," she said. "For his gift to us, Zeus punished him with eternal torture by chaining him to the cliffs of the Caucasian Mountains. There, a demonic eagle seeks him out daily and devours his liver. The eagle tears away his chest bit by bit as he screams for mercy." There was a vengeful gleam in Makara's eye as she observed Kheiron's worry over Prometheus' punishment.

"He is an immortal," she laughed. "So everyday his liver grows back and he suffers the same fate day after day. Sometimes," she added, lifting her eyes to Kheiron with a dark pleasure, "we make sacrifices for a higher purpose, despite the cost."

Keeping his distance from Makara, Kheiron watched the flame. *Stolen from the heavens*, he thought, *and for the good of humanity. Does that mean that when you act out of kindness for the good of others, without the consent of the gods, that you must pay?*

Makara stood up and looked around. Her eyes rested on a dry piece of wood. Two logs would be sufficient to make her fire hot and to replace the ember in her horn.

In the camp, Kheiron had watched her pack pine sap around the end of several branches. She didn't tell him why, but Kheiron was familiar with torches. The goddesses had used them in his cave on Mount Pelion.

"Shall we go?" Makara said, pointing the burning staff toward an opening in the hill. The daughters were familiar with every cave in the area, and because of its camouflage, Kheiron only just noticed this one as Makara disappeared into the dark hole. He followed, barely squeezing his horse body through the tight entrance.

Inside, the walls were damp and cool, just like the cave of his childhood. But the flickering shadows and smoky light gave Kheiron an ominous feeling as he walked forward.

"Will I be able to get out?" he asked Makara. But the young woman did not respond. And after a few paces the tunnel opened into a larger cavern. They continued walking until Makara finally stopped.

With a rough stone she scratched the wall, and something shiny reflected in the flickering light.

"Copper," she said, pointing out the vein of metal along the wall.

Taking a pointed tool she smacked the rock. Little pieces of the matrix fell to the ground. She hit it again and again, and did not relent until a small chunk of the metal had been exposed. Then she handed her pick to Kheiron saying, "Now it is your turn."

It took a lot of strength, and the impacts jolted his bones, but by emulating Makara's determination, Kheiron learned that the key to extracting metal from the earth involved not giving up.

Progress came slow. Makara had to light several pine pitch torches to keep their light going, and Kheiron's eyes and lungs burned with the smoke. She didn't complain though, so, neither did he.

By the time Makara was satisfied with their work, several small chunks lay on the cave floor. So much work produced so little material.

Makara took slow, shallow breaths of the smoky air and knelt down to gather the precious mineral. Few people knew the secrets to harvesting copper. Makara was one of them.

"I would not have brought you here," she told Kheiron, "but it is Artemis' will, not mine."

As part of the code of ethic, she expected Kheiron to carry the torches and tools. Everyone did their part. Though, in Kheiron's eyes, it seemed that she did not carry very much this time.

Outside, Kheiron took a deep breath of the fresh open air. There were still a few glowing embers in the small fire pit. Makara had timed herself just right. She untied her long horn and scooped up a hot coal. Among the girls, she was the main fire tender. Often, an ember from her fire would start the fire in their next camp, and she never went anywhere without it.

"You must be prepared," she said, looking at Kheiron scornfully. It was her duty to teach him even if she didn't want to.

Kheiron watched as she tucked the horn into to a tightly packed pouch.

"The ember must breathe," she said, showing Kheiron the open hole in the horn. Her method was an ingenious way to keep the ember well insulated and to ensure a fire from one place to the next. On long runs, Makara had to stop to build another fire and gather a new ember. She could boast that all of her fires came consecutively from one she built over three years previously, an achievement anyone who used fire would be proud to brag of.

It wasn't that the daughters didn't know how to start fire with a drill and a slab – each of them did and practiced the art. They always kept their eyes open for a good hearth and straight sticks with which to drill. Cottonwood was their favorite wood for this purpose. Few sticks were ever straight enough, but Kheiron learned from the daughters how to straighten fresh branches with heat so that they would harden into perfectly formed arrow shafts or drills.

"One must always have provisions or be getting them," was a common saying among the daughters.

Back at camp, Kheiron was only too happy to rest in the shade by the creek. Makara, however, was very excited about mixing her new copper with the tin she had traded.

"Now I can finish making my bronze tools," she said and turned her attention toward the fire, which was never far from her mind.

Despite Makara's intense interest in metal and the respect she earned for it, Kheiron noticed that some of the girls preferred bone, horn or flinted knives and arrow tips. The metal ones seemed thinner, sharper, and more efficient.

"Why aren't your blades made of bronze?" Kheiron asked a girl they called Cleo.

"Watch," she told Kheiron, and, using a bronze knife, she cut an elder flower. He observed as the living bush, with *drayd*, spirit fingers, retracted from the metal.

"When you cut a plant with metal," she said, "its spirit detaches. If you use your fingernails, or bone or even stone, it does not react so dispiritedly."

"Oh," Kheiron said, "perhaps I should make my blades out of stone and bone too."

167

Cleo nodded, but added, "Metal has its place though. In battle, it separates the spirit from the flesh. You know. It's more decisive."

"Have you fought in battle before?" Kheiron asked.

"No, but Makara has. She doesn't talk much about it, but she always expects danger to be hidden just beyond our view. Did you notice her bitter attitude? Don't take it personally. She hates everyone, especially Kallisto."

"Why?" Kheiron asked.

"Because she is jealous. Artemis loves Kallisto best." Cleo shrugged her shoulders. "We can't all be the favorite. At least we have a mother who cares for us."

As Kheiron watched Makara smelting the ore, a bright light shone from behind. Turning, he saw Apollo with his curly, dark hair draped over one shoulder. When the other girls realized the god's presence they tried not to stare. Artemis noticed the effect her brother had on them and quickly chided him.

"You are too lovely to grace our company, brother."

She said it kindly, but meant for him to leave. Apollo bowed respectfully and vanished into sunlight that blinded them all.

Some of the women sighed, but quickly righted their posture, trying not to give away the feelings that Apollo stirred in them. Kheiron noticed their reactions too but looked away. No one stared at him like that or sighed when he left. That was probably why Artemis let him stay among her daughters. He was not beautiful, just another animal, a deformed animal.

27

Stirrings of the Moon

On top of the hill Kheiron stood alone where he slept under the stars away from the daughters. Though he tried to sleep, the brightness of the full moon pierced through his skin, and a sense of longing, sadness and need filled him in the pale, blue light. Shadows seemed to rustle in the soft breeze. He wanted to be near someone, to be curled around a body who loved him and touched him.

He lay down wanting to snuggle against the earth. He wanted to hold the grass, something tangible in this cool, blue light that stirred his emotions. He shook himself, but the feelings did not go away. *Could it be the moon?* He wondered as he caressed the earth. He wanted to cry. He tried to hold back his feelings, but despite his efforts, tears ran down his cheeks, silently, quietly. *Alone, I am always alone.*

* * * * *

A gentle breeze lifted the fur on his horse back.

"The moon troubles the waters of the mind," Apollo whispered.

Kheiron was not surprised to see him.

"The moon stirs the depths of emotions and dredges up feelings that are otherwise invisible to the heart and eyes. What were your dreams?" Apollo asked as the blue light of the moon hovered over his shoulders.

"Dreams? I don't remember my dreams," Kheiron answered, "just this feeling of sadness and longing."

169

Apollo nodded with understanding, "Alone and afraid?"

"Maybe," Kheiron answered.

"The moon stirs dreams," Apollo repeated, "and dreams reveal disquieting truths. Everything you dream is you, the people, the landscapes. Emotions are released, but what is more important are the dramas. They are stories that tell you your true feelings. Shrouded in confusion, you must dissect them to understand."

"I dreamed I kissed Kallisto," Kheiron confessed.

"Longing for love, true love, self love," Apollo said.

"What does that mean?"

Apollo smiled. "You wonder who could ever love an animal. You, who loves everyone else?"

Kheiron shrugged. Sometimes Apollo said such provocative mysterious things, things that he was supposed to figure out.

"One day," Apollo said, "you will understand."

The full moon slid toward the western horizon as the pale light of dawn illuminated the sky.

Later that day, Kheiron thought about Apollo's words. In comparison, Artemis' teachings were more practical, survival in nature, hunting, food storage, working together as a group, and, of course, forest communications: without words.

He was learning so much, but why did this feeling linger inside him? This sadness?

28

The Red Eyed Bull

During the next year, Kheiron studied by day with the Daughters of Artemis, and at night, he watched the sheep of King Admentus with Apollo.

Apollo taught Kheiron songs and stories, made up poetry, showed him how to use his hands for healing, laughed and discussed divination, medicine and herbology.

A master with words, the golden god inspired Kheiron's imagination, and Kheiron, who listened carefully, saw and named the heroes and heroines that Apollo spoke of in the twinkling stars overhead.

"Look," Kheiron said, pointing to the northern sky, "Andromeda, the sparkling princess, with her arms and legs tied down to the rocks. She is waiting for the sea monster to come and eat her. And look at those stars. Do you see Perseus, the brave warrior who will rescue her, and Cassiopeia, her mother, sitting on the throne? And there is Cepheus, the father-king, fretting with his priests, and over there, the sea monster Cetus, coming to take Andromeda as sacrifice for his ravenous appetite."

Apollo's gaze followed the horse-boy's outstretched hand, and he laughed, "Your eyes have great powers of observation, Kheiron. And though Andromeda no longer roams the earth, she, Perseus, Cassiopeia and Cepheus continue to live in the heavens, as you see them."

"What is that cluster of stars?" Kheiron asked, pointing to a V shape."

"You tell me," Apollo answered, "you with the keen eyes. A diviner must watch the heavens and all of Nature. He must be observant of the animals that come and go and their antics. You, the diviner must pay attention to the outer portents. Everything you see in the present whispers of the past and the future. Listen to what spontaneously comes to your mind. The secrets of Nature and the messages in the stars will reveal themselves to you."

Kheiron stared at the twinkling V overhead. One of the stars shone with a red glow. As Apollo suggested, Kheiron let his mind wander. What could that constellation be? Uncertain, he watched until his eyes became heavy, and sleep carried him into a dream.

The next day Kheiron met Kallisto running from the thicket.

"Help me," she called to him. "Artemis wants us all to sew new clothes with a piece of hide from every kind of animal she has ever killed.

Kheiron shivered. "Does that include humans?"

"No," Kallisto answered, "but I suppose it could."

Kheiron trotted to keep up.

"Tell me," he asked the girl, "do you see me as more of an animal, or a man?"

Kallisto saw the look on his face and understood that her response was very important to him. "I don't think you could be categorized as either an animal or a man," she said. "But, since you ask, in my eyes you are more of a horse than a horse and more of a man than a man."

She smiled, but something lingered in Kheiron's demeanor that troubled her.

"You must not fall in love with me, Kheiron." You may love me as a sister. That is all."

"Love?" Kheiron questioned, surprised at the turn in her words.

"There are many types of love, you know," she continued. "There is the love of a child for its mother, the love of a dog for its master and the master for its dog. That is how I love Artemis and she, me, like a child and a mother, like a dog and a master. I would do anything for her as she would for me. But let's go. She doesn't like to be kept waiting. I'll show you the way."

When they came to a tall oak, Kallisto looked up. High in the branches, hanging from the limbs, were a few bundles.

"We store some of our things in the trees during the summer months," she said. "It is too high for most predators.

With that, she jumped up and grabbed a branch with both hands. She swung her body onto a lower limb and in an instant was climbing towards their secured stores.

"Here, catch," she hollered, and threw the bundles down to Kheiron who piled them at his feet. Then she scrambled to the ground as agile as any squirrel.

Kallisto hung two bundles over Kheiron's back then hoisted one more over her own. Kheiron could have carried everything himself, but among Artemis' daughters, everyone did their share.

Kheiron didn't mind being a beast of burden. He would do anything for Kallisto. But why did she tell him not to love her? Did she sense something? What were his feelings? Was his love like a child for its mother or a dog for its master? Or was it some other kind of love?

He followed Kallisto down a narrow path lined with giant ferns that scratched their legs as they passed, and soon they found themselves in a thicket with tall, maple trees draped in moss.

A sacred, unearthly feeling came over him as shafts of sunlight illuminated the under-growth. Looking up, Kheiron saw patches of blue sky framed with maple leaves and towering pines, cedars and yews. This was Artemis' woodland bower.

Like wind ruffling through the leaves, he heard the goddess' voice. "There is a man in my thicket."

"No, not a man," Kallisto replied, "but the horse-boy that you yourself have blessed with grace and tutelage. As you have told us, he is the healer who will do us no harm."

Artemis smiled. "Yes, Kheiron," she whispered. "You are welcome here, but know this: Never bring a man into my territory. I have no use for them. They dishonor women, take their sex, beat them, make them their slaves and take credit for their work."

Kheiron was silent. She spoke with such disdain that he wondered if all men were really that bad. And what did Kallisto mean when she said that he was more of a man than a man?

"Don't worry," Artemis answered his thoughts, "you will meet plenty of men, and you can decide for yourself."

Similarly to being in the presence of her brother, one could not have private thoughts around Artemis.

Her dark gaze looked beyond Kheiron. "Not all men are evil," she said. There are some who are kind and respectful, like Orion. He knew me like few others. He was a hunter beyond compare and never took advantage of my love. Yet, he died through an unfortunate event involving a scorpion. Find him for me, Kheiron, you who see the gods in the heavens. They say he is immortalized in the stars. Find him so that I can delight in his company yet again."

Kheiron laid the bundles of skins onto the ground. Artemis smiled. "Each one is so different," she said, as she un-wrapped them. Then she handed one at a time to Kheiron. "Tell me, which skin belongs to which animal?"

Am I a man? Kheiron wondered. *No, I am a deformed animal, an orphaned, deformed animal. That is why she lets me stay.*

"Which skin belongs to which animal?" Artemis repeated.

Pulling himself away from his thoughts, Kheiron looked at the animal hides and sniffed them. Immediately he recognized a rabbit and a fox hide, then a goat and a mouse. He could have named them all with his eyes closed, simply by their scents.

Artemis looked at him and smiled. "As we sew them together for our protective winter garb, I will tell their stories."

When the other women came and took up awls and sinew for sewing, true to her word, Artemis recounted each animal's birth and life, how they tracked it, where it was killed, who was there, and what meals they made of its flesh. She remembered so many details that the animals seemed honored and revered. This, Kheiron respected, because like him, Artemis honored life, even if she took it.

During the sewing, Kheiron was given an awl and the skins of a rabbit, a fox and a piece of bear to make a vest for himself, but Makara glared when he asked for a length of sinew.

"You should not be here," she whispered, "You are not a daughter of Artemis. Besides, you don't even know how to fight."

"I am learning," Kheiron whispered, trying to defend himself. But Artemis silenced them both with a reproachful stare.

175

By sundown, many sets of legging and long sleeved vests were nearly finished. Only one hide had not yet been used. It was the brown fur pelt of a bull. Kheiron touched it, and as he did so, Artemis nodded approvingly.

In his mind's eye, as she told the story, Kheiron could see the massive beast running through the brush. It bellowed and charged its pursuer, the goddess, oblivious that he was the hunted one. Bulls are like that. They have no doubt in their own abilities, and this one ran straight at Artemis.

A black-feathered arrow sped through the air and pierced the bull just behind the front leg.

"She never misses," one of the girls whispered.

"Unlike other animals," Artemis said, "this one did not run away when injured. Instead he merely paused and then stirred up a tremendous rage and charged me with everything he had. If I had been mortal, the bull would have gored me, but being the Virgin Huntress, I stepped to the side, unsheathed my long blade and sliced through his massive neck.

"The head collapsed as the bull's life fluids spurted from his throat. When the bull's knees crumpled to the ground, the earth trembled as if an uprooted tree had fallen. We ate the bull, sacred to Zeus and preserved his skin. We piled his bones in offering to Zeus and covered them with hot, succulent fat. This is the offering that Zeus, the Great God of the Heavens and earth requires. He must be thanked and adulated, or retribution will have to be paid."

Kheiron pushed the awl through the final stitches of his vest and yawned, but Artemis clicked her tongue, "You know you may not sleep here."

His head filled with hunting stories, Kheiron had been unaware when the sun had set. Silvery lights and shadows danced around Artemis' face as she smiled at him.

"You must start making your bow soon, Kheiron. After that you will begin archery practice with Kallisto."

A golden glow filled the bower as Apollo's voice echoed, "I have been teaching him archery myself."

"Of course," replied Artemis, "But he must also learn from Kallisto."

"You are right sister." Apollo conceded as his form came into focus. "Their destinies are entwined."

As with many twins, there was an understanding between brother and sister, each knew the other's thoughts with few, if any, words. However, what they said was disturbing to some, especially Kheiron and Kallisto who both questioned the comment of 'entwined destinies.'

"Everything shall unfold as it will," Apollo added when he saw their uncertain stares.

Kallisto rolled her eyes in frustration, and Kheiron pawed the dirt.

"Be gone you two," Artemis directed the two males. "Be gone."

* * * * *

On top of the hill that night, amid the cows and sheep of Admentus, Kheiron donned his vest and asked Apollo, "How do you know that our destinies are entwined? Mine and Kallisto's. Do you influence people?"

With twinkling eyes Apollo asked, "What do you mean?"

"Like did you bring us together on purpose? Are we meant to be here, or do things just happen? You can see the future, but does your seeing make it so?"

Apollo hesitated. "So many questions, like circles around a knot."

Kheiron scratched the ground with his hoof, uncertain how to say what he felt. "Do I love Kallisto as a sister? I like being around her, and I love the smell of oregano that

177

seems to follow her. I love how she smiles, but do I love her?"

Apollo grinned. "None of the daughters has anything to fear from you, Kheiron. Things seem complicated, but in reality, everything is very simple. All is unfolding as it should."

In frustration Kheiron said, "Nothing seems simple to me." "But you said that I would never hurt her, and I wouldn't. You know that, don't you?"

"Artemis knows it too," Apollo answered. She also knows that all men are not evil. She has just had some bad experiences. Men, and women alike, can be power hungry, selfish and cruel. Often this is because they were mistreated by someone else, especially when they were a child. People are born with certain natures, but no matter who you are, everyone needs a parent or mentor who demonstrates kindness and respect toward others. You were lucky Kheiron. Your mother cared for all the animals that came to her spring. Her tendencies run in your veins. Yet those of your father do as well. Kronus was and is a powerful god. And because of him, there is very little that you could not do. You Kheiron, will be a good mentor for many children."

"How do you know that?" Kheiron asked, but before he could say anything else, Apollo diverted their conversation. "Look, there is Cygnus, my swan, flying through the stars."

That was Kheiron's cue to bother him no more with questions.

What does it mean to be a good man? Kheiron asked himself as he inhaled the scent of crushed grass. The cool night breeze ruffled through his hair. A freshness floated up from the river – the smell of water. It soothed his mind with a comfort that reminded him of the spring on Mount Pelion.

Night spread across the sky, and Apollo's swan Cygnus, with its tail star shining bright, chased the path of the sun.

Kheiron saw three stars in a row, like a belt, and another three stars that could be the sheath of a knife. *Orion,* he thought. Then out loud, he said, "I think I see Orion, the hunter friend of Artemis. Was Orion a good man?"

"All men, and women too," Apollo whispered, "have dark places in their hearts and minds. That does not make them evil. Orion was not perfect. He was not always good. Artemis glorifies him too much. But people change, and I suppose he did too, especially when he saw the consequences of his actions. The hardships of life can sour a soul, or be an opening to a new way of living – with compassion for the suffering of others. Most people want to be good, but not everyone knows how. Just remember this: If you treat someone with kindness, it spreads and teaches kindness. Just be ready to defend yourself and those who are smaller than you." Then Apollo started humming a tune.

The brightest star rose above the eastern horizon. "Sirius," Kheiron said, "the dog star. Actually there seems to be two dogs, probably Orion's hunting pets, like Artemis' wolves." Kheiron didn't expect a response from Apollo, so he looked toward the western horizon where the V shape of stars still haunted him.

What is that constellation? He wondered and finally closed his eyes in sleep.

While he slept, hunting tales flooded his mind. He saw himself standing back to back with Kallisto, the strong, beautiful girl who smelled of oregano. In his dreams, he was part of the bull hunt. He was the hunter, and the bull was chasing him. When the beast was nearly on him, he pulled out his blade, just like Artemis, but, for some reason,

179

he could not kill the animal. Motionless, he stood face to face with the greatest creature he had ever met. Shivers ran down his spine, and Kheiron awoke in the dark with the bull's eyes haunting him – the bull, whose right eye glowed red. Instinctively he looked into the sky where the V shape of stars hovered above him. Then Kheiron understood what he saw, the bull with one red eye.

29

Makara

Kheiron stood in the shadows of a yew tree while he waited for the other daughters to get their dinner. He had been cooking with one of the daughters, a job he enjoyed because he loved food. He loved to touch it. He loved to smell it, and he loved to eat it. He had prepared fire-roasted deer meat and wild roots. He wanted to make sure that there was enough, so he waited for the others to eat first. The meals he helped to prepare were full of unusual flavors and textures that the girls were not always accustomed to, and maybe didn't always appreciate. Kheiron's keen sense of smell and his innate ability to discern if a plant was good to eat or poisonous, or medicinal, gave him a much wider variety of ingredients to work with.

"What is this weird root?" Makara asked him.

"Asphodel," Kheiron answered.

Makara nodded her head and ate everything in her bowl. Her attitude toward him had become more hospitable, especially now that he was cooking.

Kheiron shook his head. Their strange new relationship had developed after she attacked him one afternoon.

He had been coming down the hill from where he slept, when he saw Makara out of the corner of his eye. She ran quickly towards him with her knife in hand. Surly the one-breasted woman would have tried to kill him, but his instincts took over and he blocked her with his arm and pushed her to the side.

"You don't belong here," she had seethed and slashed his forearm. Blood spurted from the cut, and Kheiron backed up. She ran at him again, this time aiming for his face.

Kheiron reared and kicked her with his front legs, but not hard enough to hurt her badly. She fell backward, but scrambled to her feet and lunged at him. This time she cut his leg.

"Stop!" Kheiron had yelled.

"I hate you," Makara hissed and glared at him. "You are a man, a horse and a man."

Kheiron turned to the side and readied himself for her next attack. He had never really fought before, and didn't have any strategies for how to stop her. Yet, his instincts had come alive and he moved out of her way. He was much larger than her, but she was fast, and with her knife, she fought like a lion.

Kheiron could not stop her, however he succeeded in thwarting any more cuts from her knife. They fought for near an hour, until breathing hard and both covered in blood, Makara stopped.

"You are a lousy fighter," she said.

"Why did you attack me?" Kheiron asked.

"Because you need to learn how to fight and not just defend yourself, stupid, deformed horse." She had turned her back and walked away.

Since then, they had fought several more times. And Kheiron was beginning to anticipate her surprises, especially in moments when he least expected her. At first Kheiron felt afraid of these surprise attacks, but after the fourth one, he started to look forward to them. Makara, as rude and unkind as she was, taught him valuable skills. She didn't show him any tricks or moves, but over a period of time, Kheiron began to anticipate and thwart her assaults.

During dinner Kheiron watched Makara as she slyly washed her bowl in the creek before running off into the woods. He ate all the leftovers but kept a wary eye out for her.

30

The Yew Sapling

To be sure that it was still there, Kheiron patted the sheath that he wore around his neck. Though he still preferred to carry a staff, the knife inside his vest had become a valuable tool. None the less, apparently the time had come for him to make his own bow as well.

"You need to know the tree *dryad* that will infuse your bow with her life," Artemis had told Kheiron. "The wooden crescent of your weapon is not simply a tool but contains a life of its own. As you create your bow, the two of you willbecome bound in spirit, one guiding the other."

They walked along the creek, and Artemis pointed out the narrow, young yew trees that had the natural curve of a good bow.

"Heartwood will become the inside of your bow, and the wider, soft rings will form the outside curve. Trees with large branches have knots in the core that weaken the stave and make it more vulnerable to breakage. So, a younger sapling is preferred."

The wind rustled through the fronds of the trees, and a yew that Kheiron had not even noticed brushed his arm.

Kheiron turned his head to look upon the sapling and watched it move from side to side in the breeze. "I see you," he said to the tree. And it seems," he added, "that instead of me finding you, you have found me."

Artemis laughed. "I forget that you were born to a *naiad*," she said. "It normally takes a while for my daughters to speak with trees."

Kheiron smiled.

"It is customary," Artemis said, "to sit with your back against the trunk of your tree, talk to it for while and let your energies combine so that you understand one another. It is important to tell the tree what you intend to do before actually harvesting the wood."

Unlike humans, Kheiron could not sit with his spine against the trunk. Still he nodded his head and folded his legs underneath him so that he could lean his side against the sapling.

He whispered to the *dryad* in his mind. *My bow will be used for the good of everyone. When I hunt, it will be with respect for the life I take, as well as for the lives I nourish. When I fight or kill, if ever I must, it will be to protect the innocent and vulnerable. In this way, I will honor your life and the essence of my mother, the spring of Mount Pelion.*

Moisture formed in the corners of Kheiron's eyes as he thought of the cascading water on Mt. Pelion. *I miss my mom*, he told the *dryad*.

Soft breezes rustled through the branches of the tree, and yew needles rained down on his head and back. In its own way, the young sapling was speaking to Kheiron.

When Kheiron stood up, he placed mugwort flowers around the base of the tree. They were not showy flowers, but small and insignificant, yet fragrant and useful for subtle communication with the spirit world. Mugwort was one of Artemis' favorite herbs.

"Thank you," Kheiron said to the tree, "and to Grandmother Gaia, whose bones nourished you. And thank you Zeus, the new king of Heaven and Earth. May you become wise and kind, and may your rule be a blessing to all."

Kheiron cut the yew sapling with a jagged, sharp-toothed knife that he had made with Makara especially for this purpose. He did not press too hard, for fear of breaking the uneven teeth. Instead, he used a steady pressure and grated across the trunk in an even line.

He kept the branches so that later he could straighten them in his soap stone vice to make arrow shafts. The fronds and seeds he kept for making poison. The daughters of Artemis used a simmered broth of fat and crushed yew seeds for dipping their arrows. These poisoned arrows would kill their prey quickly, and this was important to Kheiron as well as to Artemis and her daughters.

31

Practice

In the camp, there was no lack of instruction on how to carve his stave.

The one problem, Kheiron learned, was that his wood needed to age for two years before he could carve it.

When she saw his sad face, Kallisto smiled in a teasing way.

"Oh poor horse-boy, don't fret. I have another stave harvested a couple of years ago. Artemis suggested that I cut a new one even though I didn't need it. She must have known that you were coming."

Eagerness returned to Kheiron's expression, but quickly faded. He had not bonded with the *dryad* of that tree, and that worried him, but Artemis assuaged his fears, saying that the *dryad* would serve him and Kallisto so long as he asked for the *dryad's* blessing. "Eeven though the wood appears to be dead, the dryad still lives in the fibers of her tree."

"But what about *my* stave?" Kheiron asked.

"You are bonded, one with the other," Artemis answered. "In two years you will be reunited and you can finish carving your bow then."

Kheiron didn't know how that would come to pass, but he trusted what Artemis said.

Makara, despite her seeming dislike, helped Kheiron by letting him use a blade with two handles. "A draw knife will give you more control over how much bark and wood you remove," she said. "You simply adjust the angle." Kheiron wondered at her generosity, but graciously accepted the use of her knife.

As he began, Artemis stood near, pointing out the image of his bow in the grain. She even drew the shape with charcoal before stepping back and allowing him to complete the work on his own.

"This is practice," she said. You cannot expect to have a perfect bow the first time that you make one."

However, Kheiron was diligent and carefully carved the bow so as not to remove too much wood, and after several weeks, Kallisto declared the bow ready for the next step: gluing rawhide to the outside curve. This would strengthen the weapon considerably, but he had to make his own glue by chewing fish skin and pine sap. That was messy. In the end, Kheiron had as much pitch on him as on the bow. Dirt and leaves stuck not only to his work, but also to his hands, legs and fur, and didn't come off for several weeks. Even then, his pleasure had to be delayed because the glue had to cure for several months. In the meantime, he continued to use the bow that Kallisto had let him use on that first day when they met.

Since the night when Apollo had declared their destinies entwined, Kheiron and Kallisto had felt shy around one another. They saw each other often but did not meet the other's gaze. What did the golden god see? It bothered each of them separately until they had an opportunity to discuss the matter openly.

"Perhaps," Kallisto suggested one day as they started off toward the practice area, "we will be known as great hunters. Or maybe we will fight the fearsome Hydra."

"Or," Kheiron suggested, "We will rescue lost children from the forest and teach them to be great warriors and healers."

Kallisto gave a small chuckle and repeated Apollo's words, "All will unfold as it will." The awkwardness passed, and Kallisto ran toward an old, skin bag stuffed with leaves and grass that hung in a tree. She gave the sack a good push.

"Go ahead," she said, "Shoot it."

With some practice, Kheiron had become much better than the first time he picked up a bow. But now, aiming at the moving target, he missed.

"That was close," Kallisto said. "Try again." She made him believe in himself, even though he failed the mark.

"Aim for where it will be, not where it is," she advised.

The bag swung high, slowing only slightly. He watched for a moment. Timing seemed to be a rhythm that he could feel in his muscles, and when next he released the arrow, it stuck.

"Yeah!" Kallisto yelled. "Do it again." He notched another arrow, paced the rhythm, and hit the mark again.

Kallisto smiled, "Do it fifty more times, and then we will practice fighting."

She was a good teacher. Kheiron wondered if it was because she made him believe in himself, or was it simply the tasks she set that improved his skills? Perhaps both were true.

As much as Kheiron enjoyed shooting arrows, he really liked sparring. Kallisto showed him how to block attacks and where to hit someone in order to paralyze them. Try as he might, he could never reproduce Kallisto's kicking techniques. Since his four legs were much different than hers. he had to figure those out on his own. In any case, he had an uncanny ability to disable someone. This may be because he understood the most vulnerable places. His most difficulty in fighting was his own attitude, because he cared more about healing than hurting.

Once when he was sparring with Kallisto, he clefted her knee, and she fell.

Kheiron knelt beside her. He felt so bad. "May I try to heal it?"

Kallisto grimaced and shook her head, yes. Kheiron put his hands over her swollen knee. His hands got hot and radiated warmth into her injury. He sniffed – oregano.

Kallisto smiled, "I like fighting with you because you know how to put someone back together after you have hurt them."

Kheiron chuckled, but Kallisto looked at his hands in awe as they became hotter and hotter and seemed to melt the pain in her knee.

"I really didn't do anything unusual," Kheiron said on the way back to camp, but Kallisto brushed past him as if she had never been injured and rolled her eyes.

Kheiron found himself trotting a little faster just to keep up with her. The smell of her sweat filled his nose with that sweet scent of wild oregano that grew in the hills. She used it for preserving meats.

"What are you doing?" she asked.

Surprised, Kheiron stuttered, "I . . .I have a strong nose. I mean I have a strong smelling nose."

They both laughed, and Kheiron tried to correct his mistake. "I mean, you smell like wild oregano."

"That's a good thing, I guess."

"It is," Kheiron nodded.

Hopefully she did not think him completely stupid, so he tried to come up with something meaningful to say.

He remembered that all of Artemis' daughters were orphans, and he boldly asked, "Tell me about your mother."

Kallisto lifted her head defiantly. "I don't remember her. Artemis said that she found me near a well in the mountains of Arcadia. That is all I know. Artemis is my true mother, and she is a very good one."

Kheiron nodded, "You are lucky to have her."

But Kallisto had already shifted her attention.

"Look," she said. "It's dittany. They say it only grows on Crete, but here it is in the Vale of Tempe." She picked a small sprig and handed it to Kheiron.

"You must never take too much, and always leave some for those who may come after."

The low growing plant with opposite leaves was, evidently, very precious. "It looks so much like oregano," Kallisto added, "but Dittany has even more magical powers. Animals that have been shot and eat of this herb can rid themselves of the arrow. It just falls out after a couple of days. Dittany is the antidote for yew poisoning. Artemis must have planted it here."

Kheiron smelled the leaves of the small herb.

"Keep it," she said. "At least get to know it. It will appear when you need it most, as do all things. That is what Artemis says."

Kheiron tucked the dittany carefully into the pouch over his shoulder next to the salted meat and dried berries that he carried with him. *I'd better not follow her too closely,* he thought. But just then Makara jumped out of the brush with her knife in hand.

32

Bow Hunting With Kallisto

The next morning Kallisto and Kheiron left early. The sky was still mostly dark, and Kheiron felt excited as they walked onto the open floor of the Vale. He rubbed his shoulder where Makara had hit him with a branch the night before.

"You are getting more agile," Kallisto said. "Makara's training is good for you."

Kheiron looked up. Above him, the stars were still bright enough to be seen. He gazed up and noticed stars that seemed to stand out more than the rest –the red-eyed bull from his dream.

"Look," he said, nudging Kallisto and pointing to the sky. "There is the bull with the red eye." He took aim with his bow and added, "I'd like to hunt a bull."

"That is too big a quarry for one who is just learning, but we could track one," Kallisto smiled. "First, we observe, learn the haunts of our prey, what it likes to eat, where it rests. We watch its seasons, when it mates and the mating rituals. We notice when the young are born, how the young are taught and protected. We observe the migration patterns. There is so much to learn."

Kheiron looked at the ground for tracks and signs of different animals. He was familiar with the habits of many different animals already, but he followed Kallisto's advice.

After a while, he trotted along beside her and asked, "Have you ever ridden on a horse?"

"No."

"You could ride on my back, and we could get there faster?"

"I am a fast runner," Kallisto said indignantly and stepped up her speed. Her feet were well protected by her shoes, pads made from the podial remnants of a bear hide.

They hurried through the rocky terrain and slowed only when they came to the vast shrubbery along the river. Willow, alder and cattails grew abundantly, and throughout them were trails, thickets and groves where almost any type of animal could be found at one time or another.

"I'll show you the way," Kallisto said, and led him through the maze of wild paths until she spied a wet dung pile. "They have been here recently," she whispered.

Kheiron had smelled the cows from a distance, but now the scent flooded his nostrils as they crept quietly through the brush. Something large moved ahead of them. A golden cow brown in color with big, dark eyes, spied them through the branches. Nervously, she turned and backed up to shield her young calf.

"Where there is one, there are more," Kallisto whispered. "But we don't kill cows, especially if they have young. However, if we find a bull . . ."

"I thought we were only tracking," Kheiron whispered.

"We'll see," Kallisto answered unresolved.

She had hunted with Artemis for years. She knew not only where to find prey, but also the etiquette about killing or not killing, especially when it came to mothers and their young.

She pointed to droppings. "See what she has been eating. I always ask myself, does the excrement have a purpose? Is it random or does it mark territory? Watch,

196

notice, listen, smell and feel. Your senses will teach you things that no one else ever could."

Absorbing Kallisto's words, Kheiron wondered if she had learned so much from observation, or did Artemis teach her? It may have been a trick of the light, but sometimes it seemed as if Artemis spoke through Kallisto, as if they were one.

"Watch, notice, listen, smell, and feel," he repeated quietly.

Kallisto motioned for Kheiron to follow. She was skirting the cow and calf intentionally trying not to disturb them any more than necessary. Defensively, however, the cow watched as they pushed through the underbrush.

In the next meadow, they found four more cows in a protective circle around two calves.

Again, Kallisto motioned with her eyes for Kheiron to follow her as she backed out of the clearing.

Kheiron enjoyed this creeping around, watching and trying not to disturb the animals, when suddenly they heard a loud bellow. Kallisto recognized the sound.

"That is a bull," she whispered. "He must have smelled us."

Curious, Kheiron wanted to see the big creature.

"Bulls can easily gore an adversary," Kallisto warned. "We must protect ourselves because he will find us."

They positioned themselves near a ravine where they could scramble down, well at least Kallisto could. The gorge would be too steep for the bull, but Kheiron thought he could make it. Then they waited, but not for long.

The crashing got louder and closer, until a huge head bashed its way through the brush and stared straight at them, ready to kill the intruders. Closer to Kheiron, the bull went after him, but Kallisto stepped in front, and the beast turned on her.

Kheiron notched his arrow and waited for Kallisto's signal.

But even with her arrow ready and aimed at the massive chest, she hesitated. Kheiron decided not to wait. With a perfect shot at the heart, he pulled the necessary tension.

"Stop!" Kallisto yelled. "He won't hurt us."

Kheiron relaxed his draw, puzzled as he watched the bull's aggressive stance soften.

As though bewitched, the bull stepped slowly toward the girl, staring with one eye, while the other kept Kheiron in its peripheral vision.

The huge creature rubbed his massive head against Kallisto's cheek, gently and sweetly as if she were a favored cow.

This was not right. Kheiron put the extra tension back on his bow and was just about to release his arrow, when the bull turned his other eye on Kheiron. It glowed red and he spoke. "Restrain yourself, Kheiron. You know not who I am."

Dumb-founded, Kheiron lowered the bow, and the bull turned toward the beautiful girl to rub against her yet again. It was all so weird, but stranger yet, Kallisto reached out her hand to stroke the bull's head, simultaneously pulling it toward her in a loving embrace. Then she pushed it away, and the bull spoke to Kheiron, "Protect her and tell no one of this meeting." Then the bull thundered away.

Kallisto seemed embarrassed. "Who was that?" Kheiron asked.

She did not respond.

"Have you seen that bull before?"

Again, she said nothing, but picked up her quiver and started away. Kheiron followed, watching the despair in her gait.

She proceeded in silence until they came to the top of the hill where Kheiron and Apollo had slept the night before. She noticed the crushed grasses and said, "I see you found my favorite place."

This time, Kheiron didn't answer. He didn't know what to say.

Kallisto sat on the hill overlooking the Vale while the four-legged horse-boy stood beside her like a sentinel. He had always looked to her for guidance, and now it was she who seemed so small and in need of protection. In fact whether she spoke or not, he would stand there. He would respect her silence and protect her, not so much because the bull had asked him, but because he must.

She broke the quiet with confusion and turmoil. "I have done nothing wrong. I have not betrayed my vows."

Not understanding what she meant, Kheiron listened.

"I have seen that bull before," she confessed, "from a distance, a magnificent creature. He has some strange power over me, and I have wanted to touch him. Today, it was as if my secret desire came true. Only now that desire is strengthened, and I want nothing more than to be near that bull. Oh Kheiron, my vows to Artemis are to her alone. *She* is my one desire. . . to be near Her, to serve Her. But, now, my heart is divided, even my vow of chastity waivers over that bull. It's sickening."

Shocked, Kheiron continued to listen. She was attracted to that bull, like a mate? It didn't make sense. He loved Kallisto. He honored her. If she was torn up over her vows to Artemis, why couldn't it be over him? Of course, he was not the bull, but he was part horse.

Frustrated, he knelt down on his forelegs and lifted Kallisto's chin so that their eyes met. "I love you," he whispered. "And I will protect you from the bull or anything else."

199

Tears filled her eyes. "You are generous, Kheiron, but that is not what I want. You should not have to protect me from myself. And if Artemis learns of this, she will not be so kind. She has sworn to kill us if we break our vows."

"But Artemis loves you, Kallisto, more than anyone else. She would not kill you."

"You do not know Artemis as I know her. She is the *Potnia Theron*, the Mistress of the Animals, Mistress of all wild nature, protector of the young. She rescued us all from abandonment, babies and young girls. She delights in the cubs of the lion, the pups of the wolf, the lambs of the ewe. She helps them find food and keeps them safe from predators. But She herself is a predator, and when they are grown, those that she loved as babies she hunts as adults.

"Yes, She loves me, but She would not hesitate to kill me, especially if I broke my vows."

Wiping the tears from her eyes, Kallisto pulled herself up. "I will be myself, no other desire but to serve Artemis. Yet," she said, sulking back down, "my heart is known to her. Oh Kheiron, you must not put yourself in danger for my sake."

Again, with resolve, she stood up and started down the hill.

A cloud of dust in the Vale caught Kheiron's attention, and he ran ahead.

"Climb on my back," he told Kallisto. She hesitated, but this time gave in and pulled herself over the natural seat in his back.

"Hold on," he said, taking off at a slow gallop.

In the distance, the wild horses stood still and watched Kheiron come towards them.

In a playful manner, Kheiron threw his head to let them know there was no threat, but still they watched him suspiciously.

200

The lead beige recognized Kheiron and whinnied loudly. Then he started to run in the opposite direction as the strange pair got close. The rest of the horses followed, including Kheiron. The thunder of their combined hooves pounded the earth and drowned out all thoughts.

Kallisto held on with hands and legs as Kheiron ran and ran. He circled around with the herd before coming back to the river. There, after the exhilarating run, the horses slowed, snorting and breathing hard. Kheiron peered over his shoulder and saw a smile on Kallisto's face. He had helped her forgot her worries, at least for a moment.

33

No Secrets

In the camp, Apollo and Artemis sat side by side, twins looking almost exactly alike except that Apollo had a golden glow and Artemis a silvery one. By allowing her divinely handsome brother to eat with them Artemis was testing her women tonight.

Apollo motioned for Kheiron to stand beside him as he laughed and smiled with the girls.

"How was your day?" the golden god asked casually.

"Fine," Kheiron answered. But no sooner had the words parted from his lips, than Artemis stared at him with an intensity that could not be denied. "Yes, do tell us about your day."

"She knows," thought Kheiron, guilty, as if he himself had done something wrong. But neither he nor Kallisto had.

"We tracked cows and saw a large bull," Kheiron answered. "And Kallisto taught me about watching, noticing, listening, and smelling the animals that you track. A lesson taught by your own wisdom through her." Kheiron bowed his head toward the goddess in a gesture of honor. Apollo nodded his approval.

"The bull," Artemis said, closing her eyes and opening them in a magical flutter, "could be fatal." She had a stern look as her eyes met with Kallisto's.

"Cows?" Apollo said, looking at Kheiron, "I would like to have cows of my own -- a herd of beautiful golden cows."

"They are there for your bidding," Artemis replied. "One hundred golden cows for my luminous brother, that he may drink fresh milk and eat cream and butter whenever he likes. My Daughters and I will guard them in your absences. Though they are rare you know. Goats and sheep are much better suited to our land than bulls and cows."

"But they are so big," Apollo gestured, estimating their tall stature with a coy smile.

Some of the women looked at Apollo with soft expressions. Apparently they did not know that Artemis was testing them.

Apollo dropped one knee and bowed to his sister, "We shall share in the bounty of the cows, my beloved sister."

"So it shall be," Artemis winked, "and we shall drink milk and eat yoghurt.

*****

Later, Kheiron stood under his familiar blanket of stars and repeated the bull's words: "You know not who I am."

Who is the bull, really? He wondered. He wanted to ask Apollo, but Kheiron's need to protect Kallisto was greater than his curiosity. So he said nothing.

Next to him Apollo gazed out over the herds that he had been guarding for the last year and whispered, "My time with Admentus is done. Tomorrow we will go to Mount Olympus. It is high time that we meet Zeus. He looked toward Kheiron and added, "the red-eyed bull."

34

Mount Olympus

Kheiron awoke while it was still dark. Overhead, amid the sparkling stars, the red-eyed bull stared down at the horse-boy who stood on top of the hill.

"Are you really Zeus?" Kheiron asked the starry bull, "my brother, my half-brother?"

The eastern horizon grew lighter, and Kheiron could see a cloud of dust in the valley below – horses. He wanted to run with them, but out of the corner of his eye, he noticed movement advancing up the hill.

Leading one of the beautiful, golden cows, the glowing form of Apollo came into view.

"See how sweet she is, Kheiron," the dark haired god called out as he stroked the cow's head.

Kheiron met them part way.

When the cow saw Kheiron's strange human-horse figure, she pulled back, but Kheiron, noticing her anxiety, stopped, looked away and shook his head to show that he was not interested in hurting her.

Curiously, she looked back at him and shook her head too.

Kheiron leaned over and nonchalantly picked some grass. The cow, followed suit and ate grass as well.

Apollo watched this non-verbal, non-threatening communication and smiled. "Perhaps you will guard my cows for me sometimes, Kheiron. "You seem to know how to make them feel at ease."

Kheiron bent his front leg and plucked a rock from his hoof. "I don't know anything, Apollo."

"You know more than you think," Apollo remarked, "and you are humble. As the fates have decreed, you will be a great teacher."

"Teacher??" Kheiron shook his head. "Why do you always say things like that? I don't know what you are talking about."

The cow, still watching Kheiron, imitated his movements and shook her head again.

Kheiron laughed at her mimicking, and Apollo smiled. The golden god knew things that others did not, and he pulled the cow forward, closer to Kheiron, who instinctively held his hand under her nostrils.

She smelled the horse-boy's fingers, then lowered her head, content that she was safe and ate more grass.

The cow seemed familiar, and Kheiron now remembered where he had first seen her. She had been among the four cows protecting the calves in the brush by the river.

From her small udders, Kheiron could tell that she was not one of the mothers. Had it been only yesterday that he and Kallisto had discovered them by the river?

Time is a strange thing, he thought. *Weeks can seem like a day, and years can seem like a cycle of the moon.*

"The cows are mine now," Apollo said, his eyes glittering with delight, "one hundred golden cows."

Apollo always seemed to get what he wanted. He wanted the cows, so he got cows. Kheiron wondered if the golden god ever felt disappointed, frustrated or confused. He watched the cloud of dust as it moved along the river and realized that his opportunity to run with the horses had passed. Sighing, he turned his attention back to Apollo with another question: "When are we leaving for Mount Olympus?"

"Now," Apollo smiled.

"We should say good-bye," Kheiron said.

"There is no need. Artemis knows everything."

Kheiron looked toward the camp and saw movement in the brush. *Makara,* he thought. *Well she won't be able to ambush me today.*

"The cow will be a gift for my father," Apollo said as he urged the placid beast toward the high mountains. Above them, the highest peaks were shrouded in mist.

As they stepped onto a foggy path, the wall of clouds parted as if drawn aside by unseen hands. Kheiron knew then that this was not a path normally traveled by mortals. He recognized the living *nephelai,* the cloud sisters of his *naiad* mother, and he whispered, "*Kali meera,* good morning." A cool mist touched his cheek, and the mystical veils closed behind him.

35

View from the Mountain

Apollo and Kheiron picked their way through large open fields of white morning glories, yellow hypericums, blue columbines and impressive outcroppings of rock. The wind ruffled the grass and tousled their hair. At one point, Kheiron turned around to see where they had come from. The top of the hill where they had slept was perfectly visible, as if they hadn't gone anywhere. And yet there were great distances of the mountains between them and the Vale of Tempe where they had begun their trek.

A large brown eagle screeched and swooped overhead. Kheiron watched as it soared through the clouds and over the Vale toward the sea.

Thinking of Kallisto, Kheiron looked toward the camp and, amazingly, he could see it.

Kallisto was cleaning a hide from a goat they had killed, and Artemis stood beside her, slicing the meat from another well-aged carcass.

What was strange was that, despite the distance, Kheiron could hear their conversation as if he were standing in the clearing next to them.

"I have taught you everything," Artemis was saying, "and you have learned better than anyone else. Of all the daughters, Kallisto, I love hunting with you best."

Kallisto bit her lower lip and wiped a tear from her eye. "I do not deserve your love, Artemis. I am most fortunate, but unworthy." Kheiron could see the pain in her face as she turned away, but Artemis grabbed Kallisto's shoulder and kissed her forehead. "I know that you have not betrayed your vows. I just want you to remember that I love you." Then, with bow and quiver over her shoulder, the goddess stepped away and disappeared into the thicket. The wolves that always accompanied her followed.

Kheiron stopped on the path to watch this scene, and Apollo walked ahead.

The golden god called, "The vantage point from Olympus is amazing, is it not?" And then he added, "Are you spying?"

Kheiron shuddered and shook his head. The cow, which now seemed to look at Kheiron for direction, shook her head too, and Kheiron smiled at her.

"No wonder the gods live here," Kheiron repled. "They can see everything."

The eagle they had been watching burst through the clouds and swooped over their heads, eyeing them with curiosity. Then it disappeared over a stone wall that encircled the peak. A golden gate glinted in the bright sunlight, and as they got closer Kheiron noticed perfectly formed leaves and grapevines that made up the grill on the closed entryway. The plants, though not living, were beautiful. Each fruit, vine and leaf was delicately crafted of golden ore, the same metal as Apollo's bow. Kheiron remembered Makara telling him about Hephaestos, the master smith who designed and constructed Zeus' lightning bolts. Fascinated, he watched as the decorative gate swung open, though no one seemed to touch it.

Soon they passed under an archway with real grapes that hung lusciously below large, verdant leaves. The scent of apples and fresh violets permeated the air. Everywhere fragrant herbs and flowers grew in abundance. Kheiron sniffed petals of deep, glowing magenta, rich shades of green, vibrant yellows, and tasted fruits at the perfection of ripeness that were asking and waiting to be plucked and eaten.

Apollo led as Kheiron trotted behind drinking in the scents, colors and textures. He wanted to touch everything, smell it, taste it, and discover the flavors and how each could be used as food or medicine.

But Apollo led them on following the giant eagle to a massive pantheon with white marble steps and giant pillars that seemed as if they were holding up the sky.

His senses overwhelmed, Kheiron lagged behind and had to gallop to catch up with Apollo and the cow.

"What do you think?" Apollo whispered over his shoulder. "Are you ready to meet the ruler of the gods? The King of Heaven and Earth? Are you ready to meet my father?"

Uncertain, Kheiron nodded apprehensively as Apollo gripped the golden rope around the cow's head and lead her up the steps. Her hooves clattered on the stone, and she looked nervously around for Kheiron's lead.

Sensing her distress, Kheiron trotted up the marble steps and rubbed his horse shoulder against her wide belly. The cow instantly relaxed as his hooves clicked against the stone in rhythm with hers.

"Let us go in together," Apollo suggested, "three abreast."

Kheiron nodded his agreement as they mounted the last three stairs. Nervously, however, under his breath, he whispered soft, gurgling water sounds.

"Glurr pluup shhhhhh

Glurr pluup shhhhh pshhhh pshhhh pshhh."

36

Zeus and the Gathering

At the top of the marble steps Kheiron could hear whispering, as if hundreds of people were speaking at the same time. He tried to hear what they were saying, and to his amazement, as he focused on one voice it became clear. It said, "Hurry, go check on the sheep. I just heard something out there."

He looked around to see the sheep, but there were none. Then he listened to another voice. This one sobbed, "No, mother, don't leave."

With these words, Kheiron was a child again, standing next to the stream, searching the meadow for Philyra. But then he heard another voice: "I'll kill you. I will search you out and kill you with all my strength and all my might." And there were more, all speaking at once.

Where are all these voices coming from? he wondered. It was enough to drive a sane person mad.

"They are the voices of all who live," a resonant voice rang out above the whispers. Kheiron looked up.

"That is my father," Apollo said softly.

The voice continued, "We've been waiting for you," but no one appeared.

A form began to appear, like a man, only bigger and more impressive. He had long curls that hung down his back and draped off his shoulder. His hair was a mixture of different colors: gold and red, white, brown and yellow. He had a beard and a mustache, and when he smiled, his eyes sparkled. He imparted a sense of ease, though in the same moment he had an air of terrible power that made Kheiron tremble.

The voice boomed as Zeus encircled them, including the cow in his massive arms.

"My son," he said kissing Apollo's forehead. And then turning to Kheiron with a momentary red gleam in his eye, "My brother. . ." With a knowing smile the great god said to Kheiron, "We were both, Kheiron and I, conceived by Kronus. Therefore, we *are* brothers."

Kheiron smiled shyly, yet felt happy that Zeus honored their kinship.

Zeus' thunderous laughter split the air as he patted Kheiron on the back. Then he turned toward the throng of assembled beings that only now, did Kheiron begin to see.

"Be welcome on Olympus," Zeus shouted. "Be welcome."

37

Hera

A mass of gods and goddesses came forward to welcome the newcomers.

Concerned about the cow's anxiety, Kheiron met the big, brown, bovine eyes, but she winked at him with an uncanny glance. She was not the same animal who had accompanied them up the mountain. Kheiron didn't have a moment to ponder what was going on with the cow because he found himself caught in the bustling embraces of unfamiliar gods and goddesses, some he had never met, but instantly knew.

"My dear little brother," a goddess whispered into Kheiron's ear. "Do you remember me? I was there when you were born with my mother Rhea and Auntie Tethys. We took care of you and sweet Philyra." A look of sympathy crossed her face as she spoke the water *naiad*'s name. "But look at you, the horse-baby grown into a horse-man."

"Hera?" Kheiron answered, remembering the young goddess who had screamed at the *hekatoncheri* in her attempt to protect him from the hundred-handed giant.

Hera, with a warm smile and plaited locks that draped around her head, kissed each of Kheiron's cheeks. She was delighted to be reunited with the horse-boy of her youth.

"Do you know what happened to her?" Kheiron asked, "My mother, Philyra? Is she still alive?"

Hera's smile receded. "I'm sorry Kheiron. All *naiad*s are immortal, and I know that in some way she must still live. But beyond that I cannot say."

"Does that mean that you know but will not tell me?" Kheiron asked.

"It means that I do not know, Kheiron. I am sorry."

Dejected, Kheiron lowered his head. If the gods were so powerful, why couldn't they help him find his mother? But Apollo had foretold that he would find her when the time was right.

Time, time, he thought. He wanted to ask Hera another question, but the goddess recoiled when Apollo and the golden cow came into view.

Startled by her reaction, Kheiron wondered what it was about them that made her so uncomfortable, but she disappeared back into the throng.

38

A Sea of Gods and Goddesses

Strange feelings surged through Kheiron as he was introduced to Zeus' immediate brothers and sisters. Poseidon caught him in a clasping embrace that sent waves through his body as if he had just gone for a swim. Demeter smiled with the warmth of the afternoon sun and smelled of thyme and ripe grapes, okra, and basil, oregano and pine, all the familiar fragrances of Mount Pelion –so many things that reminded him of home.

He watched Hestia, the goddess of the hearth fire, as she sat staring into the flames and instantly knew that she could see things that others could not. The six children of Rhea and Kronus were, of course, Zeus and Hera (sister and wife to Zeus), Demeter, Hestia, Poseidon, and Hades who, in the aftermath of the war, claimed the underworld as his domain and did not come to Olympus.

Kheiron felt at ease here on Olympus. The gods and goddesses did not look at him as deformed or strange. Here, he was accepted and treated like part of the heavenly family. And though there were so many members of this divine assembly that Kheiron had never seen before, he still felt content and welcome.

"The battle with Kronus is over," Zeus' voice boomed across the mountains. "True to Gaia's prophesy, the powerful giants from Tartarus, the *cyclopes* and the *hekatoncheires* helped in our struggle to overcome Kronus and take our rightful places as the rulers of the heavens and earth."

A loud roar filled the pantheon as all present joined in a cheer, but Zeus hushed them and continued.

"This is the time of the gathering, the coming together of the chosen twelve, those who will rule by my side on Olympus. Twelve thrones are placed in the circle. Hera will sit by my side with our sons, Ares, the god of war, and Hephaistos, creator of my most powerful lightning bolts. Poseidon will rule the seas, and Demeter will guard over the flowering, abundant earth. And that leaves six more thrones."

With palpable anticipation in the air over who the other six would be, Zeus called out, "My son and daughter," and he reached toward Apollo and the cow.

"Apollo, my son," Zeus announced to everyone. Hera glowered at him, but Zeus continued.

"Apollo is our god of sunlight, healing, prophesy, poetry, and art. He is the guardian of the Oracle at Mount Parnassus, henceforth known as Delphi. He is *Ismenion*, the seat that knows no lie. He is chosen."

Smiles and hushed whispers filled the air as Apollo's form dissolved into blinding sunlight.

"He is the embodiment of the sun, the new Helios," Zeus told the awed assembly.

Next everyone watched, surprised, but not quite as surprised as Kheiron, as Zeus called the cow.

"Come now, Artemis, show yourself," he coaxed.

A silvery form slipped from the cow's body, and there she stood, Artemis, wearing her bear-skin hunting clothes and boots. She carried her silver bow and quiver slung over opposite shoulders.

Hera frowned. But Artemis, not wanting to be gawked at, glanced around angrily.

"It is all right, my princess," Zeus told her. "You need stay only long enough to claim your place among us." Zeus spoke softly before calling out to the throng. "Artemis, goddess of moonlight. She is the *Potnia Theron*, Mistress of the Animals, Goddess of all wild things. She is pale, blue light and morning dew, *artemesia*, the pungent herb of the forest. She is the guardian and protector of abandoned and orphaned children, especially girls."

Zeus, with a sly smile, whispered to her, "I would have suspected a deer," he said, "a bear, or even a lion, but you chose to come disguised as a cow. How like your father you are. No secrets. No disguises. We can see through them all."

Artemis looked at her father suspiciously, but his smile, filled with overwhelming love and devotion, made the defiant goddess melt and embrace him as if she were a small child.

"There will always be a place for you here on Olympus, my daughter," Zeus whispered to her, "but I know that you belong in the woods, following your instincts."

Zeus understood her, and she smiled at him before looking around defiantly at those who dared to stare.

Apollo pulled his sister to the side. "You tricked me," he laughed jokingly. "You stole the excitement of my presentation for our father." He acted as if he had been deceived, but, of course, he had known immediately when she had taken possession of the cow.

Zeus, pulled the brother and sister close to him, proudly saying, "My twins."

Kheiron watched Hera step forward, her lips in a tight smile for Apollo and Artemis who shone like gold and silver. They were not her children, but Leto's, another of Zeus' many conquests, and illegitimate in her eyes.

219

A cold mist issued from her lips, "You are welcome here at Olympus," she told them.

39

Dionysus and Ares

A loud belch interrupted Hera as she was about to say something to the crowd.

Everyone turned toward the scintillating gate from whence the offending sound emanated and where a young, handsome god with budding beard and long curly hair swaggered up the steps.

"Another son, My Love?" Hera said glancing at Zeus as the young man fell at their feet.

Zeus smiled shyly.

"Intoxicated," Hera added, as the young figure pulled himself off the floor.

"'M 'here," he said slurring his words.

"Dionysus!" Zeus announced, as Hera stood up and retreated to her rooms.

Zeus roughed up the young god's shoulders. In his curly hair, so like Zeus,' a wreath of ivy had slipped to the side when he fell and now hung askew amid his tangled curls.

Zeus put his arms around the disheveled man, "This is Dionysus," he announced, "god of the vine and fermented grape."

At these words, Kheiron watched as a beautiful young maiden, a vine nymph, cloaked in layers of green leaves approached Zeus. She too wore an ivy wreath, and behind each ear hung a small bunch of grapes that draped over her shoulders and pointed to the contours of her breasts. Everyone stared as she bowed low before Zeus who, true to form, winked at the young beauty.

"Excuse me, your mightiness," she said softly, "I have brought the gifts of your son Dionysus." She held forth a large basket filled with grapes. In the middle, artistically arranged amid the ripe fruit, was a decanter.

"Permit me," she continued, revealing a goblet from beneath her verdant skirts and exposing a long slender leg.

She poured the contents of the earthen decanter into the goblet that had been handcrafted from an old vine root, and, most reverently, handed it to Zeus.

Zeus tasted as the vine nymph announced, "Made from the wild yeasts and fruit of my own tended vines."

Zeus enjoyed the intoxicating beverage, nodded his approval, and passed it toward Hera who, he immediately noticed, was not there. So, instead, he passed it to his sister Demeter. After tasting, she also nodded her approval, and the goblet made its way around to each of the gods and goddesses.

When the gnarled cup came to Kheiron, he tasted the fermented beverage. Unlike any grape, the flavor was strong, woody and fragrant like apples, grass, thyme and rosemary. It gave him a strange sort of feeling, like not having his hooves on the ground, but he liked it and added his nod of approval. Hestia, the quiet goddess, glanced at Kheiron. There was a golden glow in her eyes, reminiscent of embers glowing in the fire.

"The gifts of Dionysus have earned him his place in the heavens and, I am sure, amid the people of Earth," Zeus smiled and pointed to the throne where Hestia had been sitting. "Hestia, goddess of the sacrificial flame has relinquished her seat for you, Dionysys."

Dionysis tipped his goblet toward Hestia to honor her, and the contents spilled on the earth. Whether he intended to spill his wine on the earth or not, Hestia bowed her head in gratitude, taking the symbolic gesture as a great honor to Grandmother Gaia, to whom she was loyal.

Hera returned in time to taste the last sip of Dionysus' wine, but the sound of metal clattering against stone rattled the pillars before she could give her opinion.

Artemis' deep growl rolled between the assembled. "Do not touch me again, or I will slice you from head to toe."

Everyone turned to see the virgin huntress with her knife at Ares' throat.

"No man shall ever touch me in lust," she hissed. "Next time, avert your eyes when you know that I am near or suffer the consequences," and she jabbed her knife into the god's leg.

Ares looked to his father for help, but Zeus only laughed. "Your sister can take care of herself, and I suggest that you listen to her."

Artemis sheathed her bloody knife and stepped away from her vile half-brother, tracking him with her eyes like a fearless lion.

"The god of war is a coward," Apollo whispered to Kheiron. "As fierce as he is to others, he trembles at my sister's hand."

40

The God of Thieves

"You know," Apollo spoke softly to Kheiron, "since Artemis stole the glory of my cow as a gift, I am obliged to get a few more bovine presents to impress my father. I will return soon."

Within the time it took to inhale and exhale, Apollo was back, angry, and carrying a baby in his hands. He held it by the toe as if it were nothing more than excrement.

Raging, Apollo yelled, "Father, this thief has stolen my cows. Not just one or two, but every, single one. What have you done with them?" he yelled at the baby.

The baby sat on the floor like any baby would, not understanding a word the golden god said, only the tone which seemed to frighten him. The baby started to cry.

"What are you doing?" Kheiron asked. "He is only a baby."

Apollo stared with exasperation. "This is no ordinary baby. I found him in his cradle, innocent, with his mother sitting over him. …Innocent indeed, why you foul, little, deceptive creature."

The baby started crying anew.

Confused, Kheiron looked at Hera, the goddess of birth and small children, with hopes that at least she would do something. But her gaze showed only ambiguity.

Why wouldn't she come to the rescue of this defenseless child?

Kheiron decided to take matters into his own hands and, stepping forward, picked up the baby, who smiled and nuzzled safely into Kheiron's reassuring arms.

Zeus laughed and speaking to the infant, said, "Come now child of mine, confess your misdoings."

"I didn't do it." The baby spoke clearly. "I am too small. How could I steal a hundred cows?"

For a baby, this child spoke very eloquently, and Kheiron was beginning to realize that he may have been deceived.

Kheiron put the baby down, and the infant stood up, not even like a toddler, but more like a grown man. "I was only born yesterday." The baby's diapers drooped heavily, but he continued, "What could I want with cows?"

Again, Zeus smiled.

Enraged, Apollo hollered, "I should throw you off this mountain and into the depths of Tartarus. There you can be imprisoned with the other Titans for all of eternity."

"No, no," Zeus spoke. "This is my newest-born son, Hermes. He will not be banished to Tartarus."

At these words, the baby smiled.

Hera's eyes flashed as Hermes climbed onto his father's knee.

"My little son, so you found your way here where you belong, of course. You are tricky and clever. You made sure to be present for the gathering of the gods. Sly, you are able to slip into places unseen. In the future, I shall rely on you for many things." Zeus smiled broadly. "Come now, make peace with your brother."

At these words, the baby climbed onto the floor and made for Apollo.

"I do not want your peace," Apollo roared, "I want my cows!"

"Truly brother," baby Hermes cooed. "I did not steal your cows. No, I simply borrowed them. After all I am just a baby who needs milk. You understand, of course. You would not deny your little brother some milk."

Hermes, the baby, turned toward Hera. She had, at first, felt nothing but disgust for this other illegitimate child begotten by her philandering husband, but this baby was kind of sweet. He had, in fact, walked to her several times and laid his head on her lap, just as any tired baby would search out his mother for comfort. These actions awakened her own motherly instincts.

"You would not deny a baby milk, would you?" Hermes repeated to Apollo.

His statement, in the form of a question put Apollo on the spot. Under the gaze of the gods and goddesses, Apollo had nothing to say, but his thoughts were loud: "scoundrel, weasel, evil, vile thief."

Hermes, the small child, removed something from his shoulder. It looked like a turtle, or rather a turtle shell with horns and fitted with cordage.

"As a token of my goodwill," the baby said, "I offer you this. I made it just yesterday."

He plucked the sinew and made a lovely sound that reverberated across the pantheon. Then, continuing to pull the strings, he created various rhythms and tones and even made up a little rhyme that went along with his melody.

"Great god of light,
Healer and poet,
 Guardian of pastures,
And things yet to come,
To you, all that is hidden
Under darkness and cloak
Are revealed in the brightness of . . .dawn."

227

Apollo rolled his eyes, impressed and flattered, but not ready to give in.

"You shine like the sun," Hermes smiled.

"And breathe like the wind
No lies can unfold from your lips
For you are *Ismenion*
The truth incarnated
To you, your brother Hermes
Will always be sincere
Indeed, just know that he likes to have fun, my dear ... brother."

The baby strummed the sinew of his turtle shell instrument and ended his little song with a melody.

The gods and goddesses clapped and laughed, delighted with the baby's talents. Even Apollo smiled, amused by his little brother.

"Well Child," Apollo answered the poetic supplication, "you have appealed to my sense of art and wit, and I make you this offer: You may share my cows, drink the milk that a hungry baby needs, and even help me to care for them since you have a propensity toward herding. In exchange, I will accept your turtle shell gift if you will agree to teach me its mysteries. I am intrigued by your creation."

Apollo bowed to the baby and, in turn, to the assembled gods and goddesses.

Hermes followed suit, and handed Apollo what he called the lyre.

"We shall be friends and brothers," Hermes declared.

"So long as you know," Apollo interjected, "that you can never deceive me. And I will never pay heed to your words, but always listen acutely to your mind, your heart and intent. Of course, I will also remember that you like to play games."

The baby hugged Apollo's leg. And Apollo, bending down, whispered in his ear.

"Beware of Hera. She hates all of us born of Zeus' other lovers."

Hermes smiled and whispered back, "I have already begun to endear myself to her. Just watch."

At that, Hermes toddled over to Hera and again, as if he were tired, laid his head in her lap.

"Oh, poor little thing," Hera said, stroking his head. "Where is your mother? She is not taking very good care of you, is she? Come here." She lifted him onto her lap and held him in her arms. If she was aware of being manipulated, she didn't show it.

Hermes started to cry.

"Oh, he's hungry," Hera said and looked around. "Well, his mother's not here, and he needs to be fed." Without any concern for what others might think, the Goddess of Heaven and Earth discretely took the baby into her rooms and fed him as if he were her own.

When Hermes' belly was full, Hera lifted him over her shoulder and burped him. Then she carried him back into the pantheon. There, Hermes secretly winked at Apollo and Kheiron before falling asleep in the goddess' arms. He had indeed won her over.

"If only I could please her so easily myself," Apollo whispered to Kheiron.

Zeus laughed with delight. "I have such fine sons and daughters!" he declared, fully aware of Hermes' ploys. The baby, just newly born, had established his place as one of the twelve rulers of heaven and earth. And thanks to Hermes' ingenuity, Zeus would have one less child to protect from Hera's wrath.

41

Aphrodite

Two empty seats remained, and everyone wondered who would come next. Quiet anticipation filled the atmosphere as the sound of rustling wings broke the silence.

A young man, dressed in nothing but his dark, luminescent skin, alighted on the marble floor. Huge, radiant wings folded against his back as he stood among the assembled gods and goddesses. Naked, with tight ebony curls that hung down his back, he carried, over his shoulders, a bow and quiver. The corners of his mouth lifted slightly as he observed the affect his power had on those around him.

"E…e…eros," Zeus stuttered the name. "We do not see much of you, though, in truth, we feel your presence often."

"Especially you, Zeus," the young man smiled sarcastically. He did not seem as respectful of the sovereign as he should.

All of the gods and goddesses blushed when the dark-skinned god gazed at them.

"I come here with a purpose," the young man said, directing his voice to one and all.

"Here, at the time of the gathering, I am the messenger. I have no need to be one of your chosen few. But there is one coming whose place *is* among you. She is born of the sea foam, the frothing waters where Uranus' creative force was thrown before the old king fled to the outer heavens.

"It is from Uranus' discarded member that the elements of sea, fire, water and air blended together for her creation.

Without mother or father, swirling in the chaos just as I myself came into being at the beginning time, her gifts and powers are similar to mine and undeniable. She leaves a spell in her wake, a spell of love, desire, and passion. Prepare yourselves for her presence, for she brings controversy and disrespect of vows. She is the goddess of love.

"Some of you will hate her," he continued, "but in the same heart, you will not be able to stop yourselves from loving her.

"Some of you have the desire for power, some for wealth and accolade, some, the desire for knowledge, and some, beauty. But her only desire is to be loved. She has no other reason to exist."

Eros bowed erotically and ended his speech with a final warning: "Be gentle with her, and yet be wary."

There was a cooing of doves, and small white downy feathers floated silently among the assembled.

Seven white doves descended into the courtyard pulling a chariot of clouds. Everyone stared as the Horae, the nymph spirits of the seasons, escorted the goddess into their midst.

At first glance, her face, hidden in a cascade of golden hair, was difficult to see. But when she stepped out of her chariot and lifted her head to glance shyly at the crowd, her eyes twinkled, and her smile melted every heart. Each fell in love. The goddess was disarming. On her head, she wore a flowering crown like Dionysus, only hers was made of red myrtle flowers and small, fragrant roses. They had been warned, but one look at her beauty and all defenses were quickly gone. Everyone tried to make a place for her. Apollo even offered her his lap.

Eros lifted his hand to help her, and the goddess kissed it delicately, as she whispered his ancient name, "Protogonus."

Kheiron, who stood behind Apollo, asked quietly, "Why did she call him Protogonus?"

Artemis answered. "Protogonus is the first born. They say he was born before Uranus and even before Gaia. He is the creative urge." She rolled her eyes, but even she felt his power.

Kheiron knew what she meant. Eros was desire, lust and procreation. Kheiron had felt that longing under the full moon, but pushed it aside as best he could.

"It was Eros," Apollo added, "who brought the primordial deities together. He is the one who made Gaia and Grandfather Uranus long for one another. It was through that passion that all the elements, the gods and goddesses, plants and rocks, creatures that live on earth and below sprung forth."

Eros was not one of the honored twelve, but as he made ready to depart, Hera motioned for him. It is uncertain what she said, but Eros distinctly answered, "Some things are meant to be."

Hera looked heart-broken as the dark skinned god pressed her palm against his full, wet lips. Then, with merely a light rustling of wings, he disappeared.

Zeus called to the new goddess, "Aphrodite, born of the sea foam, we must marry you, and quickly, or I am afraid that war may break out here on Olympus."

Poseidon and Apollo each made gestures that he should have her. Ares begged Zeus to give her to him, and Dionysus, despite the gorgeous nymph who sat at his feet, stared longingly at the breathtaking goddess. Baby Hermes tried to get her to suckle, and even Zeus pondered his own rights to her before Hera spoke up.

"Zeus, there is only one here who really deserves her." She said nothing, but her eyes alighted upon Hephaistos, her son.

Hephaistos' back was turned to them. He didn't even want to be there and was completely uninterested in the proceedings.

Zeus was about to say Hephaistos' name when he caught sight of a passion already growing between the newest goddess and his other son, Ares. He looked at Hera, who didn't miss a thing. But she shook her head slowly, indicating that it would not be wise. In these matters her will prevailed, and so Zeus decreed Aphrodite wed to Hephaistos.

Disbelieving his great fortune, Hephaistos stood up. Most of his life had been spent in scorn. No one looked at his humped body, and he avoided the company of others. Once, his father, in a rage, had thrown him off Olympus for protecting his mother's honor. The event had left him forever crippled and deformed. How was it that he, Hephaistos was awarded this amazing prize?

He fumbled for what to say or even what to do, and finally came forward, limping and stuttering gibberish.

Aphrodite pulled her eyes from Ares, as Hephaistos hobbled toward her. Her face registered sympathy and then, as Hephaistos held out his hand and whispered gently, "My Lady," Aphrodite's lips melted into her ever-ready smile, and she followed him to the empty throne next to his.

Delighted, Hephaistos kept saying, "I will treat you very well. I will give you everything you want. And in my forge, I will make you the most beautiful golden ornaments."

Aphrodite smiled at his devotion, but her eyes kept drifting toward Ares, who hungrily licked his lips in her direction.

42

The Warrior Goddess

One last seat remained. Who would sit there? –A god or a goddess?

As if in response to the common question, Zeus shook his head violently and howled in pain, "Owwwwwwwwwwwww!"

He was having a strange fit, throwing his head forward, backward and side-to-side.

Overcome with agony, he crawled onto the floor and slammed his head against the marble, yelling, "Get it out! Get it out!"

"What is wrong?" Hera demanded.

"My head! My head!" Zeus screamed.

"What can we do?" Hera cried, turning toward the goddesses, and then to Apollo, the god of healing.

Apollo stood. "There are no illnesses here," he said, swooning into a trance. "No, the final Goddess is making her entrance." Then, in poetic introduction, Apollo spoke of she who was coming:

"It was foretold that, if birthed by natural means, she would be the ruler of all the worlds,

Instead, she comes forth from the mind of God,

Warrior, virgin, wise and strong.

Protector, guardian, ruthless, call to her in song.

She sees through the veil of darkness

And smites those with evil intent.

If your heart be wicked or untrue, beware her wrath

For the spear of righteousness which her right hand doth bear, will come upon you, if wrong you dare."

Apollo fell silent as Zeus screamed, "Get her out of my head!"

Everyone looked at each other in bewilderment, until Hephaistos ran to the wall and pulled loose a double-headed ax.

In disbelief, the others watched as the master smith chopped into his father's head, splitting it in half.

Was the reign of Zeus over before it had begun?

From Zeus' divided skull, split open like a ripe melon, a tiny goddess climbed out. Fully clad in silver-blue armor, she carried a spear just as Apollo had predicted.

She appeared small at first, but as she stepped to the floor her figure grew to the height of a tall tree. The stern look on her face made all feel small and naked in her sight. Every secret and intention was known and judged according to her wisdom.

Looking at her father, the seat of his mind divided in two, she set down her spear and pressed the halves of Zeus' severed brain together.

"Be whole," she whispered to her father. "Be whole and strong."

She stepped back and recovered her spear, while Zeus stood up and shook himself into completion.

"Childbirth is not for the weak," he spoke softly and bowed awkwardly before Hera.

In his weakened state, Zeus paid homage to Hera first, before his other mistresses. Hera beamed at him, delighted in her moment of glory. But Zeus, sensitive to the loyalty of other mothers and other wives, did not forget them.

"I honor all the mothers: Grandmother Gaia, the first mother of us all; Rhea, our own mother; Leto, the Hyperborean mother of Artemis and Apollo; Maia, the

Pleiadian, mother of Hermes; Semele, who perished at the sight of my true form but gave us Dionysos; and Metis, mother of Athena."

Those were the only names Zeus mentioned, but everyone suspected that there were many more.

The newly born daughter, Athena, stepped into Zeus' circle and wisely said, "And we honor the fathers, even those who eat their wives and children." She looked piercingly at Zeus. According to a prediction, his first daughter born of a goddess would become the ruler of Heaven and Earth, so Zeus had eaten Athena's mother during her pregnancy.

"There has been too much eating of children," Athena said poignantly. "I beseech you, Father, let this be the end of such traditions.

Zeus looked at her with reverent blue eyes. "So shall it be, Oh Gray-Eyed One."

The thrones were filled. Zeus sat on high next to Hera, and in a circle around them, sat Ares, Hephaistos, Aphrodite, Demeter, Apollo, Artemis, Dionysus, Poseidon, Hermes and Athena.

Zeus, the god of heaven and earth, now fully recovered from his ordeal, bellowed across the pantheon, "Let there be a sacrifice in honor of the twelve Olympian gods and goddesses."

240

43

Sacrifice

When Apollo led a bull into the midst of gods and goddess, a sinking feeling filled Kheiron's heart. Then, when the hunch-backed god Hephaistos brought out his ax and lifted his weapon to chop off the animal's head, Kheiron could not restrain himself, "No," he yelled.

A swoosh filled the air as the assembled gods and goddesses turned their heads to look at the young centaur.

Without concern for offending anyone, Kheiron said, "There is a better way."

Zeus smiled, "Show us then, Kheiron."

Kheiron lunged protectively toward to the bull, and stumbled over a rock, but having four legs, he easily righted himself. At the sound, the bull met his eyes, and Kheiron shook his head for reassurance. The bull stared at him as if unsure whether to charge or wait. Finally it shook its head at him in return.

Kheiron sniffed the bull and the bull sniffed back. "Will you give your life in sacrifice to the gods?" he whispered.

The bull's big eyes opened intently, and then, its body shivered and its head dropped in acceptance, as if it had known all along.

Kheiron poured some water into his hand from the bladder over his shoulder, and placidly, the bull licked the moisture off his palm.

During his young life Kheiron had doctored many animals, and with his natural curiosity he had dissected and begun to understand how bodies function. He was familiar with the large artery that ran through the neck, the tube that brought blood to the head. Deftly he petted the bull's neck and found the pulsing blood vessel.

A lump formed in his throat as he unsheathed his sharp knife. "Bleeding is the easiest way to die," he remembered Artemis saying. "If you sever the wind pipe," she had told him, "an animal will gag on its own blood and spend its last moments in great trauma. So long as your knife is sharp, and you slice the middle of the artery, it will die peacefully. If, however, you don't do it right, get it over as quickly as possible and cut hard and strong from ear to ear, including the windpipe. It will be better for the animal that way."

I better do it right, Kheiron thought, trembling slightly. He pet the bull's head and said, "May your life bring greatness to the gods and goddesses of Mount Olympus."

Out of character for most male bovines, the bull looked at Kheiron trustingly and only startled when the knife sliced down his artery.

"Glurrr na na pshhh pshhhh pshhh," Kheiron whispered and rubbed the bull's head while the quiet goddess Hesita brought forth a wooden bowl to catch the blood.

The bull closed his eyes and rested his head against Kheiron's chest.

"Pshhhh, pshhh, pshhhh," Kheiron whispered the calming sounds of his mother's spring, as the weight of the bull's body leaned heavily against him.

Finally, the bull's legs buckled, and it fell to the ground unconscious.

Kheiron waited until no more blood came from the bull's neck and then, wiped the tears from his eyes before he sought out Zeus. He raised his eyes to meet Zeus'. Their eyes locked, and Kheiron said, "Less suffering is better for everyone."

"Yes," Zeus admitted with a slight air of condescension. Then with solemnity Zeus added, "to honor your wisdom, Kheiron, all sacrifices to me or the gods of Olympus will be conducted in such a manner as you have demonstrated today." Zeus smiled. Then his booming voice echoed throughout the pantheon, "Let there be ambrosia, the draught of immortality, for everyone."

Kheiron returned to the fallen bull and took it upon himself to cut the meat. While he worked, he sang quietly, and when he removed the inner organs, he noticed that the heart, the liver, and the kidneys were in perfect condition.

"All is as it should be," Apollo whispered over his shoulder. With a smile he handed Kheiron a wooden goblet of fermented honey, ambrosia, the food of the gods. Kheiron took a sip, but continued to over-see the cutting and cooking of the meat. Somehow he felt responsible to make sure that the bull's life was treated with honor and respect, even in its death.

* * * * *

With the gathering of gods and goddesses complete, feasting followed. "Life eats life," Kheiron commented to Hestia as he left the cooking fire.

The goddess of the hearth, who never spoke, smiled broadly at Kheiron. She was silent but seemed to understand the deep, unvoiced sentiments of his heart.

That evening, before eating, Kheiron sent his prayers to the bull, "Thank you for giving your life as food. As I eat your flesh, may it fill me with your courage and strength and allow me to help others make our world a kinder and better place."

Kheiron filled both his bellies many times over with the rich, succulent meat. It was one of the few times in his life when hunger did not gnaw at him in some subtle way.

When the sun had gone down and the stars twinkled above, Kheiron stood near as Hermes gave Apollo lessons in the art of playing his new musical instrument, the lyre. He listened and learned and took his turn at strumming the turtle shell instrument. Together with Hermes and Apollo, they made up melodies and rhymes. All three of them laughed and delighted in their combined, harmonic creations. Up on the highest peak, among the clouds, their songs, prayers and divine supplications filled the heavens . . . with music.

44

Maia the Mother of Hermes

Under the *zodiakos kykolos*, the circle of constellations and wandering planets, Kheiron stood near the peak of Mount Olympus singing new songs that he had learned from Hermes and Apollo. Quietly, the stars listened to his familiar voice.

"Milk, milk, milk, milk
Tell me the color of milk
Sweet yellow or creamy white
Milk, milk, milk
My stomach's one delight"

Well, yes, the song was silly, but Hermes gave it a catchy tune that stuck in Kheiron's mind, repeating itself over and over.

Kheiron was happy here on Mount Olympus among family. They accepted and loved him as he was. He had not felt so content since he was young – when he had run through the meadow near his cave and sang to tadpoles and frogs with his mother Philyra. He looked to the Hyperborian star in the north, and a comfort filled his mind.

Kheiron closed his eyes. Down below, Oceanus, his grandfather the sea, lapped on the eastern Aegean shore. The full moon illuminated the celestial home of the gods, and Kheiron stood, a sleeping sentinel on Mount Olympus.

Sobbing roused Kheiron from his reverie. A woman, apparently wanting to be alone, had not realized the horse-boy's presence.

Her voice quivered softly, speaking, as if to comfort herself.

"How could he hurt me so? It is as if I never even existed. My own child has forgotten me. My own baby has deserted me for another mother."

Kheiron blinked his eyes in the darkness, trying to see who it was, but the woman's features and voice were unfamiliar.

"Who is there?" he whispered.

The sobbing stopped.

"It's all right," he continued. "I am sorry that you feel forgotten. I understand."

In the obscurity, the woman could not make out the figure who spoke to her.

"My mother left me," Kheiron told her.

"Oh," the woman responded, and began sobbing again.

Kheiron didn't mean to make her feel worse and asked, "Who is your baby?"

"Hermes," she answered.

Surprised, Kheiron said, "He is very clever for a baby. He is blessed and endowed with extraordinary gifts. I have already learned some things from him about composing songs and playing the lyre."

The woman's voice brightened. "He is special, isn't he?"

"Yes," Kheiron agreed.

"But," the woman bemoaned, "He found himself a better mother, the Queen of Heaven and Earth. Now he sits on her lap while she feeds him ambrosia from her fingers and even nurses him with her own breast. I am a sorry mother. I want nothing more than to be the one he looks to for comfort and nourishment. But he goes to her, not me." And the woman sobbed again.

Kheiron remembered the wink and smile Hermes flashed when Hera picked him up, like he had won some great prize.

"What is your name?" Kheiron whispered to the woman.

"Maia."

"Maia," he repeated. "That is a beautiful name. You must be very lovely, because Zeus only loves those who are extraordinarily beautiful."

"Beauty," the woman groaned. "What good is beauty? It does not impart happiness. It makes men and gods want and chase you. But they only take what they desire, give you a child to bear, the most precious thing that you ever held. But in the end, none of it matters. You are forgotten and left alone by both."

Kheiron was unfamiliar with the troubles of being beautiful or handsome. However, he knew loneliness all too well.

The sound of singing birds broke the silence between them. Soon the dark sky would become light. Maia spoke again. "You seem very kind. What are you called?"

"Kheiron," the horse-boy answered.

In that first glow of morning, Maia looked at his true form and recoiled from the creature that stood before her.

Perhaps she expected a god who would make her knees tremble. But Kheiron, with the body of a horse and torso and head of a man, met her gaze.

He watched the uncomfortable struggle in her mind. Yet, she had met Kheiron under the disguise of night, and now the battle between fear and her experience of him left Maia speechless.

After a long pause, she timidly extended a gracious hand.

247

"Kheiron," she said, "I am grateful to meet you. And though I didn't know you were here, I am glad that you were. It helps when someone cares."

In the pale light, she looked at the horse-boy more closely.

"Beauty," she said, "is not so special. It is kindness, care, and honor that matter most. Here, I have something for you."

Maia reached into her pocket and pulled out a stone. "I found it on a beach near a river when my sisters and I were bathing, near Mount Pelion."

She dropped the rock into Kheiron's palm. It was blue.

"Azurite," Kheiron said, turning the pithy stone over in his hands, "from my mother's cave."

"A token of our friendship," Maia said, bowing to Kheiron. Her lips parted into a smile.

"We are friends," the horse-boy replied.

"You know we may never see each other again," Maia told Kheiron," but I will watch you, kind horse-man of Mount Pelion. I live there," and she pointed to a group of fading stars above the red-eyed bull. "I am one of the Pleiadian sisters."

As she spoke the last words, a gust of wind blew by and stopped before her.

There in front of them stood the baby Hermes.

"Mama," he cooed, throwing his arms around her legs.

"Hermes, my precious boy," her voice peaked as she scooped him into her arms and held him close. "I missed you so much."

There was no reproach, no anger, or resentment. All her grief was forgotten when the object of her love appeared.

Kheiron bowed and backed up. He did not want to intrude on their reunion, but his hooves clicked against the marble stones.

"Hermes, dear," Maia said, not letting the horse-boy go without notice, "this is my good friend, Kheiron. We must always help him because that is what friends do. If you ever know where his mother is, tell him. Mothers are usually just as precious to their children, as children are to their mothers."

Hermes turned his piercing, blue eyes on Kheiron.

"Practice playing the lyre, Kheiron, and someday we will play together for your mother."

"I will," Kheiron answered eagerly, but the mother and son, engulfed in mutual adoration, appeared not to hear him. Kheiron put the azurite into the leather pouch around his neck and walked away.

45

Hera's Grief

Pale blue light spread across the sky, dissolving the starry remnants of night. Kheiron walked in the heavenly gardens touching dew covered leaves and gently stroking flower petals with the backs of his hands. Each plant was alive with a spirit that illuminated it from the inside. He wanted to meet these new plants, make friends, and learn their medicine and magic. Plants were not fearful or judgmental of his deformities.

Gently he touched a leaf and used the familiar Aegean, "K*ali merra*, good morning."

A yellow blossom bent over as if saying *"Kali meera,"* in return.

A large bird with tall, blue-green tail feathers stood in front of Kheiron, trying to intimidate him. Its tail seemed to fan out with a hundred eyes –iridescent with purples, greens, golds and indigo. As if a king among birds, the splendid creature cocked its head to one side and then to the other, looking at Kheiron with regal curiosity.

The two stood opposite one another watching until the bird dipped its head and screamed like a girl calling for help.

Kheiron gave the bird a wide girth and made his way toward another section of the garden. There, a woman stood talking to a fruit tree.

Remembering Maia's revulsion at his appearance, Kheiron ducked behind a shrub. However, this woman had already seen him.

"Kheiron," she called his name, "dear little brother, come and walk with me."

It was Hera.

Having seen the distortions of her sweetness, especially when confronted with her own jealousy, Kheiron felt timid about approaching. However, no one can ignore the requests of the Queen Goddess.

"You saw my peacock?" she called. "Isn't he beautiful? Come meet my pomegranate tree, *To Rodhi*," and she motioned to her half-brother, the young centaur.

As Kheiron came close, Hera revealed a round, dark red skinned fruit clinging to the branch.

"This is my special tree," she said, plucking the ripe fruit. She peeled away the leathery exterior, and with two hands broke it in half.

Crimson juice spread over her fingers.

"It is like blood, don't you think?" She asked catching Kheiron's eye. "The insides are like a womb. The multitude of seeds are are like unborn babies."

Kheiron saw what she meant.

"Here taste one," she said and offered him a tiny fruit.

Always hungry, Kheiron looked at the small pomegranate seed. How could such a tiny thing be satisfying? However, when his teeth split open the fruit, his mouth filled with a tangy sweetness, and he wanted more.

Hera broke off a section and handed it to him.

"Wherever the pomegranate tree is planted," she said, "is sacred to me."

Kheiron nodded his head, "I will remember that Queen Hera," and amazingly his hunger subsided.

"Come," she said with a smile. "Let us walk in the garden.

"Apollo says that you will be a great healer. Since what he says is always true, you must learn the *votana*, the herbs of childbirth."

They walked side by side. "This herb," Hera told him, "I first learned from my mother, Rhea. . . at your birth." Hera knelt down and broke a small branch from the wandering plant. "It is called *mandzurana*, marjoram. It makes a woman's womb tighten and push the baby out."

Kheiron took the herb in his hands and smelled it. The fragrance recalled the open fields where it grew wild on Mount Pelion.

Hera pointed to another plant with dark, pointy, green leaves and fine hairs.

He recognized it immediately.

"That is the stinging herb," Kheiron said, I know it all too well.

"*Tsiknida*, nettles," Hera answered with a laugh. "Its bite is painful, but it keeps the blood of a pregnant mother and her baby strong. That one too," she said pointing to a prickly, berry vine. "*Avatsinia*, blackberry."

Shaking his head, Kheiron said, "I shall have to develop tough skin to gather these plants."

"You are tough," Hera answered.

"Here is another one: *Tzourkas*, sheperd's purse."

Kheiron looked at the little weed, a favorite snack.

"It staunches bleeding," Hera told him. "And it should be part of the infusion given to a woman before her baby is due."

"Also *Agriapsithia*, yarrow... If you grind the dry, feathery leaves and sprinkle them directly into a bleeding wound, the blood will stop flowing. The flowers create fever and chase away illnesses."

Kheiron smiled quietly. He had discovered yarrow's secrets on his own.

"Most of these *votana*, herbs can be made into infusions," Hera told him, "but you can also make them into unguents with grease and beeswax. Oh, and don't forget *Artemisia*, mugwort. It pushes the afterbirth out."

Kheiron was unfamiliar with afterbirth though he guessed what it must be since he had watched goats, sheep and cows birthing. Beyond that, he didn't have any experiences with these types of womanly things.

"Isn't this women's wisdom?" Kheiron asked respectfully.

The goddess smiled. "Yes, but some of that wisdom will come through you, Kheiron. Just be sure to give credit where credit is due. And don't worry," she said, seeing the doubt cross through his mind, "when you find yourself in need of this information, I will be there to help you, in spirit if not in form."

Hera gazed at Kheiron thoughtfully. She felt comfortable with her father's son and did not mind his strange horse body. Perhaps being present at his birth made a difference in the lack of anxiety she felt with him. However, the moment passed and a scowl came over her face.

Kheiron turned to see what had attracted her attention.

Maia was holding Hermes on the lawn and feeding him as a mother should.

"What is wrong?" Kheiron asked innocently.

"It's that Pleiadian," Hera said, raising her lip. "Damn her. She is just one more pretty girl that my husband, on a whim, has taken.

"I hope you understand, Kheiron, and that you don't mind my honesty. But I suffer so much. I am devoted to Zeus. I take no other lovers.

"Before I agreed to our marriage, I asked him to promise fidelity. He agreed, but he is not honest. No sooner had I submitted myself to being his wife –thinking and hoping, expecting marital bliss – than he was out seducing someone else. The devotion and loyalty of marriage mean nothing to him. And yet, I continue in my love and fidelity. Sometimes I hate him, it is true, but only because he scorns our sacred vows. He does not respect me, and neither does she." Her gaze indicated Maia.

"And it's not just her. There has been Leto and Semele, Metis, his former wife, and others, so many others. Most recently Kallisto, one of Artemis' supposed virgins, vowed to a life of chastity. She now carries one of his children."

At the sound of her name, Kheiron's heart stopped beating for a moment. *Kallisto?* The pieces came together in his mind. The red-eyed bull... had she submitted herself to him or did she fight?

He remembered Kallisto's strange desire to see that bull.

Kheiron felt a rush of new emotions: anger and jealousy. He loved Kallisto, but he was just a horse with the upper body of a man, a deformity, not the God of Heaven and Earth. Who could resist that temptation? But how could she forsake her vows?

"I suppose it was not all her fault," Hera's words broke through his thoughts and answered his questions. "Zeus transforms himself to hide his escapades, but I am not deceived. No, when the bull disguise did not work, he made himself into the likeness of Artemis. In that form, he could get close to the young virgin and force his love on her. I know that she resisted him. And I suppose that I should have more compassion. But I am filled with a rage I cannot control, and I hate her."

Kheiron tried to listen as Hera continued. "I am not proud of my feelings," she said. "I find myself resentful of

255

young, beautiful women. Not because of them, but because I know how my husband lusts for them. I do not want to hate women, my sisters in spirit. Yet because of his lack of respect to me, I look upon all of them with distrust and disdain.

"I don't understand, but I find myself confessing everything to you. Oh Kheiron, my own worth is lacking."

Kheiron forced a smile, but his own mind was racing with thoughts of Kallisto.

"I wonder," Hera pondered out loud, "if Zeus sees me as older, matronly and unattractive. That is how I have begun to see myself. If only I were more youthful, more vivacious, happier. If only I were more lovely, then, perhaps he would lavish his attentions upon me. Oh Kheiron, my eyes are dry from crying. In fact, there are no tears left, only salty bitterness.

"Sometimes Zeus still loves me," Hera said, looking out toward Oceanus, "but it is not with that freshness of new love, not with fire and passion, not with the adoration he first showed me. He conquered me and then moved on to other beauties. At least I have the honor of being his recognized wife, the Queen of Heaven and Earth."

Imagining the red eye of Zeus' disguise, Kheiron ate the last of the pomegranate seeds, nervously thinking of Kallisto while Hera continued to share her thoughts.

"I divert my attention," she said. "I focus on the suffering of mothers in childbirth, those who bear their husband's children. I hear their moans and try to ease their pains. I listen and watch after their babies, but that does not make me any less tormented. Being a goddess is not always easy or magnificent. Sometimes it is wretched.

Kheiron put a gentle hand over hers, and she glanced up sadly. "Do not judge me harshly, Little Brother. I would not be so bitter if I were better loved and respected."

Kheiron was beginning to understand that Zeus used his power to take what he wanted. The king of Heaven and Earth didn't care whom he hurt. Strangely, everyone said that Zeus was better than Kronus, better than Uranus, but still the new ruler valued powers and pleasures over the needs of others. Dissent spread through Kheiron's mind, and he didn't know if he could look at Zeus in the same way again.

Only yesterday Kheiron had been so happy to be among family.

Hera smiled, but all Kheiron could think of, was Kallisto. Where was she? And was she alright?

46

The Price of Broken Vows

Apollo found Kheiron alone in the garden, restless and wanting to go. "Come here Kheiron," the golden god called. "There is something I want to show you."

"I don't want to see anything," Kheiron answered with agitation. Hera had just left him with troubled thoughts of his friend Kallisto. "I want to go now," he said.

But Apollo motioned insistently and pointed towards a small pool.

"I want you to look into the still waters and tell me what you see."

"I don't feel like looking, Apollo. I cannot make my mind quiet right now. I need to leave."

Not accepting anything but compliance, Apollo pointed to the pond again.

Reluctantly, Kheiron looked into the water, but all he saw was the reflection of the blue sky and the surrounding foliage.

"Soften your eyes, and ask what you want to know." Apollo whispered, "maybe something about...your friend?"

Of course, Apollo knew what troubled his mind.

"I want to see Kallisto," Kheiron said. "Is she alright?"

"Ask the water," Apollo told him, "Eventually, the ripples will clear and show you what you long to know."

Apollo disappeared into the sun's bright reflection, and Kheiron stood looking in the pool. He saw nothing exceptional. Yet, he kept watching as directed, struggling with an anxious desire to leave and the knowledge that Apollo was usually wise in his demands.

"Show me Kallisto," he asked the pool again . . . and again.

Eventually his anxiety wore down, and he became tired. His eyes grew heavy, and he drifted into semi-sleep. It was then that something moved across the still water.

Half awake, Kheiron saw the daughters of Artemis reflected. They were at the river. He knew that he should not look upon them as they bathed, yet he saw her, Kallisto, standing in the shade, saying, "No, I don't feel like bathing today."

The others teased and said, "You stink more than the rest of us." And they pulled her into the stream. She resisted.

It was then that Artemis called her, "Kallisto, I insist that you bathe."

Hesitantly, the girl took off her belt and untied the leather straps around her bearskin boots.

Undressed, she looked down, averting her eyes from the others, but there was no doubt. In her nakedness, a small, rounded belly exposed itself to the daughters and worst of all, to Artemis.

The wild women of Arcadia, those who hunted the Vale of Tempe, virgins one and all, gasped. Kallisto's vows were betrayed. She who had been the favorite of the Goddess, the envy of all the other girls, was no longer one of them.

Kallisto glanced at Artemis then lowered her eyes in submissive shame.

The goddess said nothing. She simply reached for her silver bow and one of her poison-tipped arrows.

Kallisto stood ready to take what would come next. She knew full well the consequences.

But Artemis paused in her aim, "Go," she ordered. "You do not deserve to die quickly. I will hunt you instead."

Not fully comprehending Artemis' words, Kallisto didn't move.

"Go!" the goddess ordered again.

Kallisto left her garments where they lay. It didn't matter if a man saw her now. She didn't care. Nothing mattered. In her heart, she was still devoted to the goddess, and if it gave the object of her worship pleasure to hunt, then she would give her lady a hunt, even if it was for her own skin.

As always, Kallisto was fast. She had spent most of her life running through the forests with Artemis. But this time she was alone, running for her life, if indeed it was worth anything.

No, Kheiron thought, shaking his head while the images blurred out of sight, *I have to help her.* He turned quickly and ran for the golden gates of Olympus.

"Where are you going, Kheiron?" Hera called from the pavilion.

"We have to help Kallisto," he called back.

There was no response as the gates swung open and allowed him to run onto the high mountain meadows.

Kheiron galloped down the path, but the valley came no closer. He seemed to be running and running, but getting nowhere. Apparently he could not leave Olympus on his own.

In frustration, he called Apollo's name.

A rift in the clouds separated, and he saw Kallisto running up the path. She was naked, and her belly larger than he remembered from the vision.

"Kallisto," he called.

She stopped when she heard his voice.

"Kheiron, is that you? Where are we?"

"Mount Olympus," he answered.

"Artemis is going to kill me," she said, "but I need to save the baby." Her belly had already grown to full term.

"Help me get to Zeus. He has done this to me, he will protect the child."

Anxious to help her in any way he could, Kheiron ran to her side.

"Climb on my back," he offered.

As she had done only once before, Kallisto reached around Kheiron's human waist and pulled herself onto his back. She was much heavier now than before.

Hurried by her urgency, Kheiron ran toward the golden gates.

As he ran his mind calmed, and he began to think. How had Kallisto managed to enter the forbidden lands? Apollo or Zeus must have made special allowance for her and opened the ephemeral paths. Certainly, the gates of Olympus would swing open as well. Zeus had loved Kallisto, so naturally he would offer her asylum.

But as they approached, the gates did not open.

Kheiron grabbed hold of a golden grape leaf and pulled hard, but the metal latches were frozen shut.

"Let us in," he yelled.

Hera's voice answered back. "The gates are sealed for good reason, Kheiron. Leave her there. Let her die like the beast that she is."

Beast? Hera knew that Zeus had forced himself on Kallisto, that she had not seduced him. Why was the goddess being so cold?

"Please, Hera, open the gates for me?" Kheiron called. But again there was no response.

Only this morning Hera had taught him the votana, the herbs of childbirth. Had he fallen from her graces so quickly?

Kallisto slipped off his back. "It's alright, Kheiron," she said. "I have to be brave and face my end. I just wanted to save the baby, the little one inside."

Her belly was larger than even moments before. Time passed unnaturally fast here.

"Perhaps," Kallisto said, rubbing her distended abdomen, "this is where our destines are entwined, yours and mine. You, my friend, will be here when I perish."

"No," Kheiron answered. "I will help you and your baby."

Without waiting for a response, he set off around the side of the ephemeral gates to find another opening.

With his keen ears he heard Kallisto sobbing behind him, "Please, Zeus, protect the baby."

Finding no other openings into the sacred gardens, Kheiron turned to go back. But this time he saw Artemis standing with Kallisto, her bow pulled taught.

Kheiron was too far away, but he heard the goddess' voice.

"I've always loved you, Kallisto. Despite your vows, beauty was your curse."

"Potnia Theron," Kallisto begged. "Spare the child."

Without pausing Artemis shot the girl in the chest.

Kheiron's heart sank, and he turned away. He could not bear to see his friend fall.

Why did Artemis have to kill her? Why didn't Hera open the gates? Were they all so heartless? Zeus, Hera and Artemis, they seemed to be ruled by vows, lusts and jealousies, not by what was right. Then he thought about the baby. He could cut it from Kallisto's womb and fulfill her last desire, to protect it. He could take care of the baby.

263

He ran to the place, but Kallisto's corpse was nowhere to be found – not even a trace of blood. Kheiron sniffed the air, but only the faint scent of oregano lingered.

Kheiron didn't want to be in this distorted world of gods and goddesses anymore. He didn't want anything to do with them. Without looking back, he walked down the hill, tears blurring his vision.

"Twisted, cruel, fickle and trite," Kheiron said to himself, making his way toward the Vale. He kept walking, yet he never got any closer. Still he kept moving, yelling every now and then, "I don't want to be here anymore! Let me go home!"

When the sun rested on the western hills, making long shadows across the grass, Kheiron stopped and looked toward the valley. How far was it to Mount Pelion?

In that moment, with the last orange rays of light, Kheiron realized, with complete conviction, *Kronus was a liar, just another temperamental god who destroyed lives at will. He killed my mother just like Artemis killed Kallisto.*

He wiped the tears from his face. *What good, what purpose is life without friends or family?*

Desperation filled his heart, and he wanted to get away more than anything. He noticed the bow slung over his shoulder and took it off. Then he removed the quiver filled with arrows. He had worked hard to make these tools, but that didn't matter. Finally he pulled off the sheath and knife that Artemis had given him and threw them into the brush. He didn't want anything to do with *Her* anymore.

Ahead the cliff opened into a wall of clouds. He didn't know what lay beyond the clouds, but he sensed a way out. He ran toward the mist and jumped.

It happened so quickly. One moment he was running on the solid mountain and the next he was in mid air.

Instead of falling gracefully like a bird, the harsh pull of earth yanked Kheiron upside down. His arms and legs tangled around him, and he fell hard and fast like a glacial boulder. Within seconds he would hit the rocks in the gorge below.

47

No Death

Like a tree that falls in a storm, Kheiron's limbs cracked and shattered as his body smashed against the rocks in the bottom of the gorge.

At first he felt nothing.

Am I dead, he wondered, staring at the blue sky above? *This is not Mount Pelion and not the Vale of Tempe.*

Unaware of his body, Kheiron watched the pine trees bend in the wind. Quickly, however, the numbness passed, and pain, then agony, crept into every muscle and bone. His left arm hung loose, almost separate from his body, and his legs stuck out at odd angles.

Unable to see clearly, Kheiron wiped bright crimson moisture from his eyes and felt the soft tissue of torn flesh hanging from his forehead. A sharp stone had gouged his belly, and the contents: intestinal ropes, stomach and bladder, lay exposed in a pool of blood in front of him.

In agony, he whispered painfully, "I welcome you Death."

Through long hours under the hot sun Kheiron suffered in agony. He struggled with every inhalation and waited for his breath to stop, the way it had with some of the animals he had tried to save.

He remembered the baby goat, the scruffy dead thing that he had carried around for so long. The small kid had died in the night while Kheiron stroked its soft fur and sang watery lullabies. Perhaps like the newborn goat, death would come with the shadows of night.

He waited and watched as the sun set.

But as much as Kheiron wanted to die and turn his back on the rulers of Heaven and Earth, he could not escape them.

Overhead, the stars blinked, and Zeus' eagle Aquilla, mocked his foolish desire to perish.

"Don't laugh at me, you stupid bird," Kheiron called, aching with the effort to speak. "Your master is a tormenter of humanity and gods. He has no compassion."

Kheiron expected to be shot with a bolt of lightning, but without sound or reprimand the starry, red-eyed bull rose above the eastern cliff and moved west.

Orion, the hunter, passed overhead and gazed down at the broken centaur below. Then, came the dogs and the brightest star in the sky, Sirius, the nighttime sun.

Kheiron got stronger.

Evidently, he thought, *I am like Prometheus, the immortal titan who daily suffers the talons of Zeus' eagle only to live until the next day when he suffers again – eternal torment.*

As a child of Kronus, the power of immortality mended Kheiron's bones. The gash in his abdomen gurgled, and his internal organs sucked into their rightful places.

Kheiron watched this unnatural process.

Healing hurts as much as injury, he thought, and growled in discomfort as his protruding femur righted itself.

By morning, hunger roused him from a fitful sleep, and when he looked at his belly, to his surprise, there was not so much as a scab where the sharp rocks had impaled him the day before.

48

Pomegranates and Yew

A crow perched in a cedar tree and cawed noisily as Kheiron attempted to stand. It flew up the gorge and disappeared into the thick bank of clouds.

"You didn't kill her did you," Hera asked.

Artemis ducked her head to avoid the black wings of the crow as it landed on her left shoulder. "I couldn't. I loved her too much."

"But won't she suffer longer in her present condition, ostracized and rejected even by her own kind?"

"What do you care?" Artemis snorted. "She will no longer tempt your husband."

Hera smiled wryly. "I like you Artemis. You are not coy or deceptive but speak your truth openly."

Artemis lifted her hand to the crow, which hopped onto her forearm. "I have no reason for regret. Only my heart suffers when the ones I care for are in pain. Look at her there Hera," she pointed down the mountain where they instantly saw a large animal, lifting itself off the ground. "She is lost and bewildered, walking on four legs. She will have to learn to live like that from now on."

Hera smiled, "But you caused the pain yourself. It is true that she resisted Zeus as best she could. Even she could not resist the king of Heaven and Earth for long. I couldn't, and see what misery I live in. Sometimes I just have to forget that I am queen and divert my attention with the lives of mortals. Speaking of mortals, what did you do with her child?"

Artemis rolled her eyes, "He is not entirely mortal. Zeus sucked the baby from her womb and gave it to Maia to raise as her own."

"Just as well," Hera sighed. There, look at poor Kheiron."

They turned their attention to the young centaur as he clumsily walked out of the gorge. "He thought he could rid himself of his parentage and die. He does not realize the power of being a descendant of Gaia and Uranus, or a son of Kronus. He embodies the best of us, the best of the old ways."

Artemis raised the crow to her shoulder. "He is lucky to have been so influenced by the goddesses. Yet he suffers so much, probably because he inherited his mother's disposition." The goddesses watched Kallisto and Kheiron, in two different places, each trying to re-establish their equilibrium. "Whether you live for only a short time or forever, pain is inevitable," Hera said. "Like a true healer, Kheiron turns his losses into the roots of great strength. Everyone knows there are few like him, even among the immortals. That is why no one takes offense when he scorns them."

In the gorge below, Kheiron felt the breeze drifting down from the mountain. He lifted his nose and sniffed the strange mixture of scents that filled his nostrils: fresh pomegranate and yew berries. *Hera*, he thought, *and Artemis. I wonder what they are conspiring.*

Hera took a deep breath. "I know where his mother is."

Artemis scanned the glowing skin of the goddess' face. "She is alive?"

"Of course, only transformed, like Kallisto. She still lives near her own spring. In fact the spring would have dried up if she were no longer there. Kheiron has felt her presence but couldn't figure out where she was."

"I remember," Artemis said, as she handed the crow a berry from her pouch, "when the time is right, he will find her."

Glossary of Greek Characters

Adrastia (Αδραστια)
One of the nymphs who cared for the infant Zeus in the cave on Mount Ida in Crete.

Aegea or Achaea (Αιγια)
Ancient Greece especially Thessaly (mainland Greece) and the northern coast of the Peloponnese, including the area of Corinth. It was more of a tribal/regional name, but those who marched against Troy were called Achaeans (the Roman translation). They were also called Argives for those who lived in Argolis. The Aegeans later settled in Argos and Lacedaemon (Southern Peloponnese). It makes sense to spell it Aegea since the whole eastern sea is called the Aegean Sea. Over time the ancient name was used less and less. Later the Greeks called themselves Hellenes and the land Hellas.

Amalthea (Αμαλθεια)
A nymph or she goat who suckled the infant Zeus and protected him from his father's discovery by hanging him in a tree where he could not be seen in the heavens, the sea, or on the earth. She was said to be so hideous that the gods had to hide her on Mount Ida on Crete so that she could not be seen. Zeus is said to have broken off one of her horns and used it as a gift (the horn of Amalthea or the horn of plenty) from which flowed an ever abundance of food.

Aphrodite (Αφροδιτη)
The goddess of love, beauty and intercourse. Aphrodite was one of the twelve great Olympian gods. She was born of the sea foam generated from the castrated genitals of the sky-god Ouranos or Uranus.

Apollo or Apollon (Απολλων)
Son of Zeus and Leto, twin brother of Artemis. One of the twelve great gods of Olympus, he was the god of divination, healing, music, poetry and art. Apollo plays many roles in

ancient Greece: slayer of the Python; god of the Oracle of Delphi; god of the Hyperboreans, the Iles of the Blessed; the cowherd; the lover (he had both female and male lovers). He was known as Akesios, Iatros and Phaon or Paeon, the divine healer; Nomios, the divine shepherd; Delphinios, meaning 'from the womb,' associated with Delphi the navel of the world; as well as Pythios or Pythian, having to do with the slaying of the python at Delphi.

Aquilla (Αθυιλλα)
The eagle of Zeus, sometimes a form of Zeus himself. The constellation overhead in the summer sky.

Ares (Αρες)
The god of war and one of the twelve great Olympian gods.

Artemis (Αρτεμις)
Daughter of Zeus and Leto, twin sister of Apollo. She was a sworn virgin and huntress, the Potnia Theron or Mistress of the Animals. Her life was hunting and living wild in the forests. Her arrows were said to inflict sudden death, especially if they were painless. She is associated with the roe buck hind. Artemesia plants and yew trees are sacred to her. She was the patron of the Amazon warrior women, as well as children, especially orphans, and childbirth.

Athena or Athene (Αθενε)
Goddess of war and crafts who sprung fully grown and armed from the head of Zeus. She was one of the twelve great Olympian gods. Among many things, Athena was said to have brought the gift of the olive tree to the new city of Athens and thus became the patron goddess of that city.

Kronos or Cronos (κρονοS)
Son of Gaia and Uranus, Father of Zeus, Hades, Demeter, Hestia, Poseidon, and Hera by Rhea. He also fathered Kheiron by Philyra, the water nymph. He overthrew his father Uranus by castrating him and throwing his genitals into the sea. In turn, he was defeated by his own son, Zeus in a long, ten year war called the Battle of the Titans. He was sent to Tartarus and imprisoned there, but at the end of the Age of Heros, Zeus liberated him and made him king of Elysium. There were two big wars, the ten

year war between Zeus and Kronus and a later battle with the Giants, in which the Giants tried to overtake Mount Olympus. The Clash of the Titans was the first one between Kronus and Zeus.

Kouretes or Kouretes (Κουρετες)
Servants of Rhea, a tribe of warriors, the Kouretes helped hide the baby Zeus from Kronus. Their dancing and singing, the clashing of their spears and shields so irritated Kronos that he stayed away. Thus they were able to drown out the cries of the baby Zeus.

Denarae an invented name for one of Philyra's 3000 sisters.

Dionysus or Dionysos or Bacchus or Bacchos (Διονυσος or βακκηος)
The god of wine and the son of Zeus and Semele. After spending many years wandering the world establishing his cult, the goddess Hestia relinquished her position to him when he entered Olympus.

Eros (Ερως)
The Greek god of sexual love. According to Hesiod's Theogony, Eros was Protogonus, the first born, of creation. He emerged from the sea of Chaos along with Nyx (night), Gaia (earth), Erebus (darkness) and Tartarus (the dark region, as deep below earth as the sky was above). According to the Orphic Creation Myth, Protogonus was the first god, without a mother and had both female and male sex organs with which he created Nyx. Upon her he fathered both Uranus (heaven) and Gaia (earth). Another version says that the dark bird, Nyx laid a golden egg from which Protogonus was born. The two broken halves of the egg became Gaia and Uranus. Eros, the darkest and 'most beautiful of the immortal gods: "he melts the limbs, and overpowers the reason as well as the careful plans in the breasts of all gods and men" (March-299). He is a primeval deity who embodies not only the force of erotic love but also the creative urge of ever-flowing nature, the first-born Light that is responsible for the coming into being and ordering of all things in the cosmos.

Gaia or Gaea (Γαια)
The earth and one of the first primordial gods born of Chaos with Eros, Nyx, Erebus and Tartarus. According to some, without any masculine element, she gave birth to Uranus, the heavens, the Mountains and Pontus, the masculine principle of the sea. She then coupled with Uranus and gave birth to the Titans, the early gods who Uranus kept hidden in her bowels. The other version says that the dark bird, Nyx laid a golden egg from which Protogonus was born. The two broken halves of the egg became Gaia and Uranus. One of Gaia's children was Kronus who she tutored in how to overthrow his father with a scythe. Kronus then became king of the heavens and earth only to be dethroned by Zeus, the son he believed eaten. It was through Gaia's guidance that Zeus learned of the Hundred-Handers, and with their help, was able to over throw his father.

Graces or Kharites (Κηαριτες)
Goddesses of beauty, joy and happiness.

Hekatonkheires or Hecatoncheires or Hundred-Handers (Greek: Ηεκατονκηειρες)
Briarios or Aegaeon, Cottus and Gyges or Gyes, the hundred-handers, the three sons of Gaia and Uranus. They were the most fearsome of all creatures, with fifty heads and one hundred arms and fists. They were giants, huge and strong and so ugly that Uranus refused to let them be seen in the light of day and pushed them back into their mother's womb. Even Kronus the next god of Heaven and Earth feared them and kept them imprisoned in Tartarus, deeper than the realm of Hades until they were liberated by Zeus in the Clash of the Titans. They helped him win the war against Kronus. They later became the guardians of the banished gods who were imprisoned back in Tartarus.

Helios or Helius (Ηελιος)
The god of the sun, who rode through the sky in a chariot drawn by winged horses and crowned with the aureole of the sun. He was the predecessor of Apollo.

Hephaistos or Hephaestus (Ηεφαιστος)
The hunchback son of Hera and Zeus. The god of fire, volcanism, smiths and craftsmen. None could compare with his work. He is said to have made many magical metal crafts,

including the sword of Peleus, the armor of Akhilles, the point of the ashen spear given as a gift at the wedding of Pelues and Thetis, and a delicate golden crown, also for Thetis, who nursed him(Hephaistos) when Zeus threw him from Mount Olympus into the sea in a fit of rage. He was one of the twelve great Olympian gods, and jilted husband of Aphrodite.

Hera (Ηρα)
The goddess of marriage, childbirth and protector of children. She was the daughter of Kronus and Rhea and part of the second generation of Gods. She was protected and raised by her auntie Tethys during the Clash of the Titans, and later became the queen of Heaven and Earth along side Zeus, her brother.

Hermes (Ηερμες)
The god of animal husbandry and fertility, trade, messengers, thieves and travel. He was the son of Zeus and the Pleideian nymph, Maia. He was said to escort the dead to Hades, and is famous for tricking Hera into accepting him as one of her own, as well as stealing the brown cows of Apollo and getting him to forgive him with the gift of the first lyre, made from a turtle shell and sinew.

Hestia (Ηστια)
The goddess of hearth and home. She was a virgin goddess, one of the great Olympian gods. She was also the goddess of the sacrificial flame and was so honored with every sacrifice to the gods.

Horae (Ωραι)
Goddesses of the seasons and daughters of Zeus and Themis (Zeus' first wife), sisters of the Moirai(the fates). There are three of them and they are called: Thallo (Blooming and Spring), Auxo (Increase and Summer), Carpo (Fruiting and Autumn). They were associated with justice, peace and good governance. They guard the cloud-gates of Mount Olympus. They welcomed the goddess Aphrodite into the world, dressing her in crepe myrtle flowers and escorting her to Olympus. They are associated with joy and festivities, births and weddings and are among the guests at the memorable wedding of Peleus and Thetis. Later they become four in number.

Hyperborea (Υπερβορεα)

The mythical land beyond the reaches of the North Wind. The region from which Boreas (the north wind) sends his icy blasts. Hyperboraea is an earthly paradise, where the people are untouched by disease or strife, where they spend much of their time in song and dance and sacrifice to their sun god, Apollo. Ordinary men could not come to this place, only a few such as Perseus and Herakles. Hyperboreans were said to have made a beeswax and feather temple that was brought by their priests to Delos the place of Apollo birth.

Kallisto or Callisto 'Most beautiful'(Καλλιστο)

Daughter of either King Lycaon or of Nycteus, or she was a wood nymph. In any case, she made a vow to remain a virgin and spend her days with the band of companions of Artemis. Zeus saw her and fell in love, but because she had forsaken men, he came to her in the guise of either a bull or Artemis herself. She became pregnant. When Artemis and her women were bathing in a spring, Kallisto reluctantly took off her clothes to join them. It was then that the truth of her pregnancy was made known.

Kheiron Cheiron or Chiron (Χειρων)

The son of Kronus and the *naiad* Philyra, either by seduction or rape. Kronus hid his infidelity from his wife Rhea by disguising himself as a horse to couple with Philyra. Kheiron was the progeny of this union, an immortal centaur, half horse and half human. His mother is said to have abandoned him because of his deformity and was transformed from her previous shape. Some sources say that she was there, on Mount Pelion, their home, watching over Kheiron and his children, proud of the achievements of her son. Apollo found Kheiron alone and taught him many things as did his sister Artemis. There is much more to his story, but I don't want to give away the next couple books.

Leto (Λετο)

The Titan goddess of motherhood and womanly demure. She was loved by the god Zeus, and during her pregnancy she was hounded across the earth by the goddess Hera who sent Python to make sure she had no place on earth to birth her children. Leto did give birth to twins, Apollo and Artemis on the floating island of Delos.

Maia (Μαια)
A Pleiadian star-nymph of Mount Cyllene in Arcadia. She was the mother of the god Hermes by Zeus.

Moirai (Μοιραι)
Goddesses who appointed the deaths of mortals and gods alike. Hesiod calls them the daughters of Nix(night) and later calls them the daughters of Zeus and Themis and sisters of the Horae (the seasons).   There are three Moirai: Clotho, the spinner, Lachesis, the apportioner, and Atropos, the inevitable. Clotho spun the thread of a man's life, Lachesis measured out its length, and Atropos cut the thread at the time of death.

Muses or Mousai or Pierides (Μουσαι or Πιεριδες)
Goddesses of inspiration, daughters of Zeus and Mnemosyne (Memory).   There are nine in number: Kalliope or Calliope (Lovely voice); Clio (Renown and History); Euterpe (Gladness and flute playing); Thalia (Good Cheer); Melponeme (Singer and Tragedy); Terpsichore (Delighting in the Dance, choral lyric and dancing); Erato (Loveliness, lyric poetry); Polymnia (Many songs, hymns and pantomime; and Urania (Heavenly One, astronomy).

Naiads or *Naiade*s (Ναιαδες)
Fresh-water nymphs. They were daughters of Oceanus and Tethys. There were various types: Crinaeae (of fountains), Pegaeae (of springs), Eleionomae (of marshes), Potameides (of rivers), and Limnades (of lakes).

Nymphs or Nymphai (Νψμφαι)
The beautiful female nature spirits. There were various types: *naiads*, fresh-water nymphs; *oreads* or *dryads*, tree nymphs of pine and oak; *meliae*, ash-tree nymphs; *oceanides,* cloud nymphs, bringers of rain from the river Oceanus; *haliae*, sea-nymphs; *nereids* or *nereides*, the fifty sea-goddess daughters of Nereus; *nephelae* or *nephalai,* nymphs of the clouds; and the *lampiades,* underworld nymphs.

Oceanides or Okeanides (Οκεανιδες)
The three thousand fresh-water nymph daughters of the earth-encircling river, Oceanus and the titaness Tethys. They were

nymphs of fresh water, *naiads*; clouds, *nephelai*; cool breezes, *aurai*; meadows, *leimonides*; and groves, *alseides*.

Oceanus or Okeanos (Ωκεανος)
The eldest of the Titans, son of Uranus (heaven) and Gaia (earth), the god of the great river that completely surrounded the flat earth. He fathered, with Tethys, the 3,000 rivers(sons) and 3,000 *oceanids* (daughters, the nymphs of land and water). He was the father of Philyra, Kheiron's mother.

Oneiroi (Ονειροι)
The dreams spirits. They issued forth at night, in the thousands, from the underworld, like bats from a cave.

Orion (Οριον)
There are several stories about Orion and I chose not to go into all of them. Let it be said here, however, that he was a handsome earth-born giant who, being the son of Poseidon had the unusual ability to walk on water. After being thwarted in love, he gave up and went to Crete to hunt wild animals where he became a close companion of Artemis and Leto. His hunting skills were so great that he declared that there was no animal on earth that he could not kill. In anger, Gaia dispatched a poisonous scorpion to destroy him. In another tale, it is said that he fell in love with Artemis, who considered giving up her vow of chastity in order to marry him. Apollo, jealous or simply to help his sister keep her vows tricked Artemis into killing Orion herself by challenging her to hit a mark far out in the sea. She soon discovered that the mark had been her beloved friend Orion. Artemis convinced Zeus to immortalize Orion in the stars along with his hunting dogs, and the scorpion was set there too, eternally chasing after the great huntsman (that is another possible story of his demise). The scorpion reminds all that skills are bestowed upon the living as boons from the gods and not to be taken for granted or egotistically boasted about.

Perseus (Περσιος)
A great Argive hero who slew the Gorgon Medusa and rescued princess Andromeda from a sea monster.

Philyra (Φιλυρα)
Lover of the lyre, daughter of Oceanus and Tethys and mother of Kheiron by Kronus who mated with her in the form of a horse. It is said that she so loathed being the mother of such an abomination that she begged the gods to change her into something else; and thus she was transformed. Other accounts tell of her living on Mount Pelion with her son and proudly living to see him become the wisest and most respected of living beings.

Pleiades (Πλειαδες)
Seven star nymph daughters of the Titan Atlas who were loved by the gods. They were transferred to the heavens after the lusty giant Orion chased them for seven years. To rescue them, Zeus transformed them into the stars above Taurus (Zeus), but still pursued by Orion.

Poseidon (Ποσειδον)
The King of the Sea, and the god of horses, rivers and earthquakes. He was one of the great Olympian gods who received the sea when the cosmos was divided amongst his brothers, the three sons of Kronus after the overthrow of the Titans.

Prometheus ('Forethought') (Προμηθος)
One of the Titans and a benefactor of mankind. It is said that he formed the first humans from the clay of the earth. When the gods were going to share a meal with humans at the feast of Mecone, Prometheus divided the meat of a great ox. On one plate he put the bones and covered them with the succulent fat. On the other, he placed the meat and entrails and covered them with the stomach so that it looked unappealing. He then offered the plates to Zeus to choose between the plates for the gods' portion. Zeus chose the one dripped with sweet fat and bones and set the precedence that man would take the meat and offer the bones to the gods as sacrifices. Zeus was angry and chose to withhold fire from mankind. Prometheus stole the fire, hiding it in a fennel stalk and gave it to humans anyway. In punishment, Zeus gave humanity Pandora, beautiful as she was, who unleashed all the sorrows and illnesses upon the world. Prometheus was chained to a cliff in the Caucasian Mountains, where every day an eagle would come and eat out his liver.

Every day it would grow back, and so his torture continued on for eternity until Herakles convinced Zeus to allow Prometheus take on our hero's immortality. Prometheus, a titan of the first generation of gods, is however already immortal so that doesn't really make sense, but the gods don't always follow the rules of humans.

Protogonos or plural Protogenoi
(Προτογονος or Προτογενοι)
The first born of the primeval gods who made up the very fabric of the universe – Eros (The creative urge), Kronus (Time), Chaos (Air), Gaia (Earth), Tartarus (Hell Pit), Uranus (Sky), Pontus (Sea), Nyx (Night), Erebus (Darkness), Hemera (Day), and Aether (Light).

Python (Πψθον)
A gigantic serpent born of the sludge of the earth, which was appointed by Themis or Gaia to guard the Delphic Oracle. The god Apollo slew Python with his arrows when he seized the shrine.

Rhea (Ρηια)
Daughter of Uranus and Gaia, sister and wife of Kronus, mother of Zeus, Hera, Poseidon, Hades, Hestia, and Demeter. She rescued her son Zeus from being devoured by his father and secretly hid him on Mt. Ida, where he was raised by Adrastia and Ida and a sacred goat Amalthea, whose horns were the horns of plenty.

Tartarus or Tartaros (Ταρταρως)
One of the Protogenoi (primeval gods) of the storm-wracked pit of Tartarus, which lay beneath the flat earth. His realm was the underworld and the prison of the Titan gods. He was the predecessor of Hades and yet retained the depths of his kingdom as the prison of the Titans. With Gaia, Tartarus fathered the monstrous storm-daemon Typhoeus.

Tethys (Τηθυς)
Goddess of the sea winds and tides, one of the Titans, daughter of Uranus (heaven) and Gaia (earth). With Oceanus, she was the mother of 3,000 rivers (sons) and 3,000 oceanids or *naiads* (daughters, nymphs of land and water), one of which was

Philyra, Kheiron's mother. Rhea entrusted Tethys with raising her daughter Hera.

Thea or Theia (Θεια)
The Titan goddess of sight and clear blue skies. She was the mother of the Sun, Moon and Dawn. Also the Greek word for aunt.

Themis 'order'(Θεμις)
One of the Titans, daughter of Uranus (heaven) and Gaia (earth). She was the goddess of justice and law and order. She was Zeus' first wife and bore him the three fates, the Moirai, and the three seasons, the Horae (for some reason winter was omitted in ancient times). Like her mother, Gaia, she was associated with prophetic powers and with Gaia was the original owner of the oracle at Delphi. She is the mother of Prometheus (forethought) and Epimetheus (hindsight).

Titans or Titanes (Τιτανες)
The sons of Uranus and Gaia known to have overthrown their father Uranus. They were in turn overthrown by Zeus at the end of the ten-year war of the Titans and cast into Tartarus (except for Oceanus who remained neutral in the conflict). It appears that they were later released by Zeus and settled in Elysium. Some of their sons and grandsons were also called Titans.

Titanesses (Τιτανίδας)
The daughters of Uranus and Gaia.

To-nero (το νερό)
An invented character, a frog, friend of Philyra. His name means "the water."

Zeus (Ζεος)
The King of the Gods, greatest of the twelve Olympians. He was the god of the heavens, weather, fate, and kings. His weapons were fiery thunderbolts.

About the Author

Alaria Bliss was born in a coastal town of Central California. She was raised in a multi-cultural family, where various languages, classical music, literature and art were highly valued. She was the oldest of three, with two younger brothers. As a young man, her father was a Shakespearian actor and her mother a school teacher and loving homemaker, who always told her, "You can do whatever you put your mind to."

Her grandfather was a concert pianist and orchestral conductor. When she was very young, her grandfather had musical soirees and rehearsals at his house. Along with the extraordinary musicians, there was always delicious food and lively conversation. When she got too tired from all the excitement, she would curl up with her blanket under the grand piano and fall asleep to the powerful sounds of live classical music. On quieter nights, her grandmother would read her to sleep with stories and poems. Among this rich symphony of arts, words blended together in Alaria's subconscious and created an internal music of their own.

Later in her childhood, Alaria lived with her family on the edge of a canyon in the Sierra Nevada mountains. It was there that she discovered Nature; hiking in the rain, swimming in the mountain streams, listening to the wind and talking to trees, integral parts of understanding the ancient Greek worldview.

Alaria is the mother of two grown children and now lives with her beloved on a beautiful, organic farm in Northern California.

Soon Available!
Kheiron and the Oracle

Book II -The Life of Kheiron
Wise Centaur of Ancient Greece

In *Kheiron and the Oracle,* Kheiron's fascinating life continues as he meets other centaurs who look like him but are very different in nature. He falls in love with a centauress, but realizes that he is not like the other centaurs. At the famous, Battle with the Centaurs, during the wedding of Pirithous and Hippodamea, Kheiron escapes and subsequently rescues an orphaned girl. He carries the young girl back to his cave on Mount Pelion and takes care of her as if she was his own child. Kheiron nurtures the girl's natural interests, and when she grows up, she becomes one of the most gifted oracles at Delphi.

www.ingramcontent.com/pod-product-compliance
Lightning Source LLC
Chambersburg PA
CBHW030531270626
47155CB00024B/2682